DEAD RECKONING

A novel

Other Books by Rex Owens
Murphy's Troubles
Out of Darkness

DEAD RECKONING

REX OWENS

CKBooks Publishing

CKBooks Publishing
PO Box 214
New Glarus, WI 53574
www.CKBookpublishing.com

ISBN: 978-1-949085-43-3
E-ISBN: 978-5-949085-44-0
Previously published under ISBN: 978-1-59598-601-6
LCCN: 2018936440

Cover design by Melissa Johnson

Printed in the United States of America

A GUILTY CONSCIENCE NEEDS TO CONFESS.
A WORK OF ART IS A CONFESSION.

—ALBERT CAMUS

CHAPTER 1

The room was lit with just four pillar candles that would burn until the first rays of morning light. The curtains were drawn tight. A breeze from the open window suggested Kieran Fitzpatrick's spirit was leaving his boyhood home.

It took a few minutes for my eyes to adjust; the room was blurry through my tears. Then the body, laying out on the dining table, came into full view, the rosary he received for his first Eucharist wrapped in callous, folded hands. The sting of death came only with the sight of his lifeless body.

When we first met, Kieran sported dark red hair piled on top of his head. The undertaker had combed his now-thin, sandy-colored hair straight back. The undertaker was wrong; it made him look like an American gangster from the 1950s.

I had no idea how Kieran had died. After my wife, Mairin, took the call, and drove to campus to find me; she didn't ask for the cause of death. It didn't appear that he had died by violence, but a good mortician can work miracles to make a corpse lifelike. *Should I ask? Does it matter?* My face felt wet. I rubbed my mustache with the back of my hand. *It does matter, how he died.*

What will life be like without my friend? When I bury my best friend, I will also bury my past. God, I need a whiskey.

I reached inside the side pocket of my jacket to find my rosary. It took me an entire day searching through box after box for me to find it. I dropped to my knees, clutching the rosary between both hands and whispered, "Eternal rest grant unto Kieran, O Lord, and let perpetual light shine upon Kieran Fitzpatrick. May he rest in peace. Amen."

Someone touched my shoulder. I turned to see Mairin kneeling beside me. She held her rosary with white lace gloves and prayed, "O my Jesus, forgive us our sins, save us from the fires of hell; lead all souls to heaven, especially those in most need of your mercy."

The two voices behind me recited psalm 130 in perfect harmony as one voice.

"Out of the depths I cry to you, O Lord;
O Lord, hear my voice. Let your ears be attentive to my cry for mercy.
If you, O Lord, kept a record of sins, O Lord, who could stand?
But with you there is forgiveness; therefore you are feared.
I wait for the Lord, my soul waits, and in his word I put my hope.
My soul waits for the Lord more than watchman wait for the morning,
more than watchman wait for the morning.
O Israel, put your hope in the Lord, for with the Lord is unfailing love
and with him is full redemption.
He himself will redeem Israel from all their sins."

I turned to see who had recited the traditional psalm for the dead. A woman in a black dress with a veil covering her face knelt on a pillow. Next to her was a young man with a shock of red hair, who knelt on the worn wood floor. His tie was pulled so tight, his neck was red, and his tweed jacket was too small, the buttons looked ready to pop off. Mairin leaned into my shoulder. "Don't stare, Ian."

Not wanting to offend anyone, I jerked my head back around. I suffered from incessant writer's curiosity. My lower back ached as much from the kneeling as from the long drive from Cork. The clock on the mantle had been stopped at five.

I didn't know if he had died at five in the morning or the evening the previous day.

Mairin leaned close and whispered into my ear, "I need to check on the room. You can stay here. I won't be long."

"What room?" I had no idea what she was talking about.

"I booked a room at Mai Kelly Bed and Breakfast; it's close by."

I wrapped my arm around Mairin and hugged her. I wanted to kiss her but thought it would be in bad taste, and settled for whispering a heartfelt "Thank you."

Mairin left so as to not disturb the small group of mourners. I didn't recognize any of the people surrounding his body. I couldn't imagine why there were so few. It was still early evening; I hoped there would be more later. I leaned forward to get up. Along with a sore back, my knees were stiff. I was numb, unable to grieve, but at least I hadn't sunk into my dark place once again; I hadn't been there in months. *I wonder if it is possible to live without Kieran, without a past. Jesus, I could use a whiskey.*

I almost fell forward when I got up off my knees. I broke my fall with my arms and felt an intense pang rush up into my shoulders. "Damn," I said in a muffled voice. I looked left and right. No one took notice of me, thank God. When we Irish grieve, it's all consuming and we are not easily distracted.

I stood up in short, thought-out motions, making sure I had my balance with each step. I stood straight and stretched my lower back. The car ride from Cork was nearly five hours without a single stop. My back muscles cramped. The candles flickered and filled the room with the pungent smell of burning paraffin. Behind me I could hear voices in another room. I decided to make my way to where the voices originated, guessing it would be the kitchen.

There were a few people standing and three people sitting at a white-enamel, metal table. Pots covered the stove, filling the room with the aroma of Guinness stew. My stomach growled. *I should wait to eat with Mairin.* The conversation in the room stopped and all eyes were turned toward me. I looked from face to face, not recognizing anyone. Kieran often told me of the Fitzpatrick clan's long history in County Donegal without ever sharing any details. Kieran had a reputation for cleverness, and there were so many Fitzpatrick's in the county, it would be difficult to determine specific lineage and identify mother, father, or siblings.

A man in his mid-sixties spoke first. "You must be Kieran's writer friend, Ian Murphy?"

"I am."

"Jesus, did ya hear, everyone? There is no doubt this one is from the County Cork; that twang rings in the ears. Welcome, Mr. Murphy. Cathal Fitzpatrick, Kieran's uncle. My brother, Daragh, was Kieran's da. Daragh, God rest his soul, has been gone for some time now. His ma, Fiona, passed just a year ago. So this branch of the clan is over and done with."

A family at its end in one death, an Irish tragedy. I cleared my throat. "So Kieran had no brothers or sisters?"

"One sister, Roisin. She and her boy are in the parlor with him now," Cathal said.

I looked from face to face and wondered if the people were Fitzpatrick clan, neighbors, or friends. There was a bleak Irishness about them. They all looked the same; the look of stubborn survivors hung on every face.

"I'm sure Roisin and Willie will be in directly. She's been with him since he was laid out this afternoon. Roisin, she takes her duty seriously. Can I offer you a bowl a stew, a glass of Bushmills, or a Smithwick's? You must have somethin'."

I shook my head. "We had sandwiches in the car. I'm not hungry now. My wife went to check on our room. I'll wait for her."

"Have it your way, Mr. Murphy. Roisin and Willie should be in directly. You'll want to talk with them, I'm sure. Now let me introduce the folks here in the kitchen."

Should I ask Cathal how Kieran died? It doesn't feel right. Too awkward. We just met.

Cathal was a good host; he introduced each person and their connection to Kieran. There were some family, some friends, and some from the church whose duty it was to send off the newly departed. There wasn't anyone from either the IRA or Sinn Fein. I didn't understand, but it was still early, his body had only been home a few hours.

I talked with each of the mourners, the conversation complete strangers have when they are brought together by some tragic event and will not see each other again. Mairin was gone longer than I expected. She took responsibility for the driving so it was likely she decided to take a short nap before returning. She deserved it.

Cathal jumped up from his chair, almost knocking over his whiskey glass. "Look, Roisin and Willie. This is Mr. Ian Murphy, Kieran's famous friend."

I brushed my hair back with one hand and felt the blood rise up my cheeks. I took Roisin's hand, which was thick and rough with red splotches. I grasped her hard-working hand with both of mine. "Please. Ian."

"Bless you for coming, Mr. Murphy, I mean Ian. Kieran spoke of you so often, we feel like we know you. Oh, it's been so many years. This is my son Willie. His da will come over after his shift."

Willie reminded me of the way Kieran looked the first time I met him in the pub more than thirty-five years ago. Willie had mischievous, clear blue eyes and a smile that spread across his entire face. Like Kieran, freckles dotted his cheeks and wavy red hair hung across his forehead. He couldn't be more than mid-twenties. He thrust is hand in my direction. "William Butler Boyle."

"Willie?"

"I was named for William Butler Yeats. My family doesn't want me to have a swelled head because of my namesake so they call me Willie."

Irish naming can be complex. Families can be cruel without being aware of it. I didn't have the impression from those I had met so far that anyone in the family had any interest in literature or the arts. *Why would they name their son after an Irish literary icon?* Willie noticed me pondering the enigma.

"Oh, I'm the family hope. My father gave me the name as inspiration to not spend my life in the Beleek factory. It's good work. God knows it's supported most of our family since the turn of the century."

"Interesting," I said.

"It worked too. I have a degree in theatre. I would like to do graduate work in directing."

"Outstanding. So, what name do you prefer?"

"William. My friends and teachers call me William. Family call me Willie."

"Then I will call you William."

Our conversation had captured the attention of everyone in the room. My anxiety erupted as my right hand curled up into a fist. I stuffed my hand into my jacket pocket to hide my clenched hand. I needed a diversion so turned in Roisin's direction.

"Roisin, I hope you don't mind but I've written a keen. I thought there would probably be a keen tonight."

"Of course there'll be a keen, Mr. Murphy. We'll send Kieran off in the right way. I never heard of anyone writin' a keen down on a piece of paper. It doesn't seem natural, does it?" Roisin said.

"Well, you don't have to use it. It is my tribute to Kieran."

"I am honored, sir, both for me and my brother. Not sure I know much about the family tree myself, beyond great grandfather. All's I know is Fitzpatrick kin have been in County Donegal since the beginning, and there's no more to be said. We'll read your keen this evening, Mr. Murphy." A proper keen included family history and now I may need to settle for less.

Mairin appeared in the kitchen just as we finished our conversation. "Everyone, this is my wife, Mairin."

She bowed her head and made sure to look into each face with a smile. Mairin whispered to me, "I'm sorry; I fell asleep in the room. Driving tired me."

"Mairin, thank you for collecting me. I should rest before the keen begins. Let's finish introductions later." We said our goodbye's, promising to return in several hours.

* * * * *

I lay next to Mairin, unable to sleep. I ached for a whiskey but resisted; I had to be sober to sing the keen. With Kieran dead, my past shriveled up and disappeared into eternity. How can a man have just one friend after fifty-eight years? I've never been close to my barkeep friend, Mickey, like I was with Kieran. I bore my soul to Kieran.

With Kieran gone, I was adrift. I have no reckoning point. I loved Mairin as much as a man can love a woman but she didn't understand my guilt from the Troubles. My priest continues to refuse absolution.

Kieran Fitzpatrick was the most devout Catholic I've ever known. He attended mass every day – without fail. I'd not had the faith; I didn't understand suspending disbelief. It was a form of trust foreign to me. It was unnatural for me. I had lived my adult life without faith. Maybe it's the reason I plunge into darkness without warning. The darkness wants me alone.

I knew Mairin's love rescued me, but darkness still tugged at my sleeve daily.

All Ireland knew I tried to atone for the deaths I caused during the Troubles, even though I never once pulled a trigger or set off a bomb. What was the power of words to insight hatred, violence, and death? I understood my work on the Good Friday Agreement brought an end to IRA violence, but it didn't bring peace. Ireland had turned her back on me, rejecting atonement, rejecting peace. Without Kieran, I was lost.

I turned on my back and looked up to the ceiling, wrestling with the question that has plagued me since the 1998 Good Friday Agreement: *What does Ireland want of me?*

CHAPTER 2

We returned to the Fitzpatrick home about eight o'clock. I didn't say anything to Mairin and walked directly to the kitchen, slid out the bottle I had hidden in my coat, and put it in a cupboard without anyone noticing. I left my coat in the kitchen and joined Mairin in the parlor, now filled with people, all strangers to me. The hard lesson I was learning was while Kieran was my closest friend for more than thirty years, I knew nothing about his life outside the IRA. The people in the parlor must be friends, acquaintances, and even IRA volunteers. I didn't know. My shoulders drooped as I reached into my pocket for my rosary. I dropped to my knees like the others in the room, and Mairin knelt beside me with closed eyes. Several women began singing the keen in somber, melodic voices. The longer they sang, the more their harmony increased, like Irish monks in chapel. They sang the words I had written during our drive to Ballyshannon. It was an honor they accepted the words from someone who was a stranger to them, but they knew I was close to Kieran.

The keen was repeated several times. My knees were sore from the hardwood floor; my calves ached from being in one position for such a long time. My beard was soaked with tears, even though I didn't recall crying. I felt myself sway forward and backward. I feared losing my balance and being embarrassed by toppling over on the floor. I reached out for Mairin to steady myself. She gave a faint smile and offered her hand. I couldn't smile in return. *Mairin, my strength.*

Mairin stood up and reached down to help me get up without stumbling. I stretched out with slow, deliberate moves and arched my back as I straightened out. William was kneeling on my left. When he saw me stand, he stood. I wobbled and didn't want to risk walking on my own. William and Mairin each took one of my arms and wheeled me around to walk into the kitchen.

"Are you ok, Mr. Murphy?" William asked.

"Ian?" Mairin echoed William's question.

I looked to my right at Mairin and then to my left at William. "I would be lying if I said I was fine." I winced as my right hand curled up in an intense spasm.

"I'm here, Ian," Mairin reassured me as she massaged my hand. She looked around me to speak to William. "Don't be alarmed; it's stress. He's been afflicted with it since college at Trinity."

Relief spread across William's face. "I think you could use a drink, Mr. Murphy."

"No! No, not now, thank you. At midnight I want to go back to the parlor to say the rosary for Kieran. What time is it?"

"It's almost half eleven, Ian," Mairin said. "You were kneeling for a long time."

"No wonder my legs ache."

"Here's a chair, Mr. Murphy." William nudged a middle-aged man with premature white hair off the chair and offered it to me.

"Thank you, William. Will you please call me Ian. No point in being formal at a wake, is there? Is your mother still in the parlor?"

"Yes, she must be. She is very devout. She's his only living relative. I suppose you weren't aware," William explained.

"I wouldn't have known but your Uncle Cathal told me. Kieran never, never talked about family, not even to me. I'm beginning to understand it was his way of protecting all of you."

"He was a unique man, Ian," William said.

"That's an understatement. I'll want to talk with your mother more later, after the rosary."

"You plan to be up until morning?" Mairin asked.

"I doubt if I could sleep tonight, my love."

"Your choice. I understand. After the rosary, I'm going back to our room. One of us should get some sleep."

"I understand."

"It's time, Ian," Mairin said.

The three of us returned to the parlor arm in arm. A priest with a full white beard knelt beside Kieran, holding his rosary between his hands, his elbows propped up on the table. I dropped to my knees with William and Mairin's help, made the sign of the cross, and held the crucifix with a vice-like grip in my hands.

The priest chanted, "Pray for us, O Holy Mother of God."

The mourners responded in one voice: "That we may be made worthy of the promises of Christ. Let us pray: O God, whose only begotten son, by his life, death, and resurrection, has purchased for us the rewards of eternal life. Grant, we beseech thee, that while meditating on these mysteries of the most holy rosary of the Blessed Virgin Mary, we may imitate what they contain and obtain what they promise, through the same Christ our Lord, Amen." In unison all the mourners crossed themselves.

This portion of the rosary was done. Mairin and William lifted me up with great care. Tears clouded my vision; the candles flickered in blurry light. When the candles were reduced to stubs, the priest brought new candles to replace them. I was guided back into the kitchen; we were the first of the mourners there after the rosary.

"I'm off then, Ian. You are on your own. If you need to sleep, I'm sure someone here can bring you to the bed and breakfast." Mairin touched the back of my neck and gave me a sweet kiss and was gone.

I turned to William and winked. "I have a surprise for you, young man." I reached into the cupboard on my right and retrieved the bottle of Midleton I hid earlier in the evening. I handed the bottle to William. "Glasses!"

"Midleton? I can't believe it," William exclaimed.

"It's the only whiskey your Uncle Kieran and I drank. God, you know I only live a stone's throw from the distillery. James, Daniel, and Jeremiah founded the distillery in 1825. Within just five years, they employed more than 200. The brothers were my great uncles. So not only is it the finest whiskey, it's family." I chuckled as I shared my family history.

Roisin slipped into the room without speaking to anyone. "Mother, you are exhausted. Please sit down. I'll dish up a bowl of stew. Look what Mr. Murphy has brought. He and Uncle Kieran drank it all the time," William explained, brandishing the bottle in front of her.

"I will have a seat and welcome the stew, but whiskey is too rich for my blood. A stout will go fine with the stew. Is there any bread?" Roisin asked.

"Well, I plan on drinking Midleton with Mr. Murphy, to honor Uncle Kieran, of course," William said.

"You're a grown man. Do what you want. I'll need a spoon, son."

William got the stew and beer for his mother. I put my hand on Roisin's shoulder and leaned down to talk with her. "I am sorry for your troubles, Roisin. I am ashamed I knew so little about Kieran's life. I am dumbfounded by the extent of his secrecy. I can stay for a few days and would appreciate talking with you to learn more about the mystery of Kieran Fitzpatrick."

Roisin broke into a broad smile. "I would be honored, Mr. Murphy, to talk with someone as famous as you. Maybe you could share what Kieran was like in your life. We know he was part of the Troubles in some way, and we all thought he was an IRA man, but he never said anything," Roisin explained as she ate a heaping spoonful of stew.

The room filled; alcohol disappeared down parched throats; people stood shoulder to shoulder; the banter raised to a high pitch. So many conversations were distracting to me, and I'd begun to notice background noise of any kind dampened my hearing. With each glass of Midleton, I felt warmer and wanted to take off my jacket. But to maintain the decorum of a proper wake, I left my coat on but loosened my tie.

"Ian, can you tell me how you met Uncle Kieran?" William asked.

I closed my eyes and let the first memory float to the surface of my mind. "Well, I was about your age, attending Trinity, on the path to a job in academia. In my college days I ignored current events. I studied literature and history. I liked to be alone in public places – I know it doesn't make any sense. I often wrote my papers in a pub near campus. One night your uncle appeared out of the mist with my dinner and a beer. He said he had a job for me but was very vague. Soon after I learned my best friend growing up, Timolty Doyle, was murdered during an IRA raid in the heart of Belfast. Your uncle collected me and drove me to Cork to attend Timolty's wake and funeral.

"You know something odd? I never did ask him how he knew I needed to go home. Mind you, I was reluctant to ride with a complete stranger in a car for three hours. He was very self-confident and convinced me it was the right thing to do. I don't know where he stayed in Cork. My ma asked him to stay but he refused. He attended the wake and the funeral. Several days after the burial he said he needed to return to Dublin and offered me a ride again. Of course, I accepted. I didn't see him for months after the funeral." I gulped the whiskey in my glass, which was now empty again.

"What an incredible story, Mr. Murphy."

I talked with a quiet voice so William would need to lean close. I wasn't comfortable sharing my stories with everyone in the room. "Much later I learned Kieran had recruited Timolty. The IRA leaders wanted to get support across the country and one of their strategies was to recruit volunteers from all across Ireland. Cork has a reputation for being revolutionary, and Kieran learned it was easy to recruit young men in need of a situation."

"Did Uncle Kieran always work for the IRA?"

"To the best of my knowledge. All except for the last two years, when he worked for Sinn Fein, he reported directly to Gerry Adams."

A middle-aged, heavyset man pushed through the group of people in the kitchen with his shoulder, I tightened my grip on the whiskey glass to prevent dropping it. My hands were sweaty and the glass almost popped out of my hand like a jack-in-the-box. The voices around me became an incomprehensive babble. I felt my chest heave and it was difficult to breathe.

"I can't stay in this kitchen any longer, William. I'm suffocating," I said.

"Yes, of course. We can go to my house," William offered. "Mom will be fast asleep by now. I understand, everyone is well meaning but intense. I could use a quiet place myself. Would you mind sharing stories of Uncle Kieran? I could listen until you're hoarse."

"Yes, it would be nice. I won't be able to sleep tonight. The dead only leave us with memories so I will share mine with you."

We walked for about a block and my head cleared.

* * * * *

The mantle clock struck seven as we finished the last drop of Midleton. "Well, William, you now have something more in common with your Uncle Kieran. There were many bottles of whiskey we shared to the last drop. It's a bonding. In such a short time you are my *'anam cara,'* as your Uncle Kieran was," I said as I put my glass on the table with great care.

"I am honored, Ian. You have helped me understand a great deal about my uncle. He was an expert at stuffing different facets of his life into separate boxes. He was a unique, mysterious man."

"Aye."

"It's nearly half seven. We should get back to the house to carry Uncle Kieran to the church. Knowing our priest, he will want him there at least two hours before the service," William explained.

"It's not Kieran we will be moving, it's his body only — the shell he used while he was with the rest of us living in the flesh. Oh, God, I am tired. I haven't stayed up all night since my days at Trinity and that was a very long time ago. I hope I don't embarrass myself and fall asleep during the service. Does your priest have a reputation for rousing sermons, William?"

"Certainly not, but I don't think he'll put you to sleep. Will you be speaking?"

"Oh, yes. I must honor our friendship, our struggle and salute him to heaven's gate. When called, I will speak."

A cold, light fog greeted us in the street. A chilled mist covered my beard in less than half a block. I shivered and pulled my coat collar up around my cheeks.

"Is September always this cold in Ballyshannon?" I asked William.

"It's not unusual. It's the North Atlantic."

CHAPTER 3

When we arrived at the Fitzpatrick home, there was a group of four men all wearing hand-woven, traditional Donegal tweed overcoats posted around Kieran's body. The liquor, the cold, and hunger wore me down. I tried to breathe, to fill up my lungs. I raised my head to suck in gulps of air. My knees bent and I fell to the floor. I pulled my knees to my chest and wrapped my arms around my legs and I hid my face in my arms.

"Oh, God, Ian," William whispered.

From behind me William tried to lift me up several times but each time I slumped down on the wood floor. The men surrounding us didn't know what to do.

"Do you think the four of you can carry his casket to the church? Ian isn't fit for the job, and I need to stay here with him. I'll get him some coffee and maybe a bit of porridge."

A man with streaked, white hair parted down the middle and a mustache covering his upper lip stared at me. His steel gray eyes had no pity or comprehension of my condition. *I know that man; he's Dolan Halloran, back from his self-imposed exile.* Following the vote on the Good Friday Agreement, Dolan agreed to disband the Provisional Irish Republication Army. He promoted decommissioning arms before he left, but without his iron fist, it took more than three years to enforce. There was speculation he moved to the Shetland Islands.

I looked up at William. "I want to follow the casket." With some difficulty, he finally was able to help me to my feet and led be out the door a few paces behind the men carrying the wood box on their shoulders. I wrapped my arm around William's shoulder and leaned on him, taking plodding steps. The walk to St. Joseph's Church of the Rock took less than ten minutes, even at their slow pace. The Fitzpatrick family home stood in the shadow of the church.

The men placed the casket on two sawhorses and removed the lid. They posted themselves around the body the same as they had at the house. The priest appeared by magic next to them. "Fine boys. Give the dead a rest now. I want him alone in the chapel a bit before the service. You may return at half nine."

The three men and Dolan Halloran obeyed the priest's order and left without speaking. I wanted to wait in a nearby pew. William wrinkled his brow and shook his head. "You need strong coffee and a bowl of porridge. Won't your wife be wondering where you are?"

My right hand clenched into a tight fist when he asked about Mairin, and my fingernails dug into the palm of my hand. I looked down, droplets of blood oozed underneath my nails. "She'll know," is all I could squeak out.

William wrapped his arm around my waist and guided me down the aisle and into the street. My feet slid on top of the pavement as if I were ice-skating all the way back to the Fitzpatrick home. William was stronger than he looked. "Would you mind fetching Mairin? We're at the Mai Kelly Bed and Breakfast."

"Of course. Let me help you to the sofa. I'll get you a cup of coffee and a scone from the kitchen. I'm sure Mom will drop by before the funeral." I landed in the corner of the sofa with a soft thud. My shoulders hunched forward, making it difficult for me to breath. I closed my eyes, hoping for a few moments of sleep before William returned with Mairin.

"Ian, here." I hadn't noticed William setting a cup of coffee and a plate with a scone at my feet. I smiled and whisked him off with my hand. I bent forward for the coffee but my reach was several inches short. I leaned back and thrust myself forward with all the strength I could muster. My reach was closer but not enough to pick up either the coffee cup or the scone. My stomach growled in anticipation but I couldn't satisfy its demands. I slumped back into the couch and accepted defeat.

* * * * *

"Oh, Ian!" I jolted awake to see Mairin's face within inches of mine. "Your breath is foul, Ian Padraic Murphy. I knew this was going to happen, I just knew it. When my bed was cold last night, I was sure you descended into your dark place. Thank God William was with you, otherwise I might have been picking you up in the street this morning or bailing you out of the town goal." Mairin straightened up, a scowl across her face and both hands on her hips.

I held my hands over my mouth to hide my rancid breath. "Good morning. Today is Kieran's funeral."

Mairin's eyes were like a hard frost. "Don't be obvious or insulting, Ian, and don't expect me to be understanding. I'll make you some eggs and toast. You need more than coffee and a scone. William, can you drag him into the kitchen. You look like a little breakfast would do you good too. You can both clean up after you've eaten."

"The ground you walk on is holy, Mairin," I mumbled.

Mairin turned around on her heel and walked toward the kitchen. William leaned down and wrapped his arms under my shoulders and around my back. He leaned back while pulling me off the sofa. My bones ached as I was pulled upright. William nearly toppled to one side trying to balance my dead weight.

"Shall we dance?" I said.

"I will never drink with you again, Ian. You're a sloppy, disgusting drunk."

"I am what I am, lad."

I ate my eggs and toast in silence and slurped down three cups of straight black coffee. Life surged back into my body and my head cleared. I sat straight in the chair and stretched my legs out under the table and could feel the blood rush down to my feet. *Ah, life,* I thought.

Mairin and William sat on either side of me at the table. Neither of them looked up or even attempted conversation. Mairin refused to look at me or have eye contact. I understood her anger. I fight the good fight every day to fend off the dark one. Having Mairin in my life has been my life saver but yesterday was different. She knew it was different. I lowered my head to my chest.

"You should have expected I'd honor Kieran with a bit of whiskey."

Mairin threw her napkin on top of her plate and finished her coffee. "You're not capable of one drink or even two. You know and I know. I had hope. You went almost all day without a drink." She got up and took my dishes to the sink.

"The Dark One was sitting on my shoulder all day, waiting for a brief moment of weakness. The lad reminds me of Kieran, the red hair at least. I succumbed. I've never pretended to be strong. What little strength I've developed comes from you. I will face this day cold sober, I promise."

Mairin tossed the dishcloth into the sink, dried each dish, and set them on the counter. She turned around and the scowl left her face and her eyes glossed over. "Oh, Ian, I know about loss, about being the one left behind. Honor Kieran with your words today. Don't promise me not to get drunk. Promise yourself, promise Kieran. Now go clean up and change clothes. I'll meet you at the church."

I arrived at St. Joseph Church the Rock at nine thirty as the priest instructed. Mairin, William, and Roisin were sitting in the front pew. The church had stood on "the rock" for 168 years and at the entrance was a sign listing every priest who had served the congregation. Only twenty-eight men had served Ballyshannon. The graveyard enveloped the church on three sides. As I entered the door, I could see the mound of fresh dirt from Kieran's final resting place. By the standards for a Catholic church, St. Joseph's was plain. The inside walls were plain whitewash with paintings of the saints on them. The side windows were clear glass, which flooded the sanctuary with light. There were three stain glass windows behind the alter and a wood balcony above the entrance where the choir sat. Today a lone piper stood in the balcony at attention.

The coffin sat at the center aisle in front of the altar. Kieran lay silent, listening to the final goodbyes, offering the mourners no solace. *Just like him.*

I knelt and made the sign of the cross, then scrunched in next to Mairin. The pews were wide and could have held at least ten more people but there we all sat, shoulder to shoulder. In the pew opposite ours sat Dolan Hallaron and the three other strangers. Now I was certain they were Provies. By their age I guessed these were the men who originally organized the Irish Republican Army thirty-five years ago. It was a miracle they were alive to attend the funeral of their co-founder. Kieran was directly responsible for each of them being alive today rather than victims of a firing squad.

Behind me I could hear an army of muffled voices and shuffling feet. Promptly at ten the priest began the high mass. After the mass, the priest asked if anyone had a few words for Kieran Fitzpatrick. I rose without looking around to see if others had stood. The priest nodded and waived me to come to the pulpit. I rested my hand on the chair behind the pulpit and turned toward the congregation. *All of Ballyshannon is here for you, my friend.*

I locked my arms in place, planted my feet, and cleared by throat. I took a moment to look at the somber faces, then took in a deep breath.

"Kieran Fitzpatrick was my friend. True friendship is a blessing. Kieran Fitzpatrick was also a stranger, a man of many mysteries and many secrets. Yet, I knew Kieran Fitzpatrick better than any other man alive. Like life, Kieran was a paradox. In my last year at Trinity my boyhood friend, Timolty Doyle, was killed by a British soldier during a skirmish in Belfast. Kieran appeared, drove me to Cork, and stayed by my side during the wake and burial. I begged to join the Irish Republican Army; he didn't have to recruit me. Kieran made a place for me and coaxed me to write the Green Book. After I betrayed the IRA, only Kieran stood by me. I want to reveal one of Kieran's secrets." I took a moment to look into the faces of the congregation. "I stand here before you today only because Kieran chose to turn his back on the Provisional Irish Republican Army. After the hooley on the vote, I went home early – exhausted and exulted. Kieran was waiting for me at my cottage. He sat in a dark room, chain-smoking, with a pistol sitting on the table. We shared a bottle of Midleton. He passed out before I did. I picked up the revolver, opened the chamber, and found only a single round. At the time I wasn't sure if Kieran intended it for me or for him. I tossed the bullet into the woods and then fell into a drunken sleep. The next morning Kieran was gone, but he left me a note confirming that the bullet was for me. He also left me detailed instructions on how to avoid another assassination attempt. Kieran disappeared for three years. He sacrificed himself for our friendship and my life. Nothing more needs to or should be said. I will mourn you every day for the remainder of my time on earth, Kieran Fitzpatrick. May you rest in heaven for eternity."

The priest looked toward Roisin with a question on his face, giving her the opportunity to speak. She shook her head no and used a tissue to wipe tears off her cheeks. Then the priest looked at Dolan Halloran. He sat in the pew like a stone, avoiding the priest's pleading eyes. The priest wrung his hands, and then his face brightened. "There is one thing and only one thing I know of Kieran Fitzpatrick that is certain. He was a devout man. He was a good Catholic. He attended mass every day of his adult life. In my heart I am certain, as we prepare to bury his body, his soul is resting in the hands of Jesus Christ our Lord. Amen."

"Amen," we responded in unison.

"Kieran did leave instructions for his funeral. He requested one hymn and to have the pipes played during the procession. Let's stand and sing 'Amazing Grace.'" The priest gestured with his hands to have us stand. From the balcony the organist throttled us through all four verses. I am not a singer and mumbled the words as best I could remember. The lyrics of the hymn express what I believe was the extent of Kieran's Catholic faith. He felt only God's grace could save him from his devotion to the Cause and the reliance on violence and death to gain its end. In a flash I understood Kieran's daily ritual to attend mass. Every day he asked to be forgiven for what he had done the previous day and for what he planned to do that day – amazing grace.

At the end of the song the priest knelt at the coffin, whispering a prayer only Kieran could hear. He placed the lid on top of the box. Dolan Halloran took his place at the head of the coffin and the three men who sat with Dolan followed. I took my place at the head of the coffin opposite Halloran and William took the place behind me. Without words we turned to face the door at the end of the aisle. Dolan's command rang out: "Up." In unison we lifted the box onto our shoulders. I felt William's hand on my left shoulder. Like soldiers everywhere, across time, we marched down the aisle. With the first step the piper stood at attention and played *"Flowers of the Forest."* It is a haunting lament which, by tradition, pipers played only at funerals or memorial services. *Kieran* would *choose this dirge on his journey to his final resting place,* I thought.

We set the coffin on the ground next to the burial plot. Dolan placed the tricolor on top of Kieran's coffin. We dropped to our knees, made the sign of the cross, and said our final goodbyes in silence. The priest gave the final blessing. William helped me up off my knees, and Mairin grabbed my arm to make sure I didn't topple over.

"Well done, Ian," Mairin whispered into my ear and gave me a peck on my cheek. Roisin and William left the cemetery first, walking back to the Fitzpatrick homestead. As we walked, I looked back, searching for Dolan Halloran and the other men. There were so many questions I had for them, and I hoped they would attend the noon meal being served at the house for family and mourners. I strained my neck, looking in every direction for the four men. Like the morning mist they disappeared into the day, never to be seen again.

CHAPTER 4

The house filled quickly with friends, family, neighbors, and some who appeared to be IRA volunteers. The men I suspected were volunteers all wore dark suits with shirts that were once white but now stained gray. Their shirt collars curled up and their ties were drawn tight, pinching their necks. Their haircuts looked like someone put a bowl on top of their heads and took clippers to the side and back, like whitewall tires. I also noticed they didn't speak to anyone else but nestled in a circle in the corner of the parlor. I couldn't resist the opportunity to meet a group of street fighters.

"Thank you for attending Kieran's funeral," I said, looking each man in the face. They looked at each other and then back to me, surprised they were noticed.

"It's the right thing to do for Mr. Fitzpatrick. He was like a da to me," offered one of the young men standing closest to me. "I liked what you said at the church service about Mr. Fitzpatrick. He was the finest." They all nodded their heads in agreement.

"I would've taken a bullet for 'im, I would," blurted out the young man in the corner with green eyes and scars on both cheeks.

"Aye, as we all would," they said in unison.

"What do you lads think of the peace, then?" I asked.

They looked at each other and bowed their heads to avoid eye contact with me. They shuffled their feet.

The man standing closest to me spoke up again. "Now look, Mr. Murphy, there's no disrespect, but you have no idea.

Them fuckin' Brits and RUC's don't want no peace. Jesus, they'd like to kill every one of us standin' here. Mr. Fitzpatrick, he knew. He took care of us, see. There's still fightin' every day – just more secret like. We lost two boys just last week, we did."

My ignorance was overwhelming. Maybe these men were from the Real IRA, the group of dissidents who felt the Provisional IRA had sold out so they formed their own group to continue the violence and harassment. "Well, again, Kieran would have been honored. There's a lot of food in the kitchen. It smells delicious. Please go and eat hearty – Kieran would want you to." Without another word, the men shuffled past me into the kitchen.

I looked throughout the house for Mairin and found her outside talking with William. The day had turned bright and with so many people in the house, it was very warm. There was a slight, cooling breeze coming off the River Erne just to the west. I put my arm around Mairin's waist and pulled her toward me. She tucked her head into my shoulder and put her arm around my waist. "You two found the most comfortable place. It's getting quite warm inside. I'm surprised you're not visiting with friends and family, William." William reached into his pocket and brought out a package of Carroll's Number One cigarettes and offered one to both Mairin and me.

"No, thanks, never have," Mairin said.

"No, but my pipe would be nice," I said and pulled the pipe and tobacco pouch out of my jacket pocket.

William lit his cigarette and drew in a deep breath, held it for a moment, and blew out a stream of smoke the wind turned into his face. "To be honest, I've been gone too long. I was always the odd one. I wasn't one for hurling or football in secondary school. I competed in dramatic readings, oratory, and the school play. I'm the first one in my family to attend college. I received high marks on my leaving exam and was fortunate to attend Trinity on scholarship. I couldn't afford to come home for holiday or the summers." The cigarette glowed bright red as William inhaled deeply again. "I'm a stranger in my own hometown." He threw the cigarette on the pavement and crushed it with the sole of his shoe.

Mairin looked into my face with her knowing smile. "Well, William, you have that in common with Ian. He went to Trinity on scholarship and didn't go home to Cork until after he graduated."

I knocked the ashes out of my pipe with my hand onto the pavement. I looked at William and saw myself at the age of twenty-four. "William, I believe you and I are cut from the same cloth. I think we should become friends."

The kitchen window opened and Roisin shouted out, "You three are missing it. Come in here now and have some food. Ian, I want to talk with you."

It was clear Roisin was in charge. *I'll wait until the mourners dwindle, then I'll ask her about Kieran's death.* We followed her directions and joined the small group of family members left in the kitchen. I wanted to talk with Roisin too, however, I wasn't interested in banter with the odd assortment of Kieran's relatives eating and drinking. The conversation was getting louder by the minute, which was a sign the whiskey and beer consumption was high. The only thing the group of people had in common was Kieran, and without Kieran in the room, the talk would dwindle as fast as the River Shannon flows. Roisin waved to me and led me to a small room at the back of the house. Boxes were stacked everywhere: on the floor, against the windows, and on a small, white, painted metal table. There were three metal chairs stacked in a corner. I took one each for me and Roisin. When we sat down, our knees touched.

"This is cozy," Roisin said as she blushed.

"I think it's the only quiet place in the cottage. There is no easy way to ask what I must ask, forgive my bluntness. I don't know how he died."

Roisin put her hands up to her face. "Oh, my Lord, Oh, my Lord."

I patted her on the shoulder. "If it's painful, don't – don't tell me."

Roisin straightened her back and looked me directly in the eyes. "It was like he would have wanted it. I will tell you exactly what the priest told me. He was in Ballyshannon to check on the house. I think he was considering selling it. On Thursday he attended the first mass at St. Joseph the Rock, his boyhood church. He knelt down for one of the prayers and didn't get up after the Amen. The parishioners didn't think it unusual because he was so devout. They thought he was continuing to pray on his own. Then the hymn came and he still didn't get off his knees. The two people sitting behind him rushed to his pew. He wasn't breathing. They screamed for the priest, who ran down the aisle to check on him. The priest recognized at once Kieran was being summoned. He gave Kieran extreme unction and then had someone call the ambulance. The ambulance never went to the hospital but went straight to the mortuary. I received the call from the coroner." Roisin's shoulders slumped. Her breathing was labored. Tears formed in the corner of her eyes and fell down her cheeks. "It was God's blessing he died in church. I don't know what he did in the Troubles, but I always thought he'd end up with a bullet in his head. Those two years we never heard from him, I thought he was at the bottom of the Atlantic. I'm the last then. I'm the last of this branch of the Fitzpatrick clan."

I leaned over to hug Roisin. Tears wet my mustache and fell into my beard. "He died in peace, in his church. It's a miracle of God. I think it was a symbol of forgiveness. He's probably in heaven now, looking down us and thinking – get over it, you two."

CHAPTER 5

September slipped into October and November brought the annual Cork chill, wet and raw. Mairin and I returned home after Kieran's funeral and resumed daily life. Mairin gave me a wide berth, letting me work through my troubles on my own. I knew she was always there for me should I want to talk or sit quietly or just be my companion and lover. I felt hollow inside, consumed by nothingness. I gravitated to Jean Paul Sartre and re-read his works on existentialism. At Trinity my class on twentieth-century philosophy, of course, included Sartre, and at the time, I concluded the effect of two major wars on the continent within a span of less than twenty-five years was too much for the human psyche.

I left several of Sartre's books lying on my desk, which Mairin couldn't avoid noticing. "Sartre? Ian, oh, God no, please, not Sartre." Mairin waved a book in my face as I lit my pipe, tossing the match into a glass ashtray.

"It was an accident," I said in a dismissive manner and drew pipe smoke deep into my lungs.

"Jesus, you're not supposed to inhale. I'm sure you've got lungs like a Welsh miner."

I set my pipe in the ashtray, folded my hands on my lap, then leaned back in my chair, wanting to reflect on the right words before I responded. "You worry reading Sartre will cast me down into the dark well and I won't be able to crawl back up to the light."

"I have tried to be silent and let you grieve in your own way but I love you too much to not at least share my concern with you. I don't intend to lecture and would never tell you what to do, but I do have the right to share my views with you."

When Mairin is right, Mairin is right. There was no counter argument to her statement. I smiled then winked at her. "Now is the best time. Let's take a seat and relax. Of course, I will listen."

We moved to the leather love seat to be close to each other. Mairin took both my hands into hers and smiled. Her eyes became soft and empathetic. She kissed me with tenderness. "Thank you, my love, for hearing me out. You have been despondent since Kieran's funeral. You trudge through each day without being aware of the world. You're on automatic pilot without direction or purpose. It frightens me. I know recovery is slow, but you've not even begun. You've sunk into desperation. I'm thankful you're not drinking." Mairin looked deep into my eyes, tucked her shoulder under mine, and rested her head on my chest. "You're not drinking, are you? I don't want to search your office – you relinquish your privacy – but if I get a hint you're deceiving me…"

The truth is hard to accept, especially from the person who loves you most. I slipped my arm around her shoulder and let myself enjoy the comfort of her warmth. The light in the room faded. I couldn't find words to answer her.

"Have you started your memoir yet? Maybe you could write your way out of your darkness?"

I took my time answering. I was afraid she would be upset because I hadn't even considered her suggestion. "No," I whispered.

Mairin started to move away but I held her to me. She didn't struggle.

"Did you realize Sartre says the first principle is we are all responsible for ourselves? I believe the quote is 'Man is nothing else but what he makes of himself.' His idea is so simple and straight forward, although self-evident. How would our world be different if we all just took responsibility for ourselves?"

"Ian, are you being clever and avoiding my question?"

"I answered your question. I haven't written in months. I haven't written anything – not a word. It's not there. It's not writer's block, it's writer's ennui." I slumped down and took my arm from around Mairin.

Mairin took my face in both her hands and drew me close. "I don't know what to do for you. I love you. Ask me anything and I will help."

"I've tried to atone for my life in the IRA but failed, failed miserably. Working on the Good Friday Agreement provided an opportunity to shape Ireland's future on a path of peace. It's too early to gauge if it has changed lives for the better. My soul remains adrift.

"I thought trying to intervene with the Real IRA leaders would redeem me in the eyes of Ireland. The Real IRA leadership is arrogant and uncouth. I'll never forget them laughing in my face, telling me I was just a worn out revolutionary. They ordered me to get out of their way and let them finish the job.

"I don't know where to turn. Good works to atone for past evil doesn't work. It never has."

Mairin pulled away and put her hands on my shoulders. She locked eyes with me. "Ian Padraic Murphy, you are a writer. You must write just as you must breathe. I don't understand you; you are being stubborn and unwilling to listen to me. I still think you should write your memoir. If you write your memoir, I'm certain you will find what you've been searching for. I don't want to speak on this again. You've consumed my patience and tolerance."

I wrapped my arms around her and squeezed tight to absorb her love and warmth directly into my soul. Without Mairin I would be drunk every day, barely functioning in the world. I have leaned on Mairin in my battle to avoid the first glass of whiskey. All it takes is one glass and I lose control; a glass becomes an empty bottle in a single evening. Self-medication is a coward's answer to life, it's avoidance and shame.

"I'm working on how to become responsible for myself." I straightened back up and kissed Mairin on both cheeks.

"Ian, you should go for a walk. A walk alone may help. Or you could visit Caitlin and your niece. God, we haven't seen them in months. Caitlin is probably thinking you disinherited her for not attending Kieran's funeral."

I leaned forward, resting my head in my hands. "My sister will understand. When she was living in Belfast, we didn't communicate for months, many months. I do miss Brianna, but I'm not ready for her cheerfulness. A walk is a good idea."

I bundled up against the weather with my tweed overcoat, Dubarry Donegal boots, and my Donegal tweed walking hat. I could handle any weather with this attire, my sartorial splendor. I walked directly to the River Lee, up to Popes Quay, and past the Cork Opera House. The building was closed for extensive renovation but the glass façade on the outside was attractive. The rumor was there would be a grand re-opening for the December opera season. I walked aimlessly for some time until my stomach growled, demanding satisfaction. I had wandered near Mickey's Pub. I worried Mickey might be angry with me because I hadn't visited in months.

For an early Wednesday evening there were more patrons than I expected. There were more than enough seats at the bar, so I hung my coat and hat up and took a seat. I didn't recognize the barkeep, which was unusual for me; I thought I knew all of the staff. Tonight a plain young woman, probably from Cork College, covered the bar. She pulled her brown hair straight back into a ponytail, wore no make-up, and sported thick, black-frame glasses.

"May I help you?" she asked in a businesslike manner.

"Yes, a cup of tea, please."

"Tea?" she raised her eyebrows.

"Yes, tea and a liver and onion sandwich on brown bread, if you please."

She scribbled on a small white note pad and walked through the kitchen door, returning with a steaming mug of tea. I wrapped my hands around the mug to warm them. The smell of strong, black Irish tea was reassuring to the faint of heart. I lost myself in the reflection in the tea, taking little sips to settle my stomach. There were all men sitting at the bar engaged in muffled conversation. I didn't recognize any of them, and they had no interest in me. It didn't feel like Mickey's. I was surprised he wasn't tending bar himself, especially mid-week. Having a student work meant extra expense and Mickey wasn't known for adding on cost. *God, I hope he's not ill or something. Should I ask after him? It would be bold from a stranger, but I'm not a stranger.*

The kitchen door flew open and a man shouted, "There's only one man in Cork who orders a liver-and-onion sandwich. Ian Murphy, where in the hell have you been these last few months?" Mickey's smile filled his entire face. Mickey tossed the sandwich on the bar with a side of tatoes, then reached across to shake hands.

"That, my dear friend, is a sad story. But I'm glad to be back now."

"Let's go to your regular table in the back corner. You can tell me all about it. God, I've missed yer mug," Mickey said.

The smell of the liver sandwich triggered pleasant memories. After moving back to Cork after four years at Trinity, I refused to live with my parents. I worked at a bookstore for a small wage and was allowed time to write every week. I stumbled past Mickey's one day at lunch and wandered in. Several men were sitting at the bar humped over a sandwich and a Murphy's Ale. I didn't recognize the smell of their meat sandwich but decided if so many people ordered it, then it must be delicious. In minutes the barkeep returned with a pungent mystery meat sandwich and the overwhelming smell of raw onion and yellow mustard. I looked at the other customers. They held their sandwiches with both hands and took big bites. After several bites, they slopped down a big drink of the ale. I followed their lead. In the first bite the onion crunched, the brown meat was soft and squished outside of the bread. The yellow mustard stung the back of my tongue. It was almost too much. As I took the last bite, I thought I found the food of some long forgotten Celtic god. I held up my hand for the bill and found the meal inexpensive. The sandwich and the ale came to less than a pound.

* * * * *

I looked away, not focusing, like I was in a daydream. "Ian? Ian?" Mickey asked.

I looked into his pug face and smiled. "Just recalling the very first liver and onion sandwich I had here. After that first sandwich, it became my noon meal seven days a week. You saved me, you know."

"So, where have you been these past few months, my friend?"

"Kieran died in September," I said in a bland tone.

Mickey pushed back in his chair and ran his hands through his hair. "Oh, my God, I had no idea. I didn't see it in the papers."

"No, no, it's not a death reported in the papers. Not even in Belfast. The weekly in Ballyshannon ran a traditional obituary, nothing more. The obituary was brief. No one knew much about his life, even his family. In fact, the first time I met any of his family was at the wake. Can you imagine? Not very Irish, is it? Kieran Fitzpatrick was one of the most secretive men in all of Ireland."

"Ian, I would have come if I had known. I would."

I patted his shoulder. "I know. It was such a shock. I didn't even think about telling anyone. It was only with the support of my loving Mairin that I survived the wake and funeral."

"Did you speak at his funeral?" Mickey asked.

"I did. I was the only one." I pushed the sandwich to the side of the table. "I'm not hungry now, Mickey, I'm sorry."

"No matter. Is there anything I can do for you, my friend?" Mickey's eyebrows curled up.

"God knows I am thirsty. A Midleton whiskey would be fine. I've stayed away from all liquor for three months now, a new record for me. Mairin is worried if I take the first drink, I'll slide down into the darkness and never return. I don't deserve her, you know."

"Then I won't be the one to tempt you. I'll get you a fresh cup a tea."

I looked at the liver sandwich, still not able to take the first bite. "I should be getting home. Tomorrow night Mairin and I will come for a dinner of your Guinness stew; we can call catch up then," I offered.

"Fine, fine. I'll look forward to seeing the both of yous. Speaking a funerals; have you seen today's paper? Big news from Belfast."

"No, what news now from Belfast? Did they blow somebody else up? Paisley maybe?"

"Gerry's da died."

I made the sign of the cross. Gerry Adams, Sr. was known for three things. First, he was a Republican; second, he had fathered thirteen children; and finally, his son, Gerry Jr., was the heart, mind, and soul of Sinn Fein.

"Can you fetch me the paper, Mickey?" The announcement was on the front page with a long story detailing his life and that of several of his children. I handed the paper back to Mickey. "I'm surprised I didn't get a call. Jesus, Gerry must be devastated. I remember the day my da died like it was yesterday. I can't honestly say I was close to my da. We lived in different worlds, didn't we? But he was still my da and I miss him yet."

"Ian, was Gerry close to his da?"

"I can't say he ever talked of his da. They had a falling out of some sort. They weren't on talking terms. Just the same, your da is your da. I'm surprised I didn't get a call, though I'm not eager to attend another funeral. I didn't notice in the article when services are to be held."

"The article didn't even mention services."

"Don't you find it odd, Mickey?"

"I do.

"Well, I should carry on. Thanks for the sandwich and the company, Mickey."

* * * * *

Mairin greeted me with a long, warm embrace. "Did that help, my love?"

Mairin took my hat and coat and hung them up in the hall closet. "You know walking the quay always brings me peace. It's the water, being near the water. I wandered over to Mickey's and ordered my favorite liver sandwich."

Mairin stepped back several paces from me. "I didn't smell it."

I laughed out loud, opened my arms, and gave her a bear hug. "Well, I said I ordered it, not that I ate it. Don't worry, I didn't have a drink, besides a strong cup of tea."

Mairin nestled her head on my shoulder and wrapped her arms around my waist. "I never doubted," she whispered. "Oh,

I have news for you. Someone from Sinn Fein called, he said Gerry wants to speak with you."

"I was dreading that call, my love."

"Dreading a call from Gerry? Ian, what are you talking about?" Mairin asked.

"His da died. I suppose I'm to attend the funeral."

"Well, that's surprising. The man leaving the message said it was about the elections later this month."

I pulled away to see Marin's face.

"Elections? God, I had forgotten about the elections. I think they're at the end of the month. I haven't bothered to keep up with current events in Northern Ireland. What could Gerry possibly want from me? Did the caller leave any specific instructions?"

"No, he didn't. That's strange. I didn't even think to ask. What does it mean, Ian?"

My shoulders slumped and my right hand spontaneously clenched into a fist. "It means, my love, I'm driving to Belfast tomorrow. Gerry doesn't talk to anyone on the phone."

Mairin pulled me close to her and stroked the hair on the back of my neck. "Do you want company?"

"Of course. But it's not fair to you; I don't know how long I'll be gone. Gerry is a persuasive man. My guess is he wants me to work on the election. I should do some research tonight to understand the mood up there."

"This is the part of your life that's a mystery to me, my love. You get one phone call with a vague message and you go dashing off to Belfast. What hold does he have on you? Maybe it's just to attend the funeral. This is the second time you've put your life on hold to attend to Northern Ireland. I don't understand your motivation. The war is over. You helped create the peace. What more can you want? Are you incapable of moving on? Do you even *want* to move on?"

"I don't have secrets from you, Mairin. It's the way Sinn Fein operates. I do know Gerry is desperate for the Good Friday Agreement to work. He wants to show the world Northern Ireland can handle its own affairs, be civil, and have a government. It's a noble cause, really. Maybe we can't unify Ireland but we must demonstrate to the world that Northern Ireland can rule itself—without intervention from the British. If not, the Good Friday Accord was for nothing. We must trade in our guns for the vote – we must. If I can do anything, anything at all, I must. Who knows, maybe I can find redemption by helping Northern Ireland find its place in the world."

"God, it's such a long drive. I'll get up early and be on the road by seven. I want to be in Belfast by noon at the latest. I just hope Gerry will see me tomorrow. I don't want to lounge around for him to fit me into his schedule."

"Ian, you are the Irish Don Quixote. Try to get a good night's sleep tonight."

CHAPTER 5

I drove onto Falls Road exactly four and a half hours after leaving Cork. My bones ached. I stretched when I got out of the car. The Sinn Fein headquarters on Falls Road looked the same as of any brick office buildings in West Belfast. Inside the doors was a middle-aged man sitting behind a non-descript wood desk. Behind the man was a single metal door leading to the inner offices.

The man greeted me with a smile.

"Follow me, please, Mr. Murphy."

The office was like a bank executive's with a polished walnut conference table surrounded by massive leather padded chairs at one end and the biggest mahogany desk I've ever seen at the other. A group of men stood around one man seated at the desk. Papers were piled everywhere. The men were so engaged in conversation, no one noticed my entrance. I cleared my throat. No one turned in my direction.

"I have arrived," I said in my best baritone voice.

They turned and looked, then parted from around the desk. Gerry Adams looked up. A broad smile grew across his face. "Jesus, Ian, it's good to see you again!"

"I . . . I . . . I'm sorry I missed the funeral," I stammered.

"You weren't invited. Family affair. Now, I have some fantastic news, and I need the author of the Good Friday Agreement." Gerry gestured for me and his retinue to sit at the conference table. Gerry sat at the head of the table, and everyone else took their appointed seats, leaving the seat at the end of the table opposite Gerry for me.

"God, what a brain trust," Gerry said as he looked at each man around the table. "In less than a fortnight we are going to make history, gentlemen. I want to share the most recent polling with you. Our numbers for the Democratic Unionist Party are not much more than an educated guess, but it looks like they might gain ten seats."

"Bloody bastards!" the man on my left shouted.

Gerry motioned for silence. "But there is good news too. It looks good for us to gain six. We will be the second most powerful party in Northern Ireland. God, what a long road it has been."

Clapping erupted.

"Ian, why the puzzled look?" Gerry asked.

I could feel sweat bead beneath my shirt, and my right hand clenched into a fist a fighter would relish. "If the outlook is so good, I don't understand why I drove more than four hours to attend this meeting."

Gerry Adams had a skill for knowing people and their talents. He had led Sinn Fein for years because of his unique ability to lead men and to focus the energy of the organization in one consistent direction. There was always the rumor he was also a member of the Irish Republican Army, maybe even one of their generals. In the end it didn't matter if he was or wasn't. Anyone who observed Adams over the years would learn he devoted all of his energy to a political solution to the Troubles in Northern Ireland. This was only the second election since the 1998 Peace Accord. Having elections where Catholics could vote without intervention or harassment was a miracle. Adams had used his political astuteness to position Sinn Fein to be the dominate Republican Party in just five short years.

I avoided eye contact with Gerry, I breathed in deeply and slowly released my breath through pressed lips. I hadn't expected this. "Well, Gerry, the truth is. Well, you know, you all know I'm, I'm shy. Hell, I've lived as a near recluse most of my life. I was in my late 40s when I finally fell in love, and it was a near fatal mistake. I can write. I can write speeches. I can write editorials. I could do a radio interview, but I don't want to meet a group of strangers."

Gerry leaned back in his chair and ran his hands through thick black hair. He brought his hands down on the table, slapping them with his palms. He leaned toward me and stared directly into my eyes. "This is our moment, Ian. You have the opportunity to be part of history again. Don't you want to be part of history?"

"No desire whatsoever," I whispered.

"I won't order you."

I pulled at my collar and could feel myself blush. "I . . . I just need some time to digest what you're asking of me, Gerry."

Gerry Adams bolted upright in his chair. "Time is not something we have now. The election is in nine short days."

My back stiffened. I put my hands up in resignation. "I'll need to call Mairin. Arrangements with the college might be a bit more difficult."

"I've already talked with Dean Foley; a brief sabbatical has been arranged."

Barry got up as I left Gerry's office and handed me the file. I was escorted outside where a car waited for me.

The driver had curly black hair and no neck. "Afternoon, Mr. Murphy. It's my pleasure to be meetin' you and an honor to be yer driver. Carrick is my name."

"Hello Carrick. Please call me Ian. No need to be formal."

"Wait till I tell the missus I can use yer first name God, this is a fine job. Sinn Fein, they took care of me an' my family, I can tell you fer sure. I best not linger. We don't have a long drive but I want you to rest before dinner. St. Teresa is my family church."

The tires squealed when the car stopped. "Here it is," Carrick shouted to me in the back seat. The file flew out of my hand and scattered papers across the back seat. I gathered up the papers on the floor and stuffed them into the folder. "Thank you. When will you pick me up, Carrick?"

"Half five. Dinner begins promptly at six. You'll have time for a beer and to mingle a bit, meet some of the folks."

"Should I ask for anyone in particular?" My curiosity overflowed.

"Father Houlihan will find you, no problem. Can I get you anything? Another man will bring up yer luggage."

"Luggage? Did you see any luggage? When I drove up here today I had no idea I'd be staying for ten days." I started to open the car door.

"We'll take care of it first thing in the mornin'. See you soon."

* * * * *

My room was like a prison. One average-size bed with a rail type metal headboard sat against one wall; the phone sat on a small steel table on one side of the room. No windows, of course. And the walls were painted battleship gray. Just passing the time until Carrick returned for me would be a challenge. A man named MacBride introduced himself and escorted me to my room. *When MacBride returns, I'll ask him for newspapers or magazines, something, anything to read. But first things first.* I walked over to the small table and picked up the phone.

"Mairin, it's Ian. We need to talk. This evening I'm attending dinner at St. Teresa Roman Catholic Church. I'll call again later. Of course, there's not a number I can give you here. Talk to you soon, I love you."

* * * * *

Reading a week's worth of newspapers, time did pass without boredom creeping into the room. The dinner was pleasant, not a culinary highlight; it was West Belfast, after all. Father Houlihan was a gracious host and introduced me to everyone attending the dinner, which was a blessing because it reduced the amount of time I had to speak. From my perspective the thoughts I shared with the congregation were rather obvious observations on the current political climate. The audience was true believers and my major role was simply to reinforce what they always believed and to make sure they understood how important it was to cast their vote. Father Houlihan announced that both volunteers from the church and Sinn Fein were available throughout election day to provide rides to the polling places. One call to the church office could guarantee a voter a ride within thirty minutes of the call. I was impressed with their organization, another Gerry Adams attribute.

They applauded at the close of my remarks. It was clear, from their perspective, I was someone important because I had been an IRA man and helped write the Good Friday Agreement. I was vested in their future. I didn't like being noticed and would have preferred to stay in my room and write. The evening taught me I had a greater responsibility and reminded me that words of the Good Friday Agreement meant nothing if they didn't come alive through the electoral process. Gerry Adams understood, which is why he didn't give me a choice. I had learned a valuable lesson. I hoped I was always open to learning. *Is this my path to atone for my past?*

* * * * *

Carrick's driving was getting on my nerves. He always drove as if escaping from some IRA engagement in days of old. I didn't have the courage to ask him to change his driving habits so I braced myself in the back seat and prepared for the roller coaster-like ride through Belfast. Besides, I wanted to get back to the safe house to call Mairin again.

"Do you have the time, Carrick?"

"Yes sir, nine p.m. Do you not have a watch?"

"No, I don't wear a watch or carry a pocket time piece; it's just an idiosyncrasy."

I opened the car door and looked over my shoulder toward Carrick. "Have a good evening, Carrick."

"I'll pick you up at half ten for a bit of shopping. Goodnight."

I paced back and forth, holding the receiver as the phone rang. It felt like it rang at least twelve times, but I must have been wrong.

"Hello, dear." Mairin's voice was soft and inviting.

"Mairin?"

"I've been by the telephone all evening. What has happened, Ian? Have they had the funeral for Gerry's da? I haven't seen an article in the newspapers here."

I sat down on the floor next to the little metal table and braced my back to the wall, pulling my knees up close to my chest. "I wasn't invited to the funeral. There's some sort of family row about it. I don't need another funeral, so it doesn't bother me."

"Then why are you there, and why did you attend a church supper tonight?"

"The general election is in just nine days. Gerry feels this is the moment the party has been waiting for; they can really challenge the Unionist. He wants me to stay to rally support and get Catholics to vote." There was a long moment of silence as Mairin absorbed what I was telling her.

"You're going to be gone for nine days? What about your classes?"

"Gerry arranged for a sabbatical until the end of term."

Mairin didn't speak for what seemed like an eternity. "Mairin, my love?"

"Am I to understand you didn't have a choice in all this?"

"It was an expectation. I wasn't asked to come under false pretense. No one said to come for the funeral. The message was just to come, so I did. He wants me to do this in remembrance of Kieran."

"Do you want me to come up?"

"You are adorable. Of course I would want you to join me. But it isn't practical and certainly not fair to you. They have an iron-clad schedule for me. We wouldn't have time for ourselves. Gerry's given me the challenge of bringing life to the Good Friday Agreement so it isn't just words on paper."

"The man does know how to pull your strings."

"It's his specialty."

"You didn't take clothes or anything. What are you going to do?"

"They provided some basics for tonight. They've put me in a safe house, and there's a man outside for security. Tomorrow morning my driver, Carrick, is taking me shopping. I'm being well cared for."

"No one said life would be boring with you, Ian Murphy. When do you plan on coming home?"

"The election is on the 26th. I'll drive home on the 27th. I'll insist on it."

"Once again, I don't have a choice. Do you realize how much time we've been apart since we were married? I wonder, do you care?"

"Mairin, that's not fair."

"What's not fair is your obsession with Northern Ireland."

"I could make a difference. Ireland will see me differently after the election."

"Now you've finally spoken the truth. You think working on this election will give you the redemption you've been searching for."

"Well . . ."

"Don't call again, Ian. I need some space. I'll see you on the 27th. God willing you find what you're searching for. By the way, William Boyle called and left a message. He's driving to Cork. Have you heard from him since the funeral?"

"No, not at all. That is odd. Did he mention the purpose of his visit? Did he say when he was coming?"

I waited for Mairin to say something but all she said was "You must be exhausted, good night."

"I love you, Mairin." The receiver clicked. I sat on the floor cradling the phone on my shoulder, wishing Mairin could be in my arms tonight.

CHAPTER 7

The days passed like the sluggish River Lee meandering to the Celtic Sea. My schedule was full. Each day I would have breakfast with a club like the Knights of Columbus or a similar group and dinner would be at one of the parish churches. I was certain the trip would result in me needing to loosen another notch or two in my belt. I hoped not sleeping well the first night would result in being tired beyond exhaustion and I'd have the gift of the sleep of the dead. I also thought my schedule would distract me enough to avoid loneliness, but I was wrong on both counts.

After two nights of less than four hours sleep, I was desperate. When Carrick picked me up on the third morning, I was dragging. He picked me up for breakfast at half six. I opened the car door and slithered into the back seat.

Carrick watched me in the rearview mirror. "Jesus, Ian, your eyes are bloodshot. What kind of impression are ya goin' to give my mates?"

I looked back at him in the mirror and ran my hand across my face.

"These early breakfast meetings are breakin' you. I'll see what I can do."

"Bless you, Carrick. Maybe I could meet with them after they've eaten, to give me a bit more time in the morning. Now please, pull away slowly. My stomach can't take your normal jolting take off."

Carrick turned around to look me in the eyes. "Whatever you want, Ian. I hope you get some sleep soon. Now, here we go."

* * * * *

The neighborhood association welcomed me with open arms due to my public condemnation of the peace walls which they supported. Because of groups like theirs, hope for peace still simmered in Belfast. Meeting with various groups it was clear, as Belfast went, so went the whole of Northern Ireland. Belfast alone held about 15 percent of the country's population. For hundreds of years Belfast has been the heart and soul of Northern Ireland.

I asked the members of the neighborhood association what their plans were for getting out the vote. I was surprised a detailed plan had already been developed. Flyers had been hand delivered to every home with the addresses of the polling places and a special note on which polling place to cast their vote. On the back of the flyer was a map of the polling location. At the bottom of the map a phone number was listed to call for a free ride to and from the polling place.

I waved the flyer in my hand. "This is most extraordinary. You are the most organized group I have visited so far. With your permission I will share some of your innovations with others as I visit them in the next few days."

A stern looking young man too thin for his age, stood up. "Alfred Feeney, Mr. Murphy. On election day there's a group of us who will spend the day canvassing the neighborhood to ask our neighbors if they've voted. Our goal is 100 percent turnout."

I gasped and my back stiffened. "Incredible, Mr. Feeney. I will make sure to watch the election returns in detail to see if you're successful. There is certainly nothing more to be done to ensure the vote. I will personally share your plan with Gerry

Adams. In fact, he may pay you a visit himself. Thank you all for your time and your commitment."

A loud voice came from near the door. "Mr. Murphy?" Carrick lifted his arm and pointed to his watch. I finished shaking the last person's hand. "Excuse me, I must move on to my next appointment. I am on a short leash, don't you see. I will make sure to tell Gerry what you have accomplished. Thank you. Thank you."

Once in the car, Carrick scowled at me in the rearview mirror. "I'm done."

He handed three sacks back to me containing everything on the list I had given him before the meeting. One contained the whiskey, one contained the tobacco tin and a pipe, and the third had a pile of books, all works of Yeats.

"You are a miracle worker, Carrick!"

Carrick slapped his forehead. "Oh, there's one more thing." He stretched across the front seat and dug through the glove box. "Lordy, I hope I didn't lose it," he mumbled to himself.

I stretched toward the front seat, watching him pull things out of the glove box. He appeared desperate to find something. I looked again closely, expecting to find a revolver hidden there and thought it would be an unlikely and impractical hiding place. If there was a pistol in the car, it would be under the driver's seat.

Carrick's arm flew up and he shouted, "Mercy on my soul, here it is!" He reached over the seat and handed me a plain white envelope.

"What's this?" I asked.

"Open it."

I tore the end of the envelope and blew into it, taking out some sort of a ticket. It read: "Lyric Theatre, Friday, 21 November, *On Baile's Strand*, W.B. Yeats, 8:00 p.m., Row 5, Seat 1." I yelped with joy and slapped Carrick on the shoulder.

"This is amazing! Do you know, this is one of Yeat's classics? The play is steeped in Irish mythology. How did you do this, Carrick?"

Carrick sat up straight and puffed out his chest. "I talked to Mr. Adams myself, I did. I told him you were feeling lonely, stuck in the safe house all night. I got told to wait in the outer office. In a little while a pretty red-head handed me the envelope. She told me I had to work tonight, to take you to the theatre and to get an early supper so I could wait for you."

I fell back into the seat, speechless. Tears came to my eyes, and wiped them away with a quick brush of my hand, hoping Carrick didn't notice. "I am in your debt, Carrick. I cannot express how much this means to me. There's only one ticket. Would you like to go? If Adams can get one ticket, he can get two."

Carrick shook his head back and forth with vigor. "Oh, no. Not me."

CHAPTER 8

jolted off the bed from pounding at the door. "Mr. Murphy, Murphy! Carrick is here to fetch you." MacBride shouted as loud as he could.

I threw on my tweed jacket and grabbed my ticket off the table by the bed. I rushed to the door and opened it so hard it hit the wall. "I'm off. Thanks for waking me."

"You'll be needing an overcoat, Mr. Murphy. It's more than a bit nippy outside tonight."

I waved MacBride off. "I'll be in the car, no worries." Carrick was revving the engine to make sure he got off to a jump-start.

"Evening, Ian. We'll make curtain, but just." He pulled away from the curb before I could get the back door shut.

"How much time do we have?" I asked.

"The show starts in twenty-five minutes," Carrick said.

We drove at a snail's pace. I began to fidget in the back seat. "Carrick, why are you driving at this speed?"

"We're goin' downtown, and two old IRA guys don't want to be picked up. So, easy it goes. I'd rather make you late for the show than end up in gaol."

"I thought the Northern Ireland Police Act passed earlier this year resolved the problems of the past."

Carrick turned his head to look at me, disbelief crossed his brow.

"This is Northern Ireland; give it a decade, maybe then."

There was a light fog as we approached the River Lagan. A swirling mist hung below the streetlights giving the neighborhood a mysterious look. The air was cool and the River Lagan creped along; a gray mist hung over the water. The Lyric was a brick building nestled in grayness, floodlights piercing the night sky. People were jockeying to get through the front door. I turned up the collar of my coat as I jumped out of the car. Carrick made a rolling stop, I fell forward but caught myself before toppling onto the sidewalk. The Lyric is the only performing arts theatre in Northern Ireland, which is a testimony to the culture of the country. I had read the building has received several architectural awards. Glancing up at the structure it felt familiar. I squinted when I walked into the atrium; a warm breeze struck me in the face. I walked toward the theatre doors with the ticket in my outstretched hand.

"Good evening Mr. Murphy."

I looked at the young man extending his hand to pluck the ticket out of my fist. I guessed he was a student from the Performing Arts School. He wore a white shirt with a starched collar, French cuffs and a thin black necktie. I thought I should know his name. *Why would I know his name? How does he know mine?*

The Lyric was an intimate theatre with less than 400 seats. I made my way to my aisle seat and was the last seated in the row. As I sat down, I was struck by an odd sense of nostalgia – like I was where I belonged, as if the audience was there for me. I scratched my head, shivered, and felt a tingle run down my spine. I was lightheaded and couldn't breathe. *Why was this theatre so familiar?* Everyone in my aisle nodded and said good evening.

The house lights flickered several times. We were plunged into total darkness as the purple curtain opened across the stage. Again, the overwhelming sense of familiarity washed over me like a morning shower. My chest tightened. There was a whiff of fresh paint from the set. Someone close by reeked of cheap cigar smoke. I wandered off to the netherworld and saw myself in this seat, my stage play about to be performed. I took deep diaphragm breaths and forced my attention to the stage. My right hand clenched into a boxer's fist, the fierce pain bringing me back to reality.

CHAPTER 9

MacBride snuck through the door and put a huge mug of steaming tea on the side table, turned on his heel, and walked away without a word.

"What time is my first appointment?"

"Noon today, sir. A lunch, I believe. You can have an easy morning.

I sipped my morning tea and thought about the events that brought me here. The mystery to me was why it had taken five years after the Good Friday Agreement to generate this fervor for civil involvement. In 1998 the resolution for accepting the Good Friday Agreement passed by only 60 percent in Northern Ireland. The vote in the Republic of Ireland was more than 90 percent in favor. Could the population of the Republic of Ireland be more supportive of peace than those in Northern Ireland? From my two ventures into Northern Ireland, I saw their distrust and exhaustion. History was not on the Catholic's side. Gerry Adams had fought an uphill battle to engage people and give them hope. From my experience there was less a sense of hope here than in most of Europe.

* * * * *

I didn't know what to do with myself on Wednesday, the day of the vote. It was impossible to contact Gerry, and I didn't want to bother him. I paced back and forth in the cell in the safe house. Being pent up in the room was unacceptable. I had MacBride call for Carrick. After asking for him, I wondered if it may have been a mistake; he was most likely busy driving people to the polls.

* * * * *

People in Sinn Fein headquarters were shoulder to shoulder. In the large hall a television was put on a stand and everyone watched the results. Within two hours after polls closed, the results were clear and greeted with cheers and toasts by an exuberant crowd. As Gerry predicted, Sinn Fein gained six seats. Ian Paisley's party had thirty seats and Sinn Fein, twenty-four seats and had mustered 23.5 percent of the vote. Sinn Fein would now be in a position to broker a shared governance agreement. I had a staff member rush me to the safe house to call Mairin.

"It's over, I'm coming home tomorrow, Mairin. My life without you is hollow. I want our life together back again."

"I want to hear about what you've accomplished but you sound exhausted so I'll wait until you can hold me in your arms and talk. Get some sleep. I do love you. Until tomorrow." As Mairin eased the phone into the cradle, a smile crossed her lips.

My mind reviewed the past nine days like a line in an oldie film. *Had my involvement meant anything?* This single election didn't bring me closure from the days of hammering out the Peace Accord. Change in Northern Ireland was measured in decades, not years. The people of Northern Ireland had accepted me, the Catholics at least. I didn't sense any anger or rejection because of my IRA days. It was impossible to know if they forgave me, were indifferent, or just unaware of who I was. I am, at least, done with it all. I came expecting that working on the election might atone for my days in the IRA. It didn't. My life remains hollow. *I am a simple man. I want a life with Mairin, time to write, and my work at the University of Cork. I must find a way to carry on without atonement.*

God, I need a whiskey.

It was the only way to sleep.

The little room in the safe house swallowed me.

CHAPTER 10

It was difficult keeping within the speed limit driving back to Cork. I didn't bother with breakfast because it often made me nauseous to eat before a long road trip. I limited my tea to two cups so I wouldn't need to stop for relief. I was making my way south by eight a.m., which put me in Cork by noon. I would have a few hours to gather myself together before Mairin came home from work.

* * * * *

The car clock read twelve when I drove into Cork center. I thought there was enough time to stop by O'Connaill's to pick up gourmet chocolate for Mairin. She had a weakness for chocolate and anything from O'Connaill's, though putting up with my unexpected absence for nine days deserved a lot more than candy. After purchasing the candy, I stopped by to see Mickey.

When I entered the pub there were only a few stragglers from the noon meal. One man at the bar had his faced buried in a newspaper. An older man and woman sat at a table near the window engaged in soft conversation. I didn't see any staff and waited at the bar. The doors from the kitchen flew open. Emma, one of the long-time staff, came out backwards. She twirled around with a bowl of soapy water and a towel thrown over her shoulder. "For the love of God, Mr. Murphy, it's you!"

"Emma, it's good to be back. Is he in?"

"And where else would he be? It's inventory day so you'll find him in the cellar."

The cellar stairway was notorious and had been the cause of many tumbles. I had hounded Mickey to replace the worn wood with a simple metal stair but his stubbornness knew no bounds. I took one step at a time and kept my hand on the wall for balance.

"I'm doin' inventory. Ya knows Thursday is inventory day. Now don't bother me. I'll be up soon," Mickey shouted, assuming it was someone from the kitchen.

"I need to see your ugly face, Mickey O'Shay."

"Jesus, Joseph, an Mary, there he is, Ian Murphy himself, back from savin' the people of Northern Ireland from themselves. I saw you on the news." Mickey came out from behind a stack of boxes and shook my hand so hard it was sore. "Ya look like a man who could use a drink." He rushed past me and scampered up the stairs. "Come on, then."

"Draught ale would suit me, Mickey."

"No whiskey?"

"It's early my friend, and I still have to drive home. I can only stay about thirty minutes. I want to be home for a while before the end of Mairin's day."

* * * * *

At home I unpacked, checked the mail, and called my department head to let him know I would be back in class next week. Since my leave was approved through the end of the term, he suggested I might want to take the time to research or begin a writing project. It was difficult to tell if he was being kind or maybe Mairin had told him about my recent bout of writer's block. I told him I would consider his kind offer and call him the next day. Before making a decision, I wanted to discuss it with Mairin.

I found a 1996 bottle of French wine we were saving for a special occasion, poured two glasses, and arranged the chocolates on a plate, then waited for Mairin in our bedroom. I heard the front door slam, then footsteps up the stairs."

"Oh, Ian!"

Mairin ran into my arms, nearly knocking me over from where I sat on the bed. She held my face with both her hands and kissed me with tenderness. Her magnolia scent was intoxicating. I wrapped my arms around her in a bear hug, never wanting to let go.

"I bought you chocolate, and this is the '96 we've been saving. I thought this was a special enough occasion." Her tender kisses made my pulse race. I rolled over and poured us each a full glass of wine and handed one to Mairin. Her hazel eyes were brilliant. *Ta mo chroi istigh ionat.* " (My heart is in you.)

"Ian, you know I swoon when you speak Irish."

"Mo chuisle." (pulse of my heart).

After we finished the first goblet of wine, I was light headed. Mairin giggled. "You're getting me drunk, Ian Murphy."

"No, not drunk on wine, drunk on love and ecstasy. It's hell being separated from you. I swear that will never happen again. My pain was culpable. Sleeping alone was agonizing, and I confess, many nights I slept with the bottle."

"Shhhhh. Not now, Ian. I want you. I want all of you."

* * * * *

The morning sunlight pierced our bedroom. There was an unfamiliar sound outside. I went to the window. I shielded my eyes and squinted to find the source of the noise. Living in the city was proving more of a challenge than I expected. My cottage in West Cork wasn't secluded but it was much quieter than our home. Mairin's decision to put my writing room on the third floor was brilliant. I was accustomed to being on my own and having a third-floor room let me keep the illusion.

"What's the matter, Ian?" Mairin asked.

"Just thought I heard something outside. So, did William mention why he was visiting?" I sat on the bed next to Mairin.

"The first thing you ask this morning is about William? Wouldn't you like to know how I filled my days? But to answer you, no, he didn't. He asked if he could call soon after your return, and I shared our address."

I sat on the edge of the bed, trying to organize my thoughts. Food would help since I didn't have either lunch or dinner yesterday. I felt ashamed for asking about William and not asking Mairin how she dealt with my unexpected absence. I still have awkward times with social matters, even with the love of my life. I took Mairin's hands into mine, looked her in the eyes, and leaned in close. "I apologize, my love. I had this bizarre dream about Kieran last night. He was scolding me for not taking care of William. I wonder if I'm supposed to be part of William's life? Forgive me for not asking how you managed the past ten days. I'll make breakfast and we can talk all morning, if you like."

We had her favorite breakfast of oatmeal with coddled cream and fruit. I took the time to listen and enjoy how Mairin adapted to my unexpected absence.

"Listen, I called O'Reilly yesterday afternoon and told him I could return to class next week. He said my sabbatical was approved until the end of the term. He suggested I take the time off to begin a little writing. Did you have anything to do with his suggestion?"

Mairin has never been a person capable of keeping secrets or being anything less than completely honest. Her authenticity attracted me. Mairin lowered her eyes and sheepishly looked up at me. She hid her face in her hands and moved her fingers apart to peek at me.

"I have my answer. You don't really need to say anything, my love. I understand. I had a mystical experience at the Lyric

Theatre. I'm still trying to understand, but I feel it may change the direction of my writing. You know I've been uncomfortable with the idea of writing a memoir. Who would really care or want to know about my exploits? Yet, there is something lingering inside me that I just can't grasp. Be patient. But for now, let me respond to this dream message from Kieran."

Mairin's eyes became soft and tears ran down her cheeks. "As long as we are together, everything is fine. I'll never be your judge; I am the one always and forever at your side."

Mairin decided not to go into work, we lounged around the house happy to have a day without interruption. While I wanted to contact William, I also wanted time for myself. In Belfast I was at Gerry's beck and call, a soldier drafted into his army. Even though my heart and soul believed in what Sinn Fein was doing, I was still drafted; I didn't enlist. I thought about calling Caitlin but I didn't want to engage in a conversation about Belfast and Sinn Fein politics so I decided to avoid my sister, for a few days anyway. Of course, Mairin was right. I should contact her, but not today. Maybe tomorrow. She could come for Sunday dinner.

Throughout the day my dream haunted me, and I decided the only thing to do was to contact William and learn why he urgently needed to see me. A young person's view of what is urgent is much different from a middle-aged person like myself.

He doesn't seem to fit in with the rest of the Fitzpatrick clan. I told Mickey we would stop in soon for dinner. Why don't we take William to Mickey's tomorrow? Give him a taste of traditional Cork."

Mairin got up and walked toward the kitchen. "That would be nice. I feel like a cup of French hot chocolate. Interested?"

"No, too rich for me. I'm going up to my room to read. I have several Yeats plays I picked up in Belfast calling me. I won't be long. I'll call William tomorrow."

CHAPTER 11

The next day was a classic Cork November day. It was only six degrees centigrade when I left the house and the high for the day was expected to be eight degrees. This was not weather to ride my bicycle to campus. At the beginning of the semester I turned down an assignment for a parking spot. Looking back at that decision, it was shortsighted. I remember the days when I rode my bicycle to campus every day, even in the rain. At the age of fifty-five I had to admit to myself those days were gone. I had assignments to grade, so I decided to go in before Mairin left for the day. It proved to be shortsighted. It turned out to be a day of bad decisions.

The Eireann bus was only two blocks from the house. Mairin insisted I purchase an annual pass for times like these. She packed the pass in my briefcase, which was always in my hand when I left the house. I pulled up my coat collar and walked to the bus stop. As luck would have it, the bus for campus pulled up within moments. The dampness made my hat limp and my nose began to run in a disgusting clear drivel into my mustache. Mairin also put several packs of tissue in my briefcase for times like these. It was a wonder to me how she was so detailed in the little aspects of daily survival. Her ability to organize and plan was far beyond anything I could muster on my own.

I arrived at my office, made a cup of tea, and settled in to check the mail, meeting minutes, and the administrative humdrum of college life. Several in our department are natural teachers; I am not one of them. I can't really say I "teach" in the accepted pedagogical practice. I was not teaching the students, they taught themselves. Today we were to meet at half two.

* * * * *

After class I went to my office and was mulling over our discussion when I was startled by a sharp rap on my office door. *Maybe it was a mistake.* The next knock rattled the door. "Don't damage the door! Come in!" I shouted. A short man not weighing more than sixty kilograms with ruffled blond hair rushed into the room. "Mr. Murphy, your wife called to remind you of the time." The messenger turned on his heel and left the room without another word. I rushed down the hall to the department secretary. "What time is it?"

"Half four," she said without looking up from her work.

I've done it now. I was instructed to be home by four because we have a guest arriving from County Donegal. I sprinted back to my office, snapped my briefcase shut, and plunged into my hat and coat. I was out the door and waiting at the bus stop in just a few minutes. In the early evening the buses run every ten minutes so I felt confident I could be home no later than five o'clock.

Mairin and William were having a cup of tea when I rushed into the living room. I let my briefcase drop on the carpet. "William, it is good to see you again. Forgive my tardiness. Mairin instructed me when to be home when I left for campus this morning. I'm sure Mairin has been the perfect host."

William jumped to his feet and we shook hands. "No worry, Mr. Murphy. Mrs. Murphy and I have had a pleasant conversation."

"Let's drop the formalities right now. Please, it's Ian and Mairin. Did you take the train or drive? With the stop at Dublin, I know the train takes most of the day." I slipped off my coat and hat and laid them across the closest chair.

61

Mairin planned our home to be able to entertain guests and make them comfortable with the parlor and dining room on the first floor and a small, efficient kitchen in the rear. We could host twelve guests comfortably. I learned Mairin likes to host small gatherings of folks mostly from college. This was a radical change for me from my days of seclusion in my West Cork cottage. Having William here felt right.

"I drove down. I didn't want to waste the entire day on the train. Besides, I thought it would be convenient to have a car in Cork."

I leaned forward and pulled the chair closer to William. "In Cork? Are you moving to Cork?"

"I am."

A broad smile crossed Mairin's face, a smile of both happiness and relief, which I didn't understand. "Then let us be the first to welcome you to Ireland's finest city. You know, we have the reputation for being the most European city in Ireland."

I got up and retrieved my coat. "This calls for a celebration. Mairin, I told Mickey we would come by for dinner this week and now we have the perfect opportunity. William, we're eager to learn what brings you to Cork. I confess, I can't imagine what it could be. Now, let me take your teacup into the kitchen and we can be off. If you're going to be living here, you must become familiar with the best pub in the city, Mickey O'Shay's. I have a great deal of history there. The owner and I are fast friends. Why, I've known the man for more than thirty years. Can you imagine? God knows I'm getting old when I can have a friend for thirty years. You're not even thirty years old, are you?" I didn't wait for an answer but took their cups straight to the kitchen.

"Mairin, dear, would you mind driving so I can talk with William?" I asked as I helped her put on her jacket.

"Of course I'll drive. Give me a moment to find the keys. William, has anyone ever told you that you resemble your uncle Kieran; I think it's your stunning red hair. You two chat; I think the keys must be upstairs."

I looked directly into William's face. "Mairin is right, of course, you are like Kieran in his younger days. It's more than the hair; you have his eyes too."

William blushed and averted my look. "Until recently no one except my mother ever mentioned it to me. I find it odd, really. The member of the family who was the most mysterious and led a secretive life is somehow resurrected in me. No one ever said it before the funeral. Maybe it's the sadness; people look for something to hang on to, or they need a memory. I look in the mirror and don't see it myself."

I patted William on the back and ushered him to the car park. "Don't let it worry you. They all mean it as a compliment. Your uncle Kieran was admired. They didn't know exactly what he did but they knew he was a soldier for the cause, a true Republican, and it made them proud. You have a fine heritage, young man."

* * * * *

I introduced William to Mickey, who guided us back to the Ian Murphy table in the corner of the pub. Mairin, William, and I tucked ourselves in and talked all evening without being interrupted. Mickey, as usual, was the perfect host. He brought a bottle of Midleton, setting it in the center of the table with three glasses. I knew he was being kind but I winced when the whiskey arrived. Under the table I squeezed Mairin's hand and gave her a sad puppy dog look. She tipped her head toward me and smiled. She filled each of the glasses half full. "To William and the life he will forge in Cork!" Mairin raised her glass in a toast.

I was surprised she poured me a whiskey. Every day I fought off the darkness, and I had to admit, not drinking helped me win my daily battle. When I was in Belfast, it was a lost cause. The surprise of being asked to participate in the election and the loss of privacy and control over my life while I was there were too much stress for me. Without my nightly Bushmills, I would have never slept. True, I slept in an alcohol-induced stupor but I slept. I let it slip the first night together with Mairin but she never commented. Her understanding and lack of judgment sustained me from day to day. *I don't deserve Mairin. I need to transform my life for her if not for myself. Is it possible?* Tonight was a unique celebration so the whiskey wasn't to forget or sleep, as it usually was with me.

"To William!" I echoed and clinked our glasses.

William had a broad toothy grin on his face and he blushed as red as his hair.

"Your uncle never had a such a smile! You see, William, you are your own man," I said.

William rolled his glass between both hands and breathed in the floral aroma of the whiskey. He closed his eyes and took a small sip, holding it in his mouth before swallowing. "I've heard it's the most expensive whiskey in Ireland. Is it?" William asked.

"Well, they don't give it away, do they?" I said.

"Your uncle and Ian could finish off a bottle in one sitting, and I'm afraid they did it more often than I would like to know. Ian, of course, would never admit it. We should make sure to have a decent dinner tonight. Ian, do you know what Mickey's special is tonight?" Mairin asked.

I confess I wasn't listening to Mairin. The experience of sipping Ireland's finest whiskey after three months abstinence was overwhelming. I closed my eyes, just as William had done, allowing the nose of the Midleton to permeate my senses. The first sip rested in my mouth, then I swallowed slowly, letting it glide down my throat. I forgot Mairin and William were sitting at the table with me.

"Ian!" Mairin said in a scolding tone.

I let the glass slip through my hands but caught it before it crashed on the table. With wide eyes I looked first at Mairin and then William. I couldn't find words. I stared at the glass and discovered it half gone. I thought I had sipped while in reality I gulped it down. I floundered for a response. "I'm sorry. Mickey will bring us something soon."

Mickey appeared, balancing a tray with three steaming bowls of potato leek soup, cloth napkins, and spoons. "Here yous are. This recipe has been in my family for generations. There's none better in Cork, I can tell you. Take your time; I'm havin' the kitchen make Ian's favorite main dish. It will complement the whiskey. By the end of the evening, I don't want to see a single drop in the bottle."

"Ian Murphy, you are the luckiest man. His soup does have a reputation in town, William. Ian is probably the only man in Cork who is served a delicious meal without ever having to order. I don't know how you do it," Mairin said.

I put my head over the bowl and ate big spoonfuls of soup, I was better off to busy myself with eating rather than having conversation. Mairin can get a tone in her voice that is both authoritative and challenging, and I have learned being quiet is my best defense. Just as I dropped my spoon into the empty bowl, Niahm – one of my favorite servers – and a young woman I didn't know, arrived at our table with dinner. The main dish was a whole roasted salmon with a bowl overflowing with colcannon, a plate with a stack of brown bread, and a bowl of butter. The young woman put a plate and silverware on the table for each of us, then Niahm placed the platter with the salmon in the center of the table and with incredible skill found room for the other dishes.

"May I serve you?" Niahm asked.

"Oh, so elegant. Yes, please," Mairin said.

"It's good to see you, Niahm. Let me introduce William Butler Boyle, our newest Cork resident. You should introduce the new staff, or new to me, at least," I said.

Niahm cut and served the salmon with the expertise of a person with exceptional and practiced skill. "Yes, sir. This is Shannon. She's worked here about a month. This is her first job in service, and she's shadowing me."

"Hello, Shannon," the three of us said like an acapella choir.

"Pay close attention, Shannon, there is none better than Niahm. I make sure Niahm gets a 20 percent tip; she earns it. She's put up with me for years. It's not fair for you to split the tip so I will make sure you each receive 20 percent."

"Thank you, sir. That's so generous," Shannon said.

"Not so much generous, as appreciative. Mairin, please put a large spoonful of colcannon on my plate. I'm hungry. William, take a slice of the brown bread and pass the plate, then tell us your story about why you are moving to Cork. I can't hold my curiosity in abeyance any longer."

William ate as though this was his first meal of the day. I didn't want to ask because it might embarrass him. I had no idea what his financial situation might have been, but he recently graduated from Trinity and student life was always frugal. He told me at the funeral he attended Trinity on scholarship, which meant there wasn't very much, if any, financial support from home. William wiped his mouth with a napkin and then filled each of our glasses with Midleton.

"No more for me. I plan on driving you both home this evening," Mairin instructed.

"It was delicious," William said, putting his fork down on his now-empty plate. "I think I'll make Mickey's a regular spot."

I pushed my plate to one side and pulled the glass of whiskey toward me. I stretched out my legs to get comfortable. "There's no better salmon to be found in Cork. Now, William, share your story, please."

William took a long drink of the whiskey and set the glass down with great care. "About a fortnight after the funeral, my Ma received a phone call from one of the local solicitors, Martin Gallagher. He asked when Ma wanted to come in for the reading. Ma told him she didn't understand what he was asking; she didn't know what a reading was. 'The will,' he told her, 'reading the last will and testament of Kieran Fitzpatrick.' Ma said she dropped the phone in disbelief. She told Mr. Gallagher she had no idea her brother had a will. Then Mr. Gallagher suggested I attend the reading, and in fact, it was imperative for me to attend. Mr. Gallagher explained I must attend the reading because I was the only beneficiary of Uncle Kieran's will.

"The next day we walked to Mr. Gallagher's office on Castle Street. The office wasn't impressive, about the size of a snug. Uncle Kieran left me 62,000 euros. My ma fainted in her chair and nearly toppled to the floor. It took Mr. Gallagher and me several minutes to revive her. Once she was settled again, he offered her a glass of water."

I leaned in close to William and whispered, "Euros and not Irish pounds?"

"I was surprised, too. Uncle Kieran was such a patriot. I assumed any money he had would be in Irish pounds. Mr. Gallagher explained he had taken the liberty to turn in the Irish pounds for euros with the currency exchange program last year."

"He was doing his job to the best of his ability," Ian said. "It must have been your uncle's entire life saving. Amazing.

Just amazing." I fingered my mustache, thinking about another aspect of my friend that was a surprise.

"Then Mr. Gallagher explained that Uncle Kieran had written explicit conditions for me to receive the money in a letter addressed to me. Mr. Gallagher handed me the letter, written by hand, from Uncle Kieran."

William fumbled through his jacket pockets and brought out a crumpled brown envelope. "Here. it's best if you read it, Ian."

I opened the envelope. The paper inside was torn in several places. I looked at Mairin and shrugged my shoulders. I removed the single sheet slowly so as not to tear it. The handwriting was very small and was more printing rather than cursive.

Dear Willie,

If you are reading this letter, I am dead and that is that. I want you to know how proud I am you found a way to leave Ballyshannon and attend college. Like my friend, Ian Murphy, college can be your path to a better life. I have never had any use for money so during my lifetime I just saved it for a rainy day. That day came when I had to use a bit of it when I was in hiding, and I found odd jobs to support myself. All I have is for you. All the other members of the family are doing fine and I don't think they need any more money. You have a future. I squandered my life fighting for Ireland, and in the end, it didn't matter. I've come to accept there will never be a united Ireland. My friend Ian helped me accept the sad truth. With the peace, people do have a chance again. The young people, like you, are Ireland's hope. If you accept the money, there are two conditions. First, you must use it to continue your education. I know you have talked about applying for an advanced degree. Get as much education as you can. There should be enough for you to pay tuition and your living expenses for several years. I don't want you to work. Concentrate on your studies. The second condition is that you must ask Ian Murphy to be your mentor. Ian is a good man, an educated man. He was the best friend I had in all of Ireland. When he talks, listen.

The letter dropped from my hands onto the table. A tear fell from my cheek and plopped on the paper. When I blotted up the tear with a napkin it smeared several words. I folded the letter and placed it back in the envelope. Mairin took my hand in hers. Tears swelled up in her eyes, and she rested her head on my shoulder. William bowed his head and fumbled with the whiskey glass.

"Well, your uncle gave me a new assignment, William. You are to be my charge. So be it. Raise your glass lad! *Slainte!*" A drop of whiskey splashed out of my glass as we clinked the tumblers together. "What are your plans?"

CHAPTER 12

Helping William learn Cork and the nuances of attending graduate school at University College Cork, reminded me of my first days in Trinity. I didn't have a mentor, and I relied too heavily on the advice of upper classmen, who didn't always have my best interest at heart. They played on my naiveté to pull pranks and make me the subject of their practical jokes. I had only been at Trinity for a few months when I earned the reputation for being the dunce from Cork.

I never did become accustomed to their imitation of my dialect. "There's Ian Murphy," they would say. "Soon he'll be the smartest first year in school because he ends every sentence with a question. Don't you, Ian?" I tried to ignore them but it only led to their harassment continuing unabated. I developed this special sneer by practicing in the mirror. They mimicked my sneer. Finally, I began laughing them off, trying to laugh with them. By Christmas break this strategy worked. I can't say I was accepted but at least I wasn't the target of their jest.

William's years in Dublin had transformed him into an urban man with Ballyshannon far in his rearview mirror. Like me, William spent his summers in Dublin, finding what work he could and taking the odd courses in the summer term that interested him and contributed nothing to his degree path. Learning for the sake of learning—autodidactic. (I have always enjoyed the word.) I'll never forget Professor O'Hara, my Irish history teacher. He was the first person I had ever heard use the word. "Ah, Mr. Murphy, for only the second time this month the sun blesses us with its warmth and beauty but here you are in our hallowed library. Son, you are one of the few autodidacts at our fair institution." He smiled and walked away. Of course, the fact he too was spending his sunny Sunday afternoon in the library was not lost on me. I had to use the large Oxford dictionary to look up the word. My normal trick of sounding out the spelling phonetically failed miserably. I finally had to go to the reference desk and ask.

Having William in my life meant spending a great deal of time reflecting on my years at Trinity and how I came to know his Uncle Kieran Fitzpatrick. It was pleasurable to reminisce. It was easy to forget today was the sum total of all my yesterdays, all the decisions that made both gigantic and tiny adjustments to my life path. My grief changed after William came into my life. Before William I grieved as an Irishman, forlorn at my loss and questioning how to fill the void of friendship lost by death. Each and every day was a struggle to avoid descending into my lonely, dark cave.

I tried keeping a bottle of whiskey in my desk drawer, practicing the will power not to open it. Jesus, I'm Irish through and through. It was not a successful strategy. Then I tried pouring a bottle of the golden liquid down the kitchen sink in an act of defiance and victory. That only resulted in the loss of very expensive whiskey. I also tried avoiding Mickey's. I was certain that Mickey would never understand why I didn't have a drink. Mickey never witnessed my behavior when I was languishing in my cave. I never got drunk in the pub. It was my personal rule. I also never drank alone in Mickey's Pub. In fact, it would be impossible for me to drink alone there. If nothing else, Mickey would join me, so there was always the appearance of it being just a social drink. No, the evil came from those times alone in my writing room, my pipe stocked with tobacco and my only other company, a bottle and a glass.

Three months after burying Kieran, I couldn't pick up my pen to write. Mairin suggested I purchase a new, really expensive pen. I coveted the Porsche design, pure titanium, limited edition. You could buy a small used car for the 4000 euro the fountain pen cost. It was more than an indulgence. Owning that pen would not prevent me from sliding down the well of my depression. William's presence didn't change my writing dilemma, but it did help me gain perspective. I must admit it was also some comfort that William reminded me of Kieran when Kieran and I had first met. They shared the same shock of red hair that refused to be tamed. William provided me the distraction of being concerned about someone other than myself, and he needed me. Mairin couldn't play that role in my life. Mairin didn't need me in the "I can't sort it out on my own" way that William did. Mairin bore the burden of watching her first spouse die from Parkinson's and living through grief. Mairin led an enriched life before meeting me. Our bond was our friendship, and our love was a gift.

* * * * *

William visited my school office a few weeks later. "Ian, I'm thrilled! I've been accepted into the graduate Drama and Theatre Program. I didn't realize I have to declare now whether I'll be taking the master's program or the doctorate program. Can we talk?"

To date my mentoring duties had been for mundane things like finding an apartment and being a guide around town. The question of which graduate program to undertake was significant and a choice that would set William on two very different life paths. I hid my right hand in my lap as it clenched into a fist, hoping William hadn't noticed. "You know, William, I don't have an advanced degree. I'm only a lecturer here. I may not be the right person for you to consult."

"I think you're the perfect person because you have a foot in both the publishing world and the academic world. You were never interested in graduate work?"

"I wanted to write, period. Plus your uncle kept me quite busy writing for the IRA. Lecturing takes more time than you might imagine, and I've been doing it for twenty-seven years now. Is that possible? Let me think. Yes, yes that's right it has been twenty-seven years. I was not much older than you are now when I started teaching. In fact, it was just two years ago that I learned that your Uncle Kieran was responsible for my position at UCC. I didn't get paid well at a bookstore I was working at so somehow your uncle arranged for the position at the college. I don't know for a fact but I would guess that the IRA made a financial gift to the department. Of course, no one would ever admit taking IRA money, not then and not now. Listen, let's take a walk. I always think better when I walk."

It was a rare sunny day, the crispness in the air less harsh than a typical November day. I didn't pay any attention to where we walked. Stretching my legs felt good.

"Ian, where are we going?" William wondered.

His curiosity brought me back into the moment. I looked to my left, then my right and squinted to look straight ahead. "I don't know. Sorry about that. Walking is like meditation for me. Have you ever read any Zen-Alan Watts?"

"No."

"Oh, never mind. The question at hand is your graduate direction. Do you have any interest in teaching? I don't know for sure but I don't think there's a call for research in theatre so a doctorate would mean a teaching career." I searched through my pockets for my pipe and tobacco pouch. The department had banned smoking in our offices several years ago and as a direct result, my walks became both more frequent and longer in duration. Smoking in the classroom was forbidden many years ago; I understood that because of the potential harm to those in the room. My private office was another matter, that didn't affect anyone. Someone was always trying to control aspects of my life. It was absurd. As we walked, I packed my pipe with tobacco, struck a match, and drew the flame deep into the bowl. We were surrounded in a cloud of smoke.

"I've never even thought about teaching. I'm glad you mentioned it. I can't say I have an interest in either teaching or research. Guess, the decision is obvious. Uncle Kieran was right; you have a knack for getting to the heart of things in short order. Now, I need to decide what my concentration will be. I like acting on stage but I want more than that. To be frank, I'm a mediocre actor at best, and I doubt if graduate school can help. You really need talent and passion to be a professional actor.

"I've experimented with writing some short, one act plays. It was a lot of fun. I was the dramaturge for one play my senior year at Trinity and I enjoyed it and appreciated the more subtle aspects of the play because of my research. I was also able to help the actors understand their characters and the relationships among the characters."

"What time is it, William?"

"Half three."

"I must turn around now. I have a class at four and I don't know how long we've been walking. You should spend some time making your final decision. It appears you have eliminated several paths. There's directing, of course."

"Thanks, you're a great mentor."

"I only listened. Keep track of the time for me as we walk back. I hate to be late for class; it's disrespectful."

* * * * *

I didn't see William for several days after our discussion about his graduate studies. I found my new role as his mentor had a beneficial effect on my life. I began walking to campus every day, which lifted my spirits. I developed a path around the perimeter of central campus, down Donovan Road, across College Road, past the Kane Building, toward the River Lee to the Student Center for a tea, and then to my office in the O'Rahilly Building. One morning at breakfast, before leaving for campus, Mairin made an observation.

"Ian, dear, you seem more relaxed. I notice you're going to campus earlier. Have you changed your routine?"

I sat with a piece of toast in my hand and thought about her question before taking a nibble. "I have and the habit started quite accidentally. I take a stroll around central campus before going to my office. I do find it relaxing. It's odd. I love hiking in the Dingle Peninsula but other than that, I've never really exercised."

Mairin stacked her tea cup up on top of her plate and picked up her silverware. "Well, I hope you continue with your walk. I think it's helping you. Oh, my, I hear the phone." She put her dish back on the table and went to answer the phone.

"That was William. He wants you to meet him at Fion Sweeney's office at one p.m. today."

"What did you tell him?"

She picked up her dishes again and turned toward the kitchen, talking to me as she walked away. "I told him you would, of course."

"But what if I have another meeting or something?"

"Ian, both William and I know you better than that."

I took a sip of tea and scratched my head. "Who is Fion Sweeney?" I shouted to Mairin through the kitchen door.

"Head of the Drama and Theatre Department, dear. You don't know her?"

"No. This must be serious. Why would I need to meet the head of the department?"

"You will need to go and find out. I won't be home until at least six tonight. We have a late afternoon staff meeting and I'm expecting it to be long. Maybe you want to bring some take-away home for dinner; I don't care what you get." Mairin checked her watch, put on her coat, and was halfway out the door before I could answer.

"Just meet me at Mickey's."

"All right."

I didn't need to visit my office so I took my walk, then roamed through the graduate library until it was time to leave for the meeting. I went to the Granary Theatre, assuming staff offices would be stuck in the basement. It was farther than I thought; it was nearly half way to City Centre on Western Road. I interrupted several students practicing their lines. I learned the administrative offices were in Muskerry Villas and got directions to the department head's office.

"Fion Sweeney" was printed in at least three-inch gold letters outlined in black. The door was closed so I knocked.

"Yes."

"I believe I have a meeting at one p.m. today with the department head," I shouted at the door.

"You're late. Come in."

William was sitting stiffly in a wood chair directly in front of Fion Sweeney. I looked for a place to sit and didn't see another chair.

"You can sit over there." Fion pointed to a small leather couch cracked with age.

I smiled and then offered my hand in greeting. Dr. Sweeney ignored my gesture and again pointed to the couch. I obeyed her stage direction. I guessed she was in her mid-forties, though she had premature dark gray hair swept straight back into a bun. She held both hands on top of her desk and sat in command. She wore a brown tweed jacket with a light brown blouse buttoned to the top. I noticed she didn't wear any jewelry. The office didn't have any windows, which must have been stifling. In the corner stood a small wood table with an IBM Selectric typewriter and a neat stack of white paper on one side. Both the wall behind Dr. Sweeney's desk and the wall behind the typing table were floor to ceiling bookshelves.

"Now, Mr. Murphy, our most recent graduate admission, Mr. Boyle, has made a very unusual request. He is asking that you be assigned as his graduate counselor. You are in the School of English, are you not?"

I nodded my head. "William, why did you ask for me to be your counselor?"

"Well, I don't intend to show disrespect for any of the staff but in my uncle's will he suggested Ian be my mentor, and Ian has agreed. I want to concentrate on playwriting and directing. Ian is a superb writer, known for his dialogue, which is the key to any play. If allowed, I would accept a counselor from the department for my directing studies. Would that be a good compromise?" William offered.

Dr. Sweeney pulled a pencil from her bun and scribbled notes on a yellow pad. She looked at William and then back at me. It was impossible to determine her reaction; she had a stone face, like a statue. "Mr. Murphy, you lecture in the English Department, I believe."

"Yes, for twenty-seven years."

"And in that time, you've never pursued an advanced degree?" Dr. Sweeney asked.

"No."

"Why not?"

"I don't believe that is germane."

Dr. Sweeney leaned back in her chair and looked back and forth between me and William. William sat erect with his hands folded in his lap, not willing to budge from his request. They sank into a staring contest.

Dr. Sweeney cleared her throat and leaned forward. "Mr. Boyle, we have a very talented staff. I don't deny that Mr. Murphy is a superb writer, but he is not a teacher. I have no idea why your uncle would choose him to be your mentor, though I'm sure he had his reasons. At the Graduate School of Drama and Theatre we have standards to maintain and competent, talented staff to guide you through your graduate program. No, I cannot grant your request."

William covered his face with his hands and mumbled, "Is that final?"

Dr. Sweeney stiffened and slammed the pencil on the desk. "Well, you can appeal my decision to the dean of the College. If you do, it must be in writing and turned in by the end of the week. I must also be provided a copy of your appeal. The next term doesn't begin until January so there is time to make a decision. I should advise you that the probability of having your request granted is slim, at best."

William jumped out of his chair, almost falling into Dr. Sweeney. "Fine. Let's go, Ian." He turned on his heel and stroll out of the office without saying goodbye or shaking Dr. Sweeney's hand.

I looked Dr. Sweeney in the eyes, got up, and shrugged my shoulders. I extended my hand. "Thank you for your time. I understand your position. He's young. We all were at one time." I left the office and searched outside for William. I saw him walking several blocks in front of me, unaware that I wasn't walking with him. I shouted, "William!" He stopped, looked left then right and finally behind to see me waving my arms to get his attention. He waited for me to catch up.

"William, I don't know if you're courageous or just stubborn like your Uncle Kieran. I appreciate your desire to have me help with your graduate studies but I am no playwright. You've just encountered the academic behemoth. It would be a miracle for the dean to overturn his department head's decision. I think you should think this through and reconsider your decision."

"Do you want to walk with me, Ian?"

"Yes, of course."

We walked at a pace that was difficult for me until we got to Fitzgerald Park. "You like this park, don't you?" William said.

"Yes. It brings me peace and perspective. I don't know why, it just does. Let's find some place to sit."

"Look, Ian, I'm just following Uncle Kieran's advice. You write dialogue like you're in a room listening to people. Your characters are in a scene just like characters on a stage. I can learn how to write-in stage direction; that should be straightforward. Think of a stage play as a book on stage." William looked dazed. He grabbed my arm and then wrapped his arms around me, squeezing me tight with his hug. "That's it!" he shouted at the top of his lungs.

I worked to free his grip around my shoulders and pushed away. "What are you talking about?"

"I have an idea. Let's collaborate on writing and producing a play. If I propose that to Dean O'Leary, he can't refuse. It's brilliant."

I felt my body stiffen and my right hand clenching into a fist. My nails cut into the palm of my hand. "Oh, no, I don't think so. I have no idea how to write a stage play. You really should have told me you were going to ask Dr. Sweeney for me to be your graduate counselor. I would have had the chance to talk some sense into you."

"Don't you think this project could cure your writer's block? I've read that's how some authors do it, force themselves to do something unfamiliar, something that is a total challenge."

I leaned forward on my knees to avoid looking at William. December in the park was barren, all the summer flowers gone. The sun was half-hidden by dark gray clouds. Dreary, wet winter days demand a strong soul to wait for spring to arrive. If you could count on spring arriving by a certain month or day it would be easy, but spring was the most fickle of seasons. *Maybe the boy is right. I don't know? What would I write about? What would be the plot, the theme? Oh, this is just insane. I need to be alone.*

"Ian, Ian you drifted off. Jesus, I apologize, I didn't mean to insult you. I . . . I knew you haven't written since Uncle Kieran died. I'm sorry, Mairin told me. She's so worried."

I sat with my elbows on my knees and my face hidden in my hands. I felt paralyzed and my breathing was labored. I heard William say, "Ok, I'm going to leave you alone. I promise not to write an appeal to Dean O'Leary without your agreement."

"Give me three days," I said without looking up.

"That won't give me much time to write the appeal. It's due on Friday."

"If I agree, I'll write the appeal with you. It will be our first collaboration. Now, I want to be alone, please."

William said nothing more. I listened for his footsteps before exposing my face to the world.

CHAPTER 13

I didn't intend to make William anxious but asking for three days to explore this change in the direction of my life was reasonable. I have been asked by numerous undergraduate students to serve as their mentor for their senior thesis. For years I have fended off their requests by explaining I needed time for my writing. Of course, no one knew how much time I was devoting to the IRA. I also didn't take the time to form a relationship with my undergraduate students. I didn't then and still don't feel comfortable with any relationship outside the classroom, it's inappropriate. Eileen was an exception, of course, but she wasn't a student, she just audited a lecture and she was a thirty-year-old woman. Life has exceptions, even the ones that are tragic mistakes, like Eileen.

The first thing I considered in making my decision was the yoke Kieran had given me. I was obliged, clear and simple. Yet, the obligation didn't seem like enough reason to take on a responsibility I was not suited for, had no training in, and was completely uncomfortable with. On the other hand, I owed Kieran my life. He knew when he accepted the order to assassinate me that it was a ruse, designed to save my life and jeopardize his life. Certainly, with his willingness to sacrifice himself, his request to take care of William was minor. The question was, does taking care of William entail serving as his graduate mentor? I could ask for a list of duties or responsibilities that mentors have, but our situation is unprecedented. Most likely we would be creating the rules every day. I felt like the message of the Kieran dream was him telling me to "Get on with it, for God's sake, Ian."

The other consideration was what this would mean for a change in direction of my life and my writing. I would need to mentor William on writing a play, which I've never been remotely interested in. There are or can be similarities between a work of fiction and a play. Both have character development, both have conflict, both have plot, both have dialogue. Both have scenes, although in a play the scenes are strictly visual. Both have a beginning, middle, and end. Both have pacing.

Well, my own analysis was surprising me. Ok, maybe it was just a matter of translation from one form of fiction to another. *I wonder.*

My final consideration was the eerie experience I had at the Lyric Theatre. I still don't understand how the only theatre in Belfast City Centre could feel remotely familiar. How could staff know my name? I can't deny the sensation. I can't deny that I was recognized, even by several in the audience. Life can be peculiar and events transpire to push a person in a particular direction. *Is this fate?*

These thoughts spun around in my head for three days without relief. I spent more time alone than I should have, and once again was not fair to Mairin. I guessed that William had asked her about the potential of having me as his mentor when they were having tea the other day. Normally, Mairin would ask me about the extra time alone; this time she didn't. *I wonder what Mairin advised William.* I didn't want to ask, at least until after I'd made my decision. The beauty of the future was its uncertainty. I risked complete failure again if I was not a good mentor for William. I have failed at writing, at overcoming my death dance with whiskey, with attaining atonement for IRA activities. For reasons I don't understand, I didn't feel pushed into the decision; I felt pulled into the role of mentor and that made all the difference in the world to me. I called William and asked him to come to the house as soon as he could. He knocked at the door in less than fifteen minutes.

"I'll do it."

* * * * *

After a brief supper that evening, we sat down to write the appeal. The instructions provided were not helpful. The only criteria was that the appeal could not exceed three written pages and had to be delivered at least twenty-four hours in advance of the meeting directly to Dean O'Leary's office. Typical for academia; part of the game was to deduce what the criteria for a successful appeal would be. I wanted to take the approach that it provided a unique opportunity and would be a breakthrough that would gain academic attention – if successful. William wanted to rely on whatever small reputation I had in the literary community and note the various acclaims I've received over the years.

"William, this is academia, not a television prize show. I'm certain the dean will reject any appeal based on my reputation. Besides, you are overrating my humble achievements as an author."

William brushed his hair back with both his hands and forced himself to sit still. "To meet this ridiculous deadline, we must finish tonight and hand-deliver it tomorrow morning. I just think I'm right about this, Ian."

I felt my right fist clamp up. "Maybe. Let's ask Mairin what her view is. Mairin! Mairin! We need you."

Mairin walked into my office with a cup of tea. "Did I hear you scream my name? I just sat down with a cup of tea and today's paper."

"We need your help," William and I said in unison.

Mairin swept her hair back with one hand. "Oh, this sounds dangerous. I don't know."

I jumped up and walked toward her. "My dear, we can't agree, and we're appealing to your sensibilities to help us."

"That's right," William chimed in.

"William wants to base the appeal on the advantages of working with a famous (that may be infamous) Irish writer. I, on the other hand, want to base the appeal on the uniqueness and the potential for academic recognition. What do you think?"

Mairin leaned back in her chair and sipped her tea without saying anything. She looked at me, then at William. She finished her tea and set it on the table. "Well, you both have very different points of view. And I believe there is some merit to both viewpoints. Perhaps there is a way to blend both ideas into a rock-solid argument that can't be rejected."

"How?" I sat behind my desk, pulled out a yellow pad and pen to take notes.

Mairin inched forward in her chair and spoke to both of us. "In the university world, Ian's reputation is based on having one foot in two worlds; that is to say, one foot in academia and one in the literary world. It makes Ian different; he stands out. Most academics are firmly planted and seek success in only the academic world. It means Ian has a special qualification to serve as your mentor, William. In addition, over the years Ian has gained respect from his colleagues for his teaching and the student following he manages to attract year in and year out. Meaning that Ian can teach, guide, and have a relationship with students that has been acknowledged."

I filled two pages of notes in my large scrawl on the notepaper. I set my pen on the pad and smiled.

"Mairin, you are a genius," William said, beaming.

"William, I have been in the University of Cork academic world for a very long time. I understand the world with all its quirkiness. Now, I'm going to leave you gentlemen to your task. Good night." Mairin left, forgetting her teacup on the table.

"Goodnight," we said in unison.

"Now you understand why I consult with Mairin on everything. Now, I'll knock out a rough draft, and we can work together to polish it."

Even with Mairin's guidance, the process was not easy. I learned that for a young man, William had very definite ideas and was often stubborn, which was a family trait on his uncle's side. I understood how academics thought and didn't want to be "in their face" and pose a challenge to the dean or give him any reason to reject a perfectly reasonable idea. It was close to midnight when we finished. We agreed on a final draft from exhaustion as much as anything. I suggested it was too late for William to venture out and offered him the spare bedroom. Our first collaboration was a very steep climb, which took the wind out of both of us.

I led William to the bedroom and watched him drop onto the bed face first. I was careful in getting ready for bed so not to disturb.

"Ian, it's past midnight," Mairin whispered.

"Oh, I'm sorry. I was trying not to disturb you.

"I was having a restless sleep, anyway. Did you finish?"

'Yes. Thankfully. Thank you for your sage advice."

"Oh, Ian." Mairin turned toward me and snuggled her head under my chin. We fell asleep in just minutes.

* * * * *

The dean's office looked like you would expect a dean's office to look. It was large enough for at least three faculty members in good standing. It was the office of a man who had long ago given up his profession in order to administer the institution, which from a practical day to day view, means raising money. It was curious that colleges around the world pluck administrators from the ranks of researchers and teachers. Typically they have no qualifications in management or fundraising, yet they leave the nest of teaching and research to guide and financially guard their institutions. It would be like having a writer in charge of a publishing company. Writers often didn't know anything about the business world of publishing, and being a writer gave you no qualifications to publish. My fear was that choosing administrators from academia was inbreeding and didn't allow for perspective. Regardless, William and I had to defend ourselves and our proposed mentorship/collaboration to the dean. He held William's graduate career and potentially his professional career in his hands. It was an overwhelming responsibility.

A middle-aged woman dressed in a wool suit with wire-rimmed glasses escorted us into the dean's office. "The Dean is running a bit late this morning. He's having breakfast with a group of benefactors for the Engineering School. Very important, very important indeed. May I get you both a tea while you wait?"

William and I looked at each other and shook our heads 'no.' "How long might it be?" I had the audacity to ask the gatekeeper.

She stiffened. "I have no idea. He is aware of your appointment, of course. I do not question the dean." She turned on her heel and strutted out of the office, shutting the door behind her with a slam.

William and I couldn't resist a muffled laugh.

"Do you think he will be as pompous as his secretary?" William wondered.

The door burst open. Before we could stand, he was shaking our hands. "Oisin O'Leary. Terrible name, eh? How I have wished my mother wasn't a professor of Irish Mythology. Do accept my apologies. Donors were throwing money at the Engineering Department this morning and I couldn't disengage them. It's part of the job, I'm afraid. Actually, the truth is, it's most of the job. Let's have tea and a good chat about your proposal. You can't imagine how refreshing it is to have some academic initiative.

"Helen! Tea!"

Dean O'Leary appeared average in every way a dean could. He dressed in a conservative gray suit and waistcoat with a gray bow tie. His hair was turning gray at the temples, neatly trimmed and brushed straight back. There was nothing pretentious in his dress or manner. He had the appearance of a bookstore owner. "Mr. Murphy, I am so pleased to finally meet you. I don't get around to the department socials as much as I would like. I don't think we've met before, have we? I am a fan of your work, however."

Dean O'Leary knows my work? "Please, call me Ian, and this is my friend, William Butler Boyle."

Dean O'Leary slapped his knee and laughed "Aha! Your mother did one on you, too. A Yeats namesake, I take it."

"Yes sir," William responded.

"No sirs in this room, young man. Oisin, please."

Helen arrived with a silver tray, three Belleek cups, and a matching teapot. She set the tray on the table between us as if serving the Queen of England. "Shall I serve?"

"No, no, Helen. We're quite capable. Thank you." Dean O'Leary poured each of us a cup. "I'll let you help yourselves to sugar and cream. She's efficient to a fault, really. Takes her job too seriously. Now William, tell me about yourself and why you choose University College Cork. It's not often we get someone from Trinity to come to one of our graduate programs."

William cleared his throat several times then slurped down his tea and set the cup back on the table. He looked at me for reassurance and I smiled. "Well, I'm from Ballyshannon, the first in my family to attend college. I have a keen interest in literature and the theatre. I have a dual degree from Trinity. My uncle died recently and left me a lot of money with the condition I use it for education. To be honest, I came to Cork because of Mr. Murphy – Ian. My Uncle Fitzpatrick and Ian have . . . had a history together. Along with the money, my uncle wrote me a letter instructing me to have Ian be my mentor. There is excellent faculty in the Drama Department, I know. I'm only following my uncle's wishes."

Dean O'Leary sipped his tea and smiled. "I see. And Ian, I understand you've never mentored a student. Why now?"

"Kieran Fitzpatrick was my dearest friend for thirty years. He saved my life twice, not figuratively; he saved me from my own self-destruction once and from assassination. If he wants me to mentor William, I take the yoke without a thought. It will bring new experiences to me. It was William's idea to work with him in his graduate program. He's already challenged me. He wants to collaborate in writing and producing a drama for the stage. Imagine that. A worn-in-the-heel novelist like me changing genres and art forms to write for the theatre."

Dean O'Leary poured himself another cup of tea and offered more to William and me. We both declined. It was difficult to tell if he was just being cordial or actually wanted to have a discussion about our proposal. It was my observation the dean was not a man to make hasty decisions and that he cherished his independence.

"Have you thought about a topic or theme or subject matter for your drama?" He looked back and forth at each of us, not knowing who would answer.

"No. Not yet. Dr. Sweeney wasn't pleased I decided to appeal her decision. I'm sure she thinks I'm arrogant. I didn't want to consider what to write until we had your decision. Your decision will determine my work here – one way or another," William said in a calm, respectful manner.

"Let's not presume Dr. Sweeney's judgment. I've known her for years. She's an excellent department chair. I am comfortable with her decision."

William's chest sank. He fell back into the sofa. I raised my hand and opened my mouth to speak but Dean O'Leary spoke first.

"Don't misinterpret my statement. Yes, I am comfortable with her decision, but I think it would be a travesty to not allow this mentorship program. One of our roles is to experiment, try new things, and challenge the status quo. I approve your request to assign Ian to be your mentor for your graduate program. Yet, I am not saying Professor Sweeney made a mistake or a poor decision. In her position and from her perspective, I believe she made the correct decision, which is why I am comfortable with it. In the university we need to be uncomfortable once in a while, too."

William stood up with a broad smile. His legs wobbled. He shook Dean O'Leary's hand so hard his fingers turned red. "Thank you, oh, thank you. You won't regret your decision, sir," William blurted out.

I stood by William to keep him steady. For a moment there I thought our cause was lost. I confess, I thought the dean would support his department head and not disturb the well-oiled conservative machine that is a modern university. I also realized I was getting a new lease on my writing life. Stuck in the middle of nothingness for months, I had become lazy and lethargic, without motivation or desire. With Dean O'Leary's decision, I could see clearly everything would all change now. In my mind I saw an image of Kieran. Even in his death, he was still with me. *Damn you,*

Kieran Fitzpatrick. Dead three months and the man was still influencing my life, guiding me, being the best friend a person could have. "Thank you, Dean O'Leary."

"Now, there's one condition, gentlemen. I want a front-row seat for me and my wife at your first performance."

"Done," William and I chimed together.

"Now, Ian, this is an opportunity I can't let slip through my fingers. I have several questions about one or two books. Do you have some time to stay and chat?"

My eyes widened. "Why ya . . . ya . . . ya yes, of course." I stammered. I grabbed William's arm. "William, why don't you go? Stop by Mairin's office and give her the news. Plan on having dinner with us tonight."

William walked toward the office door without excusing himself. At the door he turned back toward us. "Thank you, Dean O'Leary. Thank you." He pulled the door shut behind him without a sound. Dean O'Leary sat down and pointed to the sofa for me to take a set too.

"Well, now that that is over, certainly you would like a cup of tea. Like I said earlier, I've read most of your work. I think scholars agree, you have matured in your writing over the years. Not a criticism, mind you, an observation. In particular, I had questions about your last book, *Lost Dreams.* Dean O'Leary poured the tea.

* * * * *

When his secretary, Helen, burst into the room, she announced the dean was due downtown for a lunch meeting. We had talked for more than two hours.

CHAPTER 14

December had arrived in a fury with colder than normal days and incessant rain. The winter term didn't begin until the second week of January, and I looked forward to having no one to answer to but myself for several weeks. I failed to realize my commitment to serve as William's graduate mentor would turn my cozy little world inside out. After the meeting with Dean O'Leary, more than anything I wanted to be left alone. William called me the evening after winning our appeal, eager to begin planning his graduate career. I asked him to be patient with me; I just wasn't ready. He cajoled me to at least agree to a timeline to develop a plan.

I have never worked under a timeline. I am a planner, but all in my head, not graphs and charts or outlines. It is all too formal and too much time spent on developing something on paper and constantly changing it. By keeping it in my head, there is immediate flexibility; I can adapt to whatever happens in life. I also have never written an outline for my novels. There are those who spend months creating a detailed outline to guide them through the pain of writing a novel. I don't find it organic, in fact, for me it's the opposite – it's artificial. My novels are about the characters. They tell me their stories and I try to capture them on paper as best I can.

When I start a novel, I always know the ending. I don't write the ending but I have a final scene in mind. Knowing an end point gives me a target of where I want to end up and then my job is to write to that place. I also like to have a theme in mind, to serve as the overarching story spine. I think it was my comfort with my own way of writing which allowed me to have a dry spell and not panic. For the first time since publishing my first long work, I didn't have an idea for a story or a theme. Mairin's suggestion to write my memoir had proven to be an obstacle versus an incentive, and I was afraid to tell her. I had a deep-seated fear of sharing my life with the public.

When Eileen published her investigative report on my role in the IRA, it was devastating. I was forced into hiding, and again Kieran Fitzpatrick saved both my life and my soul, even though I tried to extinguish my life a second time. How could I write in a memoir that I had attempted suicide twice and both times directly related to my role in the IRA? Does the world need to know I risked eternal damnation? I also can't imagine anyone would be interested in reading about my life either in a memoir or an autobiography or even a biography penned by a historian. It was simply an accident of birth. I was an actor in the Troubles. An actor? *Why did I use the term actor?*

"Ian Murphy, are you going to stay hidden away in your office all day? What are you doing?" Mairin shouted at the closed door, having too much respect for me to interrupt my private time.

"Having a pipe," I shouted back. "Come in. Come in."

Mairin opened the door an inch or two, then peeked in. She hesitated for a moment before opening the door enough to come into the room. Since returning from Belfast, we have not had time just to be together. William burst into our world, self-absorbed and in need of friends, parents, and a mentor, and we were expected to fulfill all three roles. Mairin didn't have children in her first marriage, nonetheless she had a natural mothering instinct and took William under her wing on the first evening they met.

"Please, come in. I owe you an apology, my dear. We have had very little time alone together since I've been back." I moved to the couch and patted it to have her join me.

She glided in next to me and put her head on my chest. She took my hand into hers and patted my knee. She looked into my eyes for a few moments. He hazel eyes were soft and empathetic. "My dear, you look weary."

I squeezed her shoulder and pulled her closer to me. We sat without talking for a few minutes in the softness of a winter Cork evening.

Mairin pulled away from me. When she looked into my face, there was a mischievous twinkle in her eyes. "I have an idea. Let's really celebrate Christmas this year. We can invite Brianna, Caitlin and her boyfriend, and maybe even William for a traditional Irish Christmas dinner. I'll even decorate the house with a sprig of holly on the front door and candles in the window for Mary and Joseph."

I couldn't resist chuckling. "I suppose you'll want to leave a slice of mince pie and a glass of Guinness in the living room for Santa on Christmas Eve."

"Why not? Don't forget, we need to leave a carrot for Rudolph."

We laughed out loud and fell back into each other's arms. We decided to have spiced beef with other meats and cheeses from McCarthy's of Kanturk. Mairin volunteered to make her famous mince pie with brandy butter for dessert and since Santa was getting mince pie anyway, she thought we should benefit.

"Ian, I want to be serious for a moment. I would like to decorate your parent's grave with holly and ivy." A tear slipped down her cheek.

"We should also put holly and ivy on Ed's grave," I said.

Mairin sobbed then kissed my cheek. "You are a sweet man."

"Mairin, it's been six years since you lost Ed. I can't be jealous of a husband who passed, especially in his tragic way."

"I need a glass of wine. Would you mind, dear?" Mairin asked with a sad voice.

We shared a glass of wine and made more plans for the family Christmas feast. By most standards I could honestly say I have a normal life now. Every day was a day to explore and define what normal meant to me.

* * * * *

I was jolted out of a daydream by the clamoring phone. The mid-morning call was from Oisin O'Leary. He wanted to see me in the afternoon. He insisted. His demand was urgent, and I couldn't imagine anything could be so important. However, it's not like I had a schedule to keep, and I did enjoy our last conversation together, so I asked him to come by at two.

Oisin arrived promptly with a suspicious grin on his face. I invited him up to my third-floor office. "Now, Dean O'Leary, what is this visit about? You've piqued my curiosity."

The dean threw off his coat and tossed it on the chair, then went to sit on the coach. "Please, call me Oisin. No formalities. I'm escaping from the world of duties and formalities this afternoon." His grin broadened.

I joined him on the other end of the sofa, crossing my arms across my chest and taking a few moments to observe my new friend. I can count on my hand the number of colleagues from the college I've met with outside campus, and Oisin was the first to ever visit my home. It's well known I'm not social and never before has anyone been bold enough to ask to visit. I suppose it was Oisin's boldness that I responded to by allowing him to pay me a visit.

"I can see your mind is filled with wonder, Ian. Look, it's the season. I have so many social responsibilities, so much glad-handing. Helen is so damned efficient, I rarely have time for myself this time of year. The woman is relentless. Today I decided to revolt. I escaped. Can you imagine escaping from your own office and a good-intended but ruthless secretary? When she left for lunch, I snuck out the back door of the building, then took a bus here so she wouldn't notice my car was not in its parking spot." Oisin let out a huge breath.

"What an incredible tale. And you wanted to visit me?" I scratched my mustache.

"Didn't we have a fine discussion about your book?"

"Oh, yes. I enjoyed talking with you very much. I rarely, or maybe I should say, never talk with real readers. My discussions are with editors and cover designers and publishers, not normal folks who read for pleasure."

"Then I'm welcome?" Oisin asked.

"Yes, of course."

"Well then. I brought a special treat to share with you. Have you ever smoked a fine Cuban cigar?"

"No, I'm a pipe man or I have a cigarette once in a great while. I have my own blend from a tobacconist here in town."

Oisin beamed, reached into his pocket, and held two cigars in his hand. "A Cuban Montecristo No. 2 is one of the finest cigars in the world. Do you have any wooden matches?"

I went to my desk and took two boxes of matches from the drawer. Walking to the sofa, I tossed one box to Oisin. As I sat down, he handed me the cigar. It was at least six inches long. "It's shaped like a torpedo," I said. Then I slid it under my nose to take in its aroma. "Ah, like a walk in the woods."

"I knew you would appreciate it. Just wait until you smoke it. There's a very specific way to light this beauty so you don't ruin it. Now watch." Oisin lit the match and then held the end of the cigar in the flame and twirled it between his thumb and finger. Then he blew out the match and examined the end of the cigar. "You want to thoroughly singe the end so when you draw in the flame, it catches fire evenly. Now watch." He lit a second match, and I watched the cigar smolder, the smoke rising to the ceiling. The end of the cigar turned brown. Oisin blew out the match and lit another. He put the cigar in his mouth, put the match to the end, and drew in a slow, deep breath. The cigar flamed bright orange and the room filled with blue-gray smoke. "Give it a try, Ian."

I mimicked every action Oisin took in lighting his cigar. Then I drew in and held in a mouthful of smoke to savor the flavor. "It has an interesting spice flavor. I suppose it's a spice only found in Cuba. Now, this fine cigar deserves a fine whiskey to enjoy it thoroughly. Would you care for a glass of Midleton?"

"Midleton?" Oisin questioned.

"Yes, my uncles started the original distillery, although my branch of the family never worked in the business."

"That's fascinating. Of course, Midleton would be a superb pairing."

I took a two Glencairn whiskey glasses from the cabinet and opened the whiskey bottle. I set the glasses on the table, filling them to the top, and handed one to Oisin. He raised the glass to his nose.

"Oh, God. Perfect." He sipped and then puffed on his cigar. "The great escape, Ian, the great escape."

"We should toast. What should we toast to?"

"New friends, of course."

We clinked our glasses and took a sip of whiskey, swishing it around the tongue to appreciate its full depth. After finishing my cigar, I noticed the bottle was two-thirds empty. I had no idea what time it was, but I admit to enjoying my time with Oisin. "Should I get another bottle, Oisin?"

When I got up, I was lightheaded. Looking down at my feet, I couldn't focus. By good fortune I could grope my way around the office, even in the dark, and being a bit tipsy didn't hurt my ability to fetch another bottle of whiskey. I set the fresh bottle on the table and emptied the first bottle into our glasses.

"Oisin, I want to share something with you I've not talked to with another human being."

Oisin leaned forward and looked directly into my eyes. His breath was a blend of Havana and Ireland. He slapped me on the knee. "Hold forth, my friend."

"I have not been able to write since my friend Kieran Fitzpatrick died three months ago. I'm a dry well. Nothing there. Not a damn thing. And here's the scary part, no desire. Did you hear me? No desire." My words sounded slurred, even to me.

"Jesus, Ian. I had no idea. Has it happened before in your writing career?"

"No. Not once. I'm frightened. I'm overwhelmed with ennui."

"Ennui? Maybe you're just drunk. You have a reputation for being a hard drinker. From what I've seen this afternoon, you do like your whiskey."

I jerked my head back and then thrust myself into his face. "Are you calling me a drunk?"

"I didn't say that."

Silence fell between us like the tree falling in the forest with no one to hear it. We finished the whiskey in our glasses; I opened the second bottle and filled our glasses again.

"Mairin thinks I should write my memoir," I blurted out.

"She's right."

"No one wants to read about my life."

"You're wrong. Have you told your publisher about this?"

"Jesus Christ, no. He wouldn't give me any peace if I even mentioned it. Let's change the subject. I shouldn't have brought it up."

Oisin leaned back and closed his eyes. He continued to sip the whiskey. He set the whiskey glass on the table and rubbed his face with both hands as if he were trying to sober up. Then he got up and paced back and forth between the sofa and the office door.

"Have you and William made a decision on what his graduate project will be?"

"No, I've been avoiding William. I just needed time alone. The last three months have been my undoing."

Oisin sat back down on the sofa and scooted next to me. He put his arm around my shoulder. "I have an idea. You and William collaborate on writing a play that is a memoir of your life. You write, let him produce and direct. It's a perfect marriage of both your skills."

I drew back and looked him directly in his blurry eyes for several minutes. "You didn't hear me. No one is interested in my life; I'm an author, after all."

Oisin jumped to his feet, took a step, and stumbled into the table. "Pardon me. Ian, you are the original mystery man. We found out Ireland's novelist wrote the damn *Green Book* from those articles Donohue published. You kept your work in the IRA secret for thirty years. Then you have this miraculous change of heart and work on the Good Friday Agreement? Now that, my friend, is a story." Oisin filled his whiskey glass again, spilling part of it on the table. He walked back to the sofa and fell into the corner with a thud.

"And I've got the title of the play for you – *Dead Reckoning!*"

I poured myself a glass of whiskey without spilling a drop. (Years of practice counted for something.) I scratched my head and twirled the ends of my mustache.

"*Dead Reckoning?*" I asked, unsure why he suggested it.

"Dead reckoning – the art of learning where you're at right

now by knowing where you've been before. God, man – it's a navigation term. Get it?"

I was at a loss for words. Even though I was slow from the whiskey, I did understand Oisin's idea. I set my glass on the table and then searched through my desk for a pipe and tobacco. I wobbled back to the sofa and was enveloped in a cloud of tobacco smoke in just moments.

Mairin appeared in the door. I squeezed my eyes shut and hid my face in my hands.

"Ian! Dean O'Leary!"

"Hello, Mrs. Murphy."

"You two are obviously drunk. Ian, I am so disappointed. And Dr. O'Leary, half the campus is looking for you. Helen has called every department looking for you. The woman is distraught and angry. You should call her. No, you shouldn't. I don't think you could use a phone now. I'll call for you."

"Tell, tell, tell her I'll be in tomorrow," Oisin said.

Mairin stood in the doorway staring at us for what seemed like an eternity. "You'd better stay here, Dean, and call your wife! Tell her I insist. We have a spare bedroom. I'll order take-away for both of you. Maybe with food you can sober up a bit. Ian, you find someplace to sleep tonight – maybe on your sofa. I don't want you in my bed. I'll be going out. When the door-bell rings, it will be your dinner. I hope you can make your way to the door and pay the delivery person a nice tip. Goodnight!" She slammed the door.

CHAPTER 15

I woke the next morning curled up in a backbreaking position on the sofa in my office. I stretched out my right leg. A stabbing pain ran up my spine. My arms were tucked underneath my chest. I moved my arms to brace myself to get into an upright position. I pushed up. My arms slipped, and my head bounced on the arm of the sofa. Panic raced through my mind. I wanted to call out for help but my ego blocked my vocal cords from working. I tried again, this time stuffing my left shoulder into the corner of the sofa for support. In one Herculean push I became upright. There were two empty Midleton bottles on the table, one upright and the other on its side. I only saw one glass. I looked at the floor and saw the other glass upside down next to the sofa. The overbearing stench of spent whiskey made me dizzy. I straightened up and propped myself into the back of the sofa. Morning sunshine streamed into the office; it was impossible for me to even guess what time it might be.

It took me a few minutes to muster the courage to leave my office to find Oisin and Mairin. Bones creaked and my lower back screamed its disapproval of my trip. My knees were stiff and I walked like Frankenstein toward the door. I opened the door without making a sound. As I walked down the hall, my knees loosened somewhat and my gait became a swishing side-to-side motion. The door to our bedroom was shut; I couldn't remember it ever being shut in the past. I opened the bedroom door a crack, just enough to peek in without being noticed. The bed was made, the window partly open, a soft breeze moved the curtains. I couldn't decide if Mairin had slept in our bed or not. It looked perfect.

I stumbled down the stairs, holding onto the railing for support to guide my descent. The door to the spare bedroom was open. I looked in. The bed there was also perfect, like it hadn't been slept in. I seem to remember Mairin offering Oisin the bedroom. Maybe he stayed over, maybe he didn't. I would call him in the afternoon.

I made my way back upstairs by grabbing onto the railing and pulling myself up hand over hand. I distinctly remember Mairin telling me she was disappointed in me. I was ashamed. Would she be able to distinguish me from my behavior, decrepit as it was? I could recover from her being disappointed with my behavior, but if I have damaged our relationship, I don't know if I could survive the self-inflicted blow. I could gather myself together and go surprise her for lunch. If I were honest with myself, I was not sure I could be so bold in such a short time. For three months I had controlled my screaming desire for whiskey and my body had begun to recover, my head had been clear, and I felt in control. Now, in a single night, I had demolished all my progress. With Oisin's help, I drank twice as much as I would normally drink in an evening and the affects were quadrupled. Both my forehead and the back of my neck throbbed in sequence, battering me into a useless pulp.

I fell into the chair behind my desk and dropped my head onto my folded arms. I closed my eyes against the morning sun because it felt like it was searing my eyes, blinding me. Somehow, in this awkward position, I fell back to sleep. When I raised my head next, the sun was no longer in the window, which meant it was afternoon. It was then I noticed how the cigar smoke from last night permeated my office. There was a definite foreign-land earthiness I feared might be a permanent attribute of my workspace. Mairin wouldn't be pleased, and to be honest, I couldn't blame her.

When I sat back in my chair fragments of my conversation with Oisin popped up in my mind. We talked about my struggle with the idea of writing my memoir. My ego, by most standards, is overwhelming but not so large that I think anyone would be interested in my memoir. More important, I am a private person and I'm not inclined to share with anyone my experiences with the IRA or what I felt were the justifiable reasons for the extreme actions we took during the Troubles.

Oisin suggested I work with William to create a new genre – the stage play memoir. The notion was intriguing because, to the best of my knowledge, it hadn't been done before. It was a suggestion which enticed the writer in me. I had to remember to be fair to William. Oisin's suggestion that my play be titled *Dead Reckoning* felt subtle and suggestive. He comprehended the internal purpose of the play would be for me to determine how I got to where I am today because, I had to confess, I had a certain lack of self-awareness on this point. *How can Oisin have this much insight? I've only talked with the man twice and he's pierced my soul with his intellect and heart at the same time. There are some events in life that must be listened to, and in my gut, I'm feeling this is one of those moments.*

The path for me to finally address my demons would be to accept the creative challenge, mentor William, and have the audacious bravery to share myself with the world. In the short term, I had to prepare myself to talk with Mairin.

I took a scalding shower to awaken all body and mental functions deadened by the whiskey. I made myself eggs with several slices of brown bread. As is my habit, I took a walk along the quay. I walked without purpose or direction. My entire life I've been drawn to the quay when I needed balance in my life. There was solace in the water, always flowing, always changing while always the same, day in and day out. *Walking the quay reminds me I am of Cork; I am of Ireland.*

I checked the phone book for a home cleaning service. I thought I should have something done to my office to overcome the Cuban cigar and whiskey mixture. I wouldn't have any idea what product to use or how to use it. I was willing to pay a premium for the work to be done before Mairin came home from work that afternoon, assuming Mairin would be coming home after work.

The person I talked with on the phone heard the urgency in my voice and was very kind. They agreed to send a crew of three people to the house and promised to be finished by four that afternoon. They guaranteed to eliminate any residual odor in the carpet, sofa, and curtains: The true definition of a modern miracle. For this level of service I agreed to pay the full bill in cash plus a thirty percent tip to each of the workers. It was more than a fair bargain. At least Mairin would acknowledge I knew the situation needed rectifying, and I took the initiative to resolve the problem.

It was important that I wasn't too eager to reconcile with Mairin. She was very independent and would seek me out when she was ready to talk. After the cleaning crew left, I worked in my office to research how to write a stage play. Since the revival Yeats began, the Irish theatre had been robust, but I had to admit, I hadn't paid much attention. I had attended maybe one performance a year, with someone usually inviting me. I enjoy theatre as entertainment, not as a serious art form. It was likely my own parochialism. I was so absorbed by writing straight dramatic fiction, I hadn't allowed myself to indulge in other art forms, even when they had a literary foundation. Besides writing, I read. It was what I did. I read science fiction, drama, history, historical fiction, and a bit of poetry to quench my soul's thirst.

The first thing I must do is read current playwrights. I'll need help in choosing who will be helpful to me to teach me how to translate scenes and action into pure dialogue to tell a story. Mairin could help me develop a reading list. I didn't hear Mairin come into the house. There was a soft rap, rap, rap on my office door.

"Yes?"

Mairin came in and let the door swing full open. She walked to the center of the room, looked left then right. She took a deep breath and exhaled through her mouth. A faint smile crossed her face. I intentionally didn't speak but waited for her.

"What did you do? The stench is gone. I know you don't know how to clean. You hired a professional cleaner, didn't you?" She placed her hands on her hips and stared directly at me.

"Yes. It was necessary." I lowered my head to avoid her piercing gaze.

"I'm glad you figured it out on your own." She walked to behind the desk and glanced at the various papers I had spread out, covering the entire surface. Mairin took my face into her hands. Her eyes became soft and tears gathered in their corners. "Oh, Ian, I do love you. God, how I wish you could wrestle your demons into submission. You were so close, so close. What happened?"

I pulled Mairin close to me, inhaling her magnolia fragrance, which always felt reassuring. I tossed her hair with my hand. I didn't have a simple answer for her, or maybe I did.

"Oisin O'Leary happened. In just two visits he's become a dear friend, not a Kieran Fitzpatrick but a friend with incredible insight. He challenges me intellectually."

Mairin pulled away, her expression turning to a puzzled look.

"In some strange way he knows me, Mairin. In our very first conversation we discussed several of my novels with a depth I've never experienced with a reader before. Last night he suggested I write a play as a memoir. With William's help, it could be his graduate project to cast and direct it. That's what you see spread out across my desk, my initial research. I'm intrigued. I sense this is the right direction for me. It's a challenge, and I need a challenge again in my writing life."

I pulled Mairin toward me again. She buried her head in the side of my neck and wrapped her arms around my shoulders in a big hug. I felt forgiven, even though she said nothing. Silence was the best forgiveness between lovers. Although I was a man of words, words weren't always the answer. I hated to admit it because words were my life. With Mairin I have learned the gentleness and power of silence; it was healing, and in this moment, I was beginning to heal.

"How will you start? Your desk is in disarray," Mairin said.

A broad smile flashed across my face, and I twirled the end of my mustache. "I'm going to read. I want to read Irish playwrights from the twentieth century, especially those who have written either historical plays or political plays. I'm going to unmask myself; Ireland will see the real Ian Murphy – oh, God, it's frightening. I can't let fear influence me in any way. I just can't. I must bury heart and soul in the writing, exactly as I do when I write fiction. It's my way; it's the only way."

"Well, Ian, you are married to a librarian. I could help. I want to help."

"You have an interest in the theatre?" I asked.

"Yes, of course. I'm not interested in musical theatre, unless I just want a night of romping entertainment without engaging the brain, but a well-acted drama appeals to me."

"Why haven't you ever said anything?"

Mairin pulled back and examined my face. "Ian Murphy, we've been a bit busy with your intrigues. First, it was your rush to snuff out the fires of the Real IRA and their bombing frenzy. Then there was your Don Quixote-like fight against the Peace Lines in Belfast. It's only been months since Kieran's death and now you've just returned from helping Gerry

Adams finally have a voice that must be listened to in Northern Ireland. So when were we going to have the time to attend the theatre?"

I hung my head in shame. "Point taken."

I don't know how long we sat together. Mairin jerked back, a broad smile on her face and the gleam back in her eyes. "I'm starving. Let's go out."

"What are you hungry for?"

"Mmm. Oysters, I'm hungry for oysters." Mairin winked at me.

"Oysters. Well then, oysters it is. I never turn down shellfish."

"Oh, Ian, over dinner let's finalize our family Christmas meal. I have a few other ideas."

"Good. I was counting on you. Could we invite Oisin and his wife?"

"Ian!"

"It wouldn't hurt to ask."

"Well, they probably have plans. A man in his position, you know," Mairin said. "It won't exactly be a family event, then."

"Well, William isn't technically family and we're including him. Didn't you also mention asking Caitlin's boyfriend?"

"Rory, Rory Burke. I wouldn't call him a boyfriend. At forty-five a woman doesn't have a boyfriend. For a mature woman, he is a true friend or it's just about sex or they're developing an emotional relationship," Mairin explained.

"Oh, my ignorance is massive. When did you become an expert?"

"Ian, I've lived it. Remember how we met? I made it clear I wasn't interested in a male companion. We were attracted to each other sexually but not to fulfill physical desires. I needed love in my life again and then you stumbled into my library and here we are."

Typical for me, I had never thought very much about our relationship and how it had developed. Our relationship was natural, based on friendship, with a deep engaging love that would not waiver with time. It may have been trite but I was comfortable with Mairin. At middle-age, I think it is a critical aspect of a relationship between a man and a woman.

"Well, of course we should invite Rory, if he isn't returning to Galway for the holiday. Do you want me to ask Caitlin or would you like to talk with her?" I asked.

"It would be nice for you to talk to her, Ian. It would mean something special coming from you."

Mairin is a stickler for etiquette in social events. I've avoided social events, both family events and all others. I have no sense of what is appropriate. Why should it make any difference if I invited Caitlin and Rory or Mairin invited them? I suppose it had something to do with the fact it was a family dinner. I had never defined family only as those with a blood relationship. We were all part of the human family, and that is enough for me.

"So, we'll have Rory and Caitlin, William, Brianna, of course, with us makes six. We would have room for Oisin and his wife."

"It's not a matter of having enough room. We don't know them. I don't even know his wife's name. I'm sure they have family to be with or for certain he has some university events like the annual madrigal dinner. Do you even know his wife's name? Do they have children?"

I didn't expect Mairin's resistance to my suggestion; it was uncharacteristic of her. I persisted. "No, I don't know his wife's name. Does it matter? I also don't know if they have children. We haven't talked about such things. There are always numerous holiday events to attend on campus. You know, I sense Oisin tires of attending university events because there is an underlying requirement or expectation he attends. *I* would certainly revolt against it."

Mairin wagged her finger at me. "You've being ridiculous now, Ian. You would never be in a position like Oisin O'Leary."

I crossed my arms over my chest and stared at my wife. "That's not the point. I like the man. I want to have him be a part of our lives. Jesus, the one time I want to be gracious and want to open up, you slam the door."

"Ok, Ian, point made. Invite them."

* * * * *

Quinlan's was the perfect restaurant for a quiet dinner with gourmet food. During the festivities, Mairin gave me instructions on how to host a traditional Irish Christmas dinner. It was embarrassing but I'd never participated in a traditional dinner. While my parents were alive, we had a small dinner with just my parents, my sister, and myself. My mother would make a mince pie and we would have some sort of boiled meat with potatoes. It wasn't much different from any other Sunday dinner. I didn't recall decorating the house, although. I needed to ask Caitlin what she remembered. Mairin demanded real candles be placed in the windows and lit throughout the dinner to welcome Joseph and Mary. I couldn't believe she insisted on such traditional Christian symbolism. I scratched my head in disbelief but nodded my head in agreement. I agreed to have a large sign reading "Happy Christmas" to be hung in the entrance to the dining room for all to see, but I insisted the sign must be in traditional Irish – *Nollaig Shona Duit.*

* * * * *

The weeks before Christmas passed quicker than I expected. Oisin and his wife, Clare, agreed to attend our Christmas extravaganza. He was actually relieved to accept our invitation to avoid another university event. I learned they didn't have children and were tired of the university social events. Caitlin giggled with joy when I told her we wanted Rory to join us for the holiday. He didn't have plans to visit Galway, and she was afraid he would be lonely. Brianna was surprised we were having a big holiday dinner and gave Mairin all the credit for converting me. She looked forward to the day and even expressed some interest in meeting William.

William was uncertain if he would be in Cork to attend our big event. He hadn't heard from his mother on what the family plans were, which he said was unusual. During college he often would return home for only a portion of the holiday because he had adopted Dublin as his home. Now he was adopting Cork as his home, but he wanted to be careful and not offend his mother. Several days after I called him, he let me know he would be in Cork through Christmas day and then return to Ballyshannon through the New Year.

I felt this Christmas was a turning point in my life. For the first time ever I had a home that I shared with a woman I was passionate with, and I felt open to others. Our guests were an eclectic group of people. I expected many stories, fine food, good wine, and the joy of friendship. It would also be the first time Oisin, William, Brianna, and I would be together. My plan was to share with William and Brianna my decision to write a memoir play for William to use as his master's project. Brianna had earned her master's in arts administration from Trinity just two years ago. Currently she was an assistant in theatre production. I wanted to ask her to produce our project, hoping William would support me.

CHAPTER 16

Mairin filled my days with preparation for the Christmas Eve dinner of the century. I kidded her; we had failed to invite the mayor of Cork or the chancellor of the University College Cork. As usual, she failed to appreciate my dry wit. I did find time to create a list of twentieth-century playwrights to read. Mairin granted me an hour of her time one evening and shared with me her impressions of each author. She asked if Tom Murphy was at Trinity College when I was in school. I couldn't remember for sure but I thought he was a writer in residence at the time. Mairin was sure he produced *The House* in 2000 and was certain he had published a novel in the mid-1990s. To check her facts, she promised to research it when she returned to campus after the holidays. I wasn't in a rush. The idea of writing a play was still swirling about my subconscious, and I wanted to let it rest there.

Christmas Eve dinner was set for eight. Of course, Caitlin arrived with Rory in tow about seven and offered to help Mairin with any of the final preparations.

"Don't you think I do anything around here?" I complained. "Look at these hands, raw from the tedious work she gives me every day."

"My darling brother, you should kiss the ground Mairin walks on. If she's put you to work, you deserve it."

"Rory, it's time for you and me to have a drink. You look like a whiskey eggnog man to me," I suggested.

Mairin had set up a table in the parlor with a variety of wines, drink mixes, and of course, my whiskey. I followed Rory into the room, noticing his military like bearing. Every detail of his suit was perfect. I was surprised he wasn't wearing a waistcoat. On other occasions, he dressed fairly formally or, more to the point, much more formally than me. The back of his neck looked like he had gotten a trim, maybe even today. His hairline receded just a bit with no hint of gray yet. I had to remember he was still in his late forties or maybe mid-forties like Caitlin. He had some sort of administrative position on campus, in central administration. He and Caitlin had been seeing each other for – I'm not sure – sixteen to eighteen months.

"Fine, Ian. I'm surprised you mix whiskey and eggnog."

"Oh, I don't, Mairin does. I always drink my whiskey . . . neat, as the good Lord intended." I chuckled.

"Ian! Come greet the O'Learys!" Mairin shouted.

"Do you know Oisin and Clare O'Leary, Rory?"

Rory sipped his spiked eggnog. "Mmmm, I've met Dr. O'Leary at several campus social functions. Just idle talk."

"Tonight it will be Oisin and Clare. Come with me."

Clare O'Leary is just the type of spouse I imagined Oisin would have. She was trim and wore a gray suit, very similar to Oisin's gray suit. They had reached the magic time in marriage and began to look like each other, dressing like they were twins. Clare had an engaging smile, and I'm sure she was an excellent conversationalist. I could imagine a future where the Murphys and the O'Learys would be fast friends.

"Oisin, you are in charge of making sure Ian stays on his best behavior tonight. I hope you didn't bring any of those wretched cigars," Mairin said.

"Cigars?" Clare asked and gave Oisin a puzzled look.

"Trust me, you don't want to know," Mairin explained.

Oisin directed his wife to the parlor. "Right, dear, you don't want to know. Wouldn't you like a tricolor drink? I'm sure they will have one for Christmas Eve."

The six of us gathered in the parlor, each selecting a special Christmas Eve drink, except me; I remained traditional – my tradition. Brianna let herself in and joined us for a drink. Now a beautiful young woman of twenty-five, she was the perfect blend of her father and mother. Brianna's father, Brian, had died in an IRA bombing before she was born. He was a mason by trade, and she had his traits of accuracy and detail with just a bit of creativity. She hasd inherited her Spanish black hair from her father as well. Caitlin gave her a light complexion and stunning light-blue eyes with a smile that disarmed most men. Caitlin also gave her self-confidence and independence, both by nature and by how she was raised. Working in arts administration was a perfect fit for her.

"Brianna, this is Oisin and Clare O'Leary."

"It's a pleasure to meet you."

"Ian, when do you expect William?" Mairin asked.

"Who's William?" Brianna said.

"He's a graduate student at UCC. He's Kieran Fitzpatrick's nephew," I said. "He'll be studying in the Theatre Department next term. I'm going to be his mentor for his master's thesis. He'll be here any time."

"You're his mentor in theatre? I thought you avoided mentoring students? What brings about this change?" Brianna asked.

"Well, William is special. I feel attached to him because of Kieran. I got to know William in a short time during Kieran's funeral. Kieran even managed to talk to me from the grave. In his last will and testament, Kieran asked me to take care of William, and I'm glad to do it."

Brianna brushed her long black hair back over her shoulder. "Uncle Ian, you always surprise me. I'm looking forward to meeting him."

"Oh, you just wait. Before the evening is over, I have another surprise for you. I hope it's one you'll find fascinating and engaging."

We all talked in the parlor and enjoyed our Christmas cocktails. William arrived just before we were ready to sit down to dinner. Mairin ushered us into the dining room. I was surprised to find little cards with names at each of the seats. "Mairin, what are those?"

"Name tents, dear."

"You're seating us? This wasn't supposed to be a formal dinner, friends and family," I pointed out.

"Ian, darling, just follow my lead on this."

Mairin placed me at one end of the table. To my left sat Rory, then Caitlin and next to her Clare O'Leary. Oisin sat across from me. On my far right sat William, then Brianna and Mairin next to me. It was clear why Mairin had positioned each and every one of us. William and Brianna would have an opportunity to meet and talk throughout dinner. Mairin is both clever and subtle. I hoped Brianna and William wouldn't notice the intentional seating arrangement.

I stood and raised my glass. "To our family and our friends. Welcome to our very first traditional Irish Christmas feast. All of the credit belongs to the lovely Mairin Murphy. In particular we would like to welcome Rory Burke and the O'Leary's – Clare and Oisin. From Ballyshannon we welcome William Butler Boyle, a first-year student in the Graduate Theatre Program at our own University College Cork. Also greetings to our family: my sister Caitlin and her beautiful daughter Brianna. *Nollaig Shona Duit* (Happy Christmas)."

The chatter was continuous during dinner, as anyone would expect at an Irish Christmas dinner. I couldn't hear their conversation but William and Brianna appeared to be having a good time, laughing and exchanging glances. Mairin was a born matchmaker, and Brianna was an intelligent, bold, and exciting young woman. William was more reticent but he was independent and enjoyed challenging authority, as our recent history demonstrated. If I recalled, everyone around the table offered a toast. Mairin had provided both red and white wine during dinner and promised champagne later in the evening.

I found Rory an interesting man to talk with. He wasn't the "cut out of a mold bureaucrat" I expected. I should have known Caitlin would never be attracted to a cardboard-box man. I confess, I worried twenty-five years of widowhood might have changed her personality dramatically. Rory was engaging and, I learned, an amateur history buff. He had a keen interest in Irish mythology. Clare O'Leary sat too far away from me to engage in conversation that wasn't shouted across the table, but she appeared to be enjoying herself. Of course, Oisin had no difficulty engaging in animated conversation. Oisin could have a dialogue with the Devil if we had invited him to the table. Several times during the meal I touched Mairin's knee with mine to let her know I felt her love and tenderness, even at a crowded table.

Mairin brought several bottles of French champagne to the table after we finished our mince pie. I handed one off to Rory. "Please do the honors, Rory. If I pop it, the cork is likely to hit poor Oisin in the chest." The second bottle I passed down to Oisin. "If you please, honorable sir, show us your cork-popping skills." The champagne bottle corks popped out simultaneously. Everyone clapped, then we held up our glasses to be filled.

"I would like to make a toast and announcement. Raise your glasses, please.

"May peace and plenty be the first to lift the latch on your door, and happiness be guided to your home by the candle of Christmas. *Nollaig Shona Duit.*"

Everyone stood up and clinked glasses before we took a sip. There were broad smiles and a feeling of shared joy around our Christmas table. Growing up, Ma and Da made sure we always celebrated Christmas dinner but it was only with our small family, friends or other relatives were never invited. Our Christmas dinners were more somber and private. I don't really remember them very well. Although I do remember Ma making sure we attended Christmas Mass. By the time I was ten or twelve, I thought Christmas Mass was a cruel trick to make sure I would sleep in on Christmas Day and not get my parents up too early. Ma assured me it was to give Santa enough time to visit all the children around the world in one night, which I had to admit, was a mighty job.

"Now, for my announcement. As you all know, William is starting his graduate studies in theatre in the January term. The gracious Oisin O'Leary has approved my serving as William's mentor for his program; a first for me. I have had some difficulty these past few months putting words on paper, which has been a new experience for me. Most of my life my beloved fountain of words has flowed across the yellow tablet in the first draft of my manuscripts. My inkwell dried up more than five months ago. In an effort to drag me out of the dark, Mairin suggested I write my memoir to extricate the demons that plagued me. Of course, as you might expect, I fought against her suggestion.

Then, several weeks ago my friend Oisin and I spent a night smoking Cuban cigars and drinking more Midleton whiskey than I like to admit. In a volcanic explosion of creativity Oisin suggested an idea that has turned my world inside out. He suggested I collaborate with William to write a stage play that is a memoir of my experience in the Provisional Irish Republican Army. William and I have had many hours of discussion, and he agreed to the collaboration, directing the play will be his master's thesis. Now, this evening I would like to publicly invite Brianna to join us in our adventure, to serve as artistic director and producer for the play. Brianna?"

I looked toward Brianna. She blushed from the collar of her dress to the top of her forehead. She fiddled with her napkin. Her head fell to her chest. She jerked her head up, looked at Mairin, and then her mother. Brianna turned in her chair to face William. "Would you work with me?"

With the broadest smile I've ever seen on a man, he said in a clear voice, "Yes."

Brianna turned back toward me, our eyes locked. "I couldn't say no."

Cheers went up around the table and we all clinked our glasses again. Mairin jumped up, gave me a bear hug, and whispered into my ear, "You clever man, you."

Mairin turned toward our guests. "Let's finish our evening together in the traditional Irish way. Let's be off to Christmas Mass. We have a great deal to be thankful for."

No one objected, although I wanted to tug on Mairin's sleeve and ask if I had to go too. It was a fleeting thought. We walked to church together. Even I said a little prayer during mass. I hadn't prayed for years.

CHAPTER 17

r. Sweeney's decision was overruled. I was allowed to mentor William, which may have put him at a disadvantage. Mairin suggested I contact Dr. Sweeney before the winter term started to ask how I could work with the department and benefit William. She also suggested I share with her our idea to collaborate in writing a memoir stage play and be sure to mention Brianna would serve as the artistic director and producer. As part of her arts administration degree, Brianna had worked closely with the Theatre Department and throughout her college years taken on many jobs in the theatre, including acting, set decoration, sewing costumes, lighting design, assistant directing, stage managing, and producing. I would need to tap all of her skills and experience to make my play a reality.

My only experience with the theatre was limited to being in the audience. I faithfully attended every production she worked on. I thought Brianna was a competent actor and thought her path might be on the stage. She said she had no passion for acting but wanted to experience the production from the actor's perspective. Brianna told me she learned the technical staff often were disrespectful of actors and didn't appreciate their craft. There was one set designer at the university who even referred to actors as living props. I agreed with Brianna the characterization was unfair and harsh.

Talking with Brianna at her graduation party from Trinity College, she shared her viewpoint. "Theatre requires many different type of people with very different skills to join together for one common cause, for one specific purpose. Theatre is a classic example of the adage – the whole is more than the sum of the parts. When the curtain is raised, magic happens, it's simple." This sage perspective came from a woman of twenty-four at the time.

I found myself drawn into the maelstrom of writing a play, and like the eye of a tornado, there was a haunting calm. I spent hours in my office studying the twentieth-century master Irish playwrights. I looked for similarity in form, use of words, how dialogue alone could push along a story, and the art of storytelling by the performing arts.

Against both Mairin's and Oisin's advice, I didn't attend the theatre before beginning writing my play. I did accept Oisin's suggestion to title the play *Dead Reckoning*; it was appealing and the public would understand what it meant. Oisin also suggested I interview the Dublin playwright Tom Murphy. He arranged a meeting with him in Dublin. I wouldn't have been able to arrange such a meeting on my own. I researched his history before meeting with him. His first play, *On the Outside,* was presented in 1959. He was prolific, with twenty-three plays to his credit. It was the equivalent of a play written and produced every two years. From a fiction writer's perspective, it was a prodigious amount of work in a short period of time. In 2001 the Abbey Theatre honored him by presenting six of his plays in a single season. His work had recurring themes of searching for redemption and hope in a desolate world. I felt drawn to his work because it reflected my own life experience, especially the search for redemption, which I had found elusive. I was surprised to learn he had even written a novel in 1994 called *The Seduction of Morality.*

A library assistant led me up three flights of stairs to Thomas Murphy's office. They expected him soon, and I was told to wait in his office, which made me uncomfortable, but

I followed instructions. When I entered his office, I began coughing. There was an overpowering stench of stale cigarette smoke embedded in the walls and furniture. Ashtrays were placed all around the room and all were overflowing with discarded cigarette butts. I couldn't imagine how he had survived to age sixty-eight as a chain smoker.

His office was stuffed into a small room with a vaulted ceiling on the third floor of Trinity College Library. There was an oversize oak desk opposite a ten-foot window with stained glass at the top. On the wall opposite the desk was a leather couch, which appeared to date from the Easter Rising. All three walls had floor to ceiling bookshelves. In one corner there was a stack of literary magazines at least four feet tall. There were piles of books leaning against the bookshelves around the entire room. By the placement of his desk, Murphy read by natural light.

I didn't feel comfortable enough to sit down; I stood in the center of the room with my hands folded in front of me. I waited. I heard someone climbing the steps, coughing, almost choking with each trudging step. The steps stopped, following by labored breathing. The door opened. A very thin man in a worn tan suit with an open shirt walked in. He stopped and stared at me, brushing back a few strands of thin hair.

"You must be my namesake."

"Ian Murphy, sir."

"No sir bullshit. We're both writers – we're equal, and we're both members of Aosdana. Years ago I took the stipend. It gave me a year to write *A Whistle in the Dark*, and without it, we might not be talking today. Cigarette?"

"No, I do a pipe but have lost the taste for it recently." We both stood in the center of the room, sizing each other up. I didn't want to sit down before I was offered. I had no idea how much time he would share with me.

"You look uncomfortable, Ian. Sit on the couch. I'll call down for tea. You would like tea, wouldn't you?"

I backed up toward the sofa and sat down, sinking into the stuffed leather cushion. Thomas Murphy searched his pockets and pulled out a package of Carrolls. I noticed his hands were stiff and his fingers yellow from years of tobacco use. The end of the cigarette glowed like the morning sun. He breathed in deeply and blew the smoke toward the ceiling. I watched the smoke rise and could see the brown stain on the once-white ceiling. "So, you've got a notion to write a play? Did you take the stipend, you didn't say?"

I leaned forward, placing my elbows on my knees. "Yes, like you, when I first began writing. My only income was from working part-time in a bookshop in downtown Cork. I lived in a three-room cottage west of town. I rode my bicycle everywhere. Like you, the income gave me the most precious gift – time. Later, I was lucky to be hired at University College Cork as a lecturer. Actually, many years later I learned it wasn't luck at all. My friend in the IRA, Kieran Fitzpatrick, arranged the whole thing."

Thomas walked to his desk and leaned on the edge. "I remember reading about you. That Donohue woman raked you over the coals. I also remember reading your defense of the Good Friday Agreement – eloquent!"

"You are the only playwright I know who has written a novel. I hope to be a novelist who writes a play, so we have something in common, and I would like to learn from you."

Thomas gazed right though me. He drew several heavy puffs on his cigarette, then smashed the butt into the nearest ashtray he could find. "Do you want the play produced or is this just a literary exercise?"

"Produced. Within a year or fifteen months at the most."

Thomas raised an eyebrow and looked down his nose at me. He began searching through the room for something, throwing books everywhere. He tossed several bundles of paper bound in brown twine in my direction. I used my hands to defend myself from getting hit in the face.

"Pick those up," he ordered.

I picked them up and stacked them on the cushion next to me. "Those are draft manuscripts for: *The Sanctuary Lamp, Conversations on a Homecoming,* and *The House.* You can get the published scripts from the librarian downstairs. I'll call and have them get them ready for you. Take them for as long as you want. Study the draft and the final. The draft is me in the raw. The published version has been on the stage. Here's the secret, Ian; the playwright should only be concerned with the dialogue. Your characters become real flesh through the actors; let them do their job. You set the scene, of course, but only in the broadest terms. Let the director do his job with the other professionals you know: scenery, costumes, lighting, etc., etc. Your only job is to write the damn words. Understand?"

I let myself sink into the cushion a bit more. I studied Tom as he pulled out another cigarette and lit it. There was a knock on the door. A library assistant brought the largest pot of tea I had ever seen, hidden in a tea cozy. Without being asked, he poured two cups of tea and handed each of us one.

"Very nice, Jeremy. Thank you for trudging up all those flights of stairs. I didn't mean to interrupt your day," Tom said.

Jeremy backed out of the door, not saying a word, and closed the door.

"I suppose it's not very different from writing fiction. Relying totally on dialogue to reveal the characters and tell the story is daunting to me right now," I explained.

"My understanding was you had another twist. The play is actually going to be your memoir. Is that right?" Tom came and sat on the opposite end of the coach and locked onto my eyes.

"Yes."

"Why not just write your damn memoir – why a play? It's bold. I like bold, of course. I could help, but it wouldn't be right. You need to do this yourself."

I sipped at my tea to give myself time to think before continuing our conversation. "For the first time in my life I've not written for months. It's just not there. It scares the hell out of me. I might be done, I don't know. I desperately need the challenge. Does that make sense, Thomas?"

I got up and poured myself another cup of tea and offered to fill Thomas's cup. He waved me off with his hand. He got up and looked through a number of desk drawers until he found another pack of cigarettes. He lit up again and then turned his back on me and stared out the window for what felt like hours. He smashed the cigarette into an ashtray on the windowsill. Cigarette butts flew onto the floor by his shoes. Thomas turned toward me in a military about-face.

"I know fear. I think every writer has. Look, just read and then you can ask questions. I'll give you my private phone number so my gatekeeper won't interfere. I am with you, Ian, really, I am."

I stood and shook hands, tucked the manuscripts under my arm, and began the long descent to the entry floor of the library. When I reached the main floor, Jeremy greeted me with a stack of scripts in book form. "Mr. Murphy? Mr. Murphy asked me to have these ready for you."

"Thank you, Jeremy. Don't I need to sign them out?"

Jeremy shook his head. "Oh, no, Mr. Murphy gave explicit instructions. Please, they are yours for as long as you like."

I smiled at Jeremy and shook his hand.

During the train ride back to Cork I placed the three manuscripts on the seat next to me. I didn't feel like sharing the trip with another rider. Though Thomas Murphy had been very generous, he was not a teacher. I wasn't looking for a teacher;

I just wanted to be shown the path. I have read extensively, however, I'd never read the script of a stage play, either in manuscript form or produced. *Thomas believes I can learn from reading, so I must trust his judgment.*

Ireland rushed past me. The clickity clack, clickity clack, clickity clack: mesmerizing. The conductor announced, "Cork City next. Cork City – fifteen minutes."

CHAPTER 18

Soon after the term began, Mairin and I invited William and Brianna over on a Friday evening for a light supper. I had Mairin warn them that following dinner I wanted to discuss our collaboration to produce the play. As Thomas Murphy predicted, I did learn a great deal by reading both the draft manuscript and the final stage production of the three plays he had me read. I marveled at how he manipulated dialogue and interaction among characters to tell a story with traditional plot development. He wove scenes from emotional struggle and snared the reader (the audience). Comparing the manuscript draft to the produced script, it was evident the contributions the theatre professionals made. The set designer, costumer, lighting tech, and stage manager all made notes in the script. Their magic was to be able to read the words and bring them to life on the stage. I didn't have a script used by an actor; at some point I would ask for one just to learn how actors interpreted the words.

I stepped up to Mairin in the kitchen. "Mairin, can I souse for you?"

"Absolutely. Is this the new Ian Murphy? Working in the kitchen with me?"

I felt my cheeks blossom rose red. "I don't know why I never offered before. It just feels right, now."

"Well, would you like a glass of wine while we cook? It would be very French."

"No, I don't trust myself to use a sharp knife and drink a glass of wine."

Mairin laughed out load. "Such honesty is quite becoming. I've done it for years; please pour me a glass of Malbec, dear. I've noticed you haven't been having your traditional evening whiskey lately."

I looked at her with a tinge of surprise. "I haven't, have I?"

"My darling, Ian, I notice everything about you. Nothing slips past me. I'm not judging, just observing. I must confess, I believe drinking less is an improvement. Oh, God, I don't want to lecture. Forgive me. Here, peel these carrots and the julienne them, please."

I let her comment slip past me, picked up the knife, and scraped the thin skin off the carrots. "Julienne?" I asked.

"Yes, here watch." Mairin cut the length of the carrot into four equal pieces, then cut each piece into four thin strips. "Julienne."

"Julienne."

Mairin was comfortable in the kitchen and allowed a novice like me to contribute whatever I could. She put a large chicken in the oven to roast and boiled potatoes and cabbage for colcannon. My carrots were added to a green salad. She also toasted almonds, which she added later to green beans swimming in a delicate butter sauce. Mairin knew how to prepare a warm, welcoming meal.

Brianna arrived first and offered to help Mairin with the dinner. For a person her age, I found her thoughtful and considerate, a trait of the Murphy women, including her mother and grandmother.

"Brianna, your Uncle Ian helped so there's nothing to do now but let the chicken roast. It will be about seventy minutes, then we can finish making the colcannon," Mairin explained.

I led Brianna into the parlor and offered her a cocktail or a glass of wine. As I walked with her, she looked over her shoulder directly into my face. "You helped Mairin with dinner?"

I patted her shoulder and directed her into the parlor. "I am capable, you know. It's not earth-shattering. Even at my ripe old age, I can learn."

Brianna sat on a chair in the corner of the room where she could see William enter from the front door. "Uncle Ian, I am impressed. I can't wait to tell Ma. She'll have to call Mairin to confirm this development, of course. A glass of white wine would be very nice, thank you."

Mairin joined us, her glass half full, which I topped off with the Malbec we opened in the kitchen. She sat on the sofa and patted the cushion to direct me to join her. As I watched Brianna sip her wine, I noticed for a twenty-five-year-old, she wasn't particularly fashionable in dress; she wore practical, attractive clothes. While her mother Caitlin made a reasonable salary at University College Cork, there was rarely enough for any small extravagance or travel. The Murphy family, by tradition, were not travelers. Brianna took a conservative path to the arts. Recognizing her own performance talents were not exceptional, she had found a place for herself in administering the arts in a variety of capacities. I'm sure her father would have been proud of her. I was never comfortable asking Brianna how it felt to be raised only by her mother and to not have known her father at all. Hailing from a traditional Irish Catholic family, my understanding of any other way to be raised was limited.

"Uncle Ian, before William arrives, I need to ask you a question and I demand an honest, straightforward answer," Brianna commanded.

"You would never get anything else from me."

"Did you invite me to participate in your stage play debut to have me meet William and maybe hope for some romantic development?"

I leaned forward and looked her directly in the eyes to respond. "Absolutely not. I need your skills, your talent, and your contacts with the theatre community to bring my play to life."

Mairin looked at me, chuckled, and patted my knee, then looked toward Brianna. "Trust me, dear, such a devious notion would never, and I mean never, come from your uncle. Remember, this is the man who married just two years ago."

Brianna pouted. "Well, I'm sorry, but I had to ask. Ma thinks I'm an old maid at twenty-five. When she was this same age, I was already six years old. I don't know how we survived in Belfast, especially after Grandpa disowned us."

I shook my head and wagged my finger in Brianna's direction. Your grandfather NEVER abandoned you. Your mother was a free spirit, and he didn't understand. From his viewpoint, after you were born, you should have continued to live with them. It's the traditional Irish way. Once your mother decided to move to Belfast, your grandfather was distraught and couldn't find a way to communicate with your mother, so he gave up. I wish he would have lived long enough to see you move back to Cork."

Silence fell between the three of us, separating us like the Peace Walls in Belfast separating the Catholics and the Protestants. Silence is never neutral. Brianna avoided looking at either of us and concentrated on sipping her wine.

"I never thought about it from Grandpa's point of view," Brianna confessed in a hushed tone.

"So, Brianna, what's your first impression of William from our little Christmas dinner soirée?" I changed the direction of our conversation intentionally.

"It was just one evening. I don't know."

Mairin straightened up. "I will tell you one thing, he's the odd duck in his family. He is the first person in the entire extended Boyle clan to attend college. Attending graduate school nearly makes him a freak of nature. The rest of the family has worked in the Belleek factory for generations. I don't think William has ever worked in the factory. Ian, do you know?"

"He and I had quite a bit of time to talk at Kieran's funeral. Kieran also sent money to William's mother for his education. No, he never worked at the factory."

I was beginning to doubt my effort to create a team with me, Brianna, and William. I failed to consider she would accept because I asked her, not because it presented a professional challenge or could help her career in even the smallest way. The editors, book designers, and marketing professionals I've worked with over the years to help me bring my fiction to the world evolved over time. I worked with three different editors before Liam Noonan, and we had found a natural way to work with each other.

Relationships in the arts were too often temporary; it was the nature of the work. Liam had been my editor for twenty-two years. I would have to submit his name to the Pope for sainthood after working with me. He could be the patron saint of modern Irish authors. The man had more patience than any three editors combined. His command of the language was extraordinary. In all our time together, I had never argued with him, despite having had nearly tragic differences of opinion. We respected each other's skills and knowledge. Ours was a once in a lifetime relationship, yet he wasn't a friend, not in the way Kieran was a friend.

"Well, for you, Uncle Ian, I'm willing to try. I accept he has credentials. I checked with a few people I know at Trinity, and he has a very good reputation. What can I say?"

There was a sharp knock at the door. "William, I'm guessing," Mairin said. "Ian, get the door. Brianna, you and I can check the chicken."

* * * * *

Dinner went well. Over time I had become more accustomed to having guests for dinner or appetizers and wine. Mairin had dropped hints we should invite some friends we had gotten to know well over for card games or a board game. I absolutely refused each and every time she brought it up. First, I didn't know any card games, and at my age, I didn't have any interest in learning. Having people for cocktails or wine would be acceptable, but I'd rather meet in a pub.

Mairin guided our conversation at dinner because she knew I wouldn't do it. I've never been a conversationalist; it was not natural for me to express myself verbally. The written word was my medium. I did enjoy listening to how

Mairin would pose questions to Brianna and William designed to get them to learn about each other in a casual, indirect manner. Mairin had a real talent for putting people at ease. She wasn't playing matchmaker but she was very close. I couldn't tell if Brianna and William had a natural attraction for each other, and I made a note to myself to ask Mairin her view when we snuggled into bed later.

Mairin suggested we have dessert in the parlor. I surprised everyone by volunteering to help clear the table. Mairin chided me. She said I was just trying to impress William with my good manners but assured him he was witnessing a first. I stacked dishes and let Mairin put them in the dishwasher. She looked at me and winked as I handed her the glasses. "You're a coy old man."

"Coy?"

"Yes. We let Brianna and William have a few minutes alone. Very coy, I would say. I do appreciate your help clearing the table. I could get used to this, Ian Murphy."

I patted Mairin on the back. "Darling, I am not obtuse, nor am I coy. I didn't even think about our guests being alone. I was just expressing my appreciation for an excellent dinner and you being a superb host, a role I am and will always be uncomfortable with."

"If you insist, dear. I know you want to have a planning meeting on your stage play. Go ahead, I can finish."

"You must join us. You're a part of our team, too. I never would have considered a memoir, exposing my life, without your influence. Forgive me, but I assumed you would contribute to the entire production. I need to show you more respect. Mairin, would you please be part of our team?"

Mairin slammed the dishwasher door shut, leapt into my arms, and held me very tight. Her sweet fragrance made me lightheaded. She kissed my cheek and whispered into my ear, "You want me?"

I drew her close. "I wouldn't have it any other way." We walked arm in arm into the parlor to join Brianna and William, who were so engaged in conversation athey didn't notice us walk into the room.

"Hmm, can we start talking about the stage play? I want to let you know what I've been working on."

William and Brianna jerked their heads up and gave a faint scowl at being interrupted. "Dessert?" William asked.

"Later, William, later."

"I'll make coffee with dessert, too," Mairin offered in perfect hospitality.

"First, you both need to understand our endeavor is not my original idea. As you know, Mairin suggested months ago I write my memoir to help me overcome writer's block. She thought I needed to tell my story of the Provisional Irish Republican Army and how I changed direction in my life and participated in the Peace Accord. I shrugged off her suggestion for months; thank God she isn't the type of person who nags. She simply planted the seed and let it rest."

"The concept of writing a stage play definitely wasn't mine. I am a novelist. I also told you that Oisin O'Leary came up with the idea of me collaborating with William on a play about my life. He actually came over to hide from some of his social responsibilities, and, we ended up consuming a bottle of

Midleton, or maybe a bit more. He was suggesting ways I could mentor William in his graduate studies, and without warning he told me I should write a memoir stage play and have William direct it as his master's project and write a thesis about the experience. I laughed in his face. It might have been the whiskey that laughed in his face – one of those belly-heaving laughs that makes your stomach hurt afterward. It took me a few moments to regain my composure and I saw Oisin wasn't laughing – he was serious. Of course, I expressed my complete ignorance of the theatre and how to even begin to write a play. His honesty was brutal. He told me I needed the challenge, and I had a unique opportunity to share my story with Ireland. He even told me I had a moral responsibility to share my story because I was a symbol of how Ireland once embraced war and evolved to a country working daily to create peace."

I fell back into the sofa, exhausted from sharing my experience and path to this point. I felt relief to share with those who understood and cared for me. Mairin rubbed my shoulders, releasing the tension in my back.

William stared at me like he had seen a ghost. "This is the kind of thing Carl Jung wrote about, all the elements coming together in synergy. Brianna, how likely is it that your degree is in arts administration, Ian is your uncle, and the good friend of my uncle? This is extraordinary."

"I'm beginning to understand too," Mairin said.

"Uncle Ian, how are you going to make the transition from writing a novel to writing a script?" Brianna asked.

I explained I would learn the only way I knew, to read. I told them about my meeting with Tom Murphy and how I had buried myself in reading play after play to try and capture the craft. Since Christmas I had distracted myself to the point I was shedding bad habits like oak leaves falling in the fall. I still had my pipe after dinner but I didn't drink as I read. I felt I had to remain clear and able to comprehend what I was reading. Many nights I would become so absorbed in reading plays, I would set my pipe in the ashtray and let it grow cold, only half smoked. Often, when I couldn't sleep, I would just get up and read a magazine or read a novel to distract my mind from play reading. I don't know why I didn't have a whiskey on those sleepless nights. It could have helped, I suppose.

"Writing the play was forcing me to look back on my own life. In telling the story it is important that I not be judgmental while at the same time revealing the truth about my motives and my role in the Provisional Irish Republican Army. The play unfolded before me like one of my novels. I imagined the curtain opening and on the front stage right would be a middle-age man sitting at a desk, writing on a yellow pad, smoking a pipe, with a half full bottle of whiskey and a large tumbler of whiskey in front of him. The character would take a few sips, blow smoke at the ceiling, and then write furiously on the pad. The image I wanted to convey is me drafting the play, which would segue to the main curtain opening on scene 1, act 1."

"Uncle Ian, that is the perfect image, just perfect," Brianna gushed.

Mairin squeezed my shoulders and gave me a peck on the cheek. "Ian, I am impressed, too. You're creating a vision exactly like you were beginning a novel."

I caught my breath, looked at Mairin, then Brianna and back at Mairin. "I am, aren't I?" The moment of self-realization often occurred by surprise and came with a certain innocence. Before writing a single word I always envision an entire novel with plot, characterization, location, and most important, themes. I was subconsciously applying the same method to drafting the script.

"Do you have any more details about the script you can share with us now?" William wondered.

"Darling, would you like a whiskey? I can run up to your office and get it," Mairin offered.

My face scrunched up into a question mark. I found her offer out of character and a bit odd since we had guests. "No, I don't think so. A cup of Barry's would be refreshing. William? Brianna?"

"Yes," they said in unison.

Mairin beamed. "I would be delighted to make us tea. Now, hold off on our discussion until I return."

I jumped to my feet. "I'll help. You kids entertain yourselves." I followed on Mairin's heels. Once in the kitchen she turned and gave me a bear hug, burying her face in my chest. I became lightheaded with her magnolia scent. I didn't understand her embrace, but it was so warm and loving, I didn't care. Mairin looked into my face. Her eyes were damp, and she smiled.

"Your path through life is to write, Ian. It's the only path for you. I'm realizing myself; writing is not just what you do, writing is who you are. You experience life through self-expression. I am so proud of you."

I pulled her close to me. I was speechless. It didn't happen often but it did happen. For a moment I forgot we were in the kitchen to make tea for William and Brianna. My mind wandered off and I recalled something Picasso said that I thought was profound. I shared this with Mairin. "Later in his life a reporter asked Picasso about the purpose and meaning of life. He said, 'The meaning of life is to find your gift. The purpose of life is to give it away.' I am just now beginning to understand what he meant."

"I think you were fortunate, you found your gift when you were very young and your entire life has been about giving it away," Mairin whispered.

It was like a fairy cast a spell as we stood in the kitchen holding each other. From the parlor I heard Brianna's voice. "Tea?"

We were jolted out of our solitude and back into our kitchen in 2004. It was a harsh return. Mairin and I giggled at each other and worked in harmony to make the tea as fast as we could. Mairin sent me back into the parlor with a plate of biscuits and a few chocolates.

"Uncle Ian, what were you and Mairin doing?"

As I sat the plate down in front of them, I snapped my head up to look at her. "Oh, nothing. Never mind. Chocolate?"

Just as I was sitting down, Mairin came in with four steaming mugs of tea. Warm tea gave a sense of well-being and the feeling that all was right with the world, even if it was only an illusion.

"Your first image is spot on, Ian," William said. "Have you thought about the structure of the play, you know – how many acts, how many scenes, locations, you know?"

I sipped my tea and gathered my thoughts before answering his questions. "Yes, I have a broad panorama. I want four acts. The first will be how I joined the IRA; it was a combination of your Uncle Kieran's recruiting and circumstances. The second act will cover when I wrote the Green Book. The third act will be about Eileen's betrayal and my encounter with self-destruction. In the final act I will share my experience with drafting the Peace Accord. I don't know how many pages the script will be or how long the performance will be. I suppose there will need to be an intermission."

Mairin patted my knee. "Ian, you have been working on this harder than I imagined. You really have envisioned the sweep of the play."

"Brianna, William do you have any questions? Oh, yes, I want you to understand my expectation is you two will be in charge of the production. I have neither the time, inclination, or interest in being involved in the production. In fact, I intend to be an observer – a member of the audience, if you will. I will consult on the script once you are in rehearsal. Are we clear?"

They looked at each other. "Sure," they said together.

"Uncle Ian, you're giving a couple of novices a lot of responsibility," Brianna said.

"I am giving you the opportunity."

Mairin glanced at her watch, which was intended as a signal for me, but I am never alert to such subtle nuances. "Well, young people, it's time to call it an evening. It's been very exciting. Ian will need some time to write now. I'll be in charge of communicating with you as Ian develops the script. Ian, you'll need to coordinate with the Theatre Department so you are aware of the timeline William will have to share his project, and you will need more detail for your job as his mentor."

I shot up to my feet. "Yes, Ma'am! That's it, kids, she has spoken. Off with you. It's been a rewarding evening. Maybe we should do this weekly. Mairin?"

"An excellent idea. I'll be in touch with both of you to schedule our meeting next week."

"Mmmm. Maybe two weeks, dear," Ian said.

"Yes, Ian, I understand."

William turned toward the door and then did an about-face to shake my hand. "I don't know how to thank you."

"There will be an immense amount of work for you; no need to thank me. I must confess, I feel Kieran's presence with us on this undertaking."

Brianna hugged both Mairin and me. "I'm going to make my ma proud."

CHAPTER 19

For the first time since I began teaching at University College Cork, I was not eager to begin the spring term. I was completely absorbed by writing my play and any activity, no matter how small, felt like an evil distraction. Mairin reminded me, in conjunction with the play, I had a responsibility to William to participate in his graduate program as his mentor. Two weeks had passed since our dinner with William and Brianna. The term officially had begun a week ago Monday but my first class wasn't scheduled until a week from Thursday. Mairin was surprised I had not been contacted by either the Theatre Department or William to initiate my duties as his mentor.

A note came in the day's post; a meeting had been scheduled for next Monday at ten a.m. in the Theatre Department Conference room for all graduate mentors. The graduate students were exempt from this meeting; however, there would be meetings in the future for both mentors and students in an attempt to create a collegial atmosphere for the students. I called William to inform him of the meeting and to assure him I had not abandoned him even before classes began. William assured me Brianna was taking excellent care of him and helping him get acclimated to University College Cork, the Theatre Department, and the city.

"We took a great walk through Fitzgerald Park Sunday evening. She's been my guide to campus. She even took me to the house where you grew up," William said.

"Interesting. As you saw, it's nothing special."

"I shouldn't ask, but I will. Have you been to her apartment? No, never mind, none of my business. Look, why don't you stop by for dinner Monday evening and I'll share with you what I learn at the mentor's meeting."

"Thank you. What time?"

"Let's say half six."

"Is it too early to ask you where you are at in the manuscript?" William inquired.

"Yes, it is. We'll look forward to seeing you Monday."

"Can Brianna come? I'm seeing her tonight; we're going to a hooley at Rearden's. Brianna says it's the best."

"Of course, Brianna is always invited. Rearden's is a classic. It's not Mickey's, of course, and I suppose Mickey's is more for my age group."

"I like Mickey's but Brianna says Rearden's rocks."

"Well, enjoy yourself. Give Brianna my love. Goodbye."

* * * * *

There were five mentors including me, the department head, Dr. Sweeney, and the department administrator, Siobhan Sheehan. The Sheehans had been in County Cork for centuries, and she shared my mother's first name. My guess was Siobhan was the glue holding the department together, and she made sure all the graduate students stayed on the right track for their chosen specialization. Besides the department head, she was also the only other woman in the group. She appeared to be in her late forties, short hair, and wore a suit with an open-neck blouse. She didn't wear any jewelry at all. Her bright blue eyes caught your attention when she looked at you. All the men were, as I was, a non-descript academic sort, except one, the senior lecturer, Dr. Hurley, another traditional County Cork name. Dr. Hurley had wavy silver-gray hair touching the top of his shirt collar, and he looked like he spent a great deal of time each morning brushing it straight back. He wore

W.B. Yeats-style glasses high on his nose, a hand-tied bow tie with a stiff, starched collar shirt, and a Donegal tweed suit. I couldn't decide if he dressed like the stereotypical mid-century academic to express himself or to elicit a specific response.

Dr. Sweeney made the introductions and in particular welcomed me into their department enclave. Following introductions, Siobhan Sheehan took over the meeting. Everyone displayed notepads and a pen, except me. No one had suggested I should take notes. My right hand bound up into a fist. I pushed it under the table to hide it from everyone and cleared my throat several times.

"Sorry, I didn't know I was expected to take notes. I don't attend these meetings in my department, I'm only an adjunct lecturer – don't even have a graduate degree," I explained to the group.

Dr. Sweeney shook her head in disbelief. "You could have asked how to prepare, Mr. Murphy."

"Yes, you're right, of course, I should have asked."

"You can meet with me following the meeting and I'll give you some additional materials. What matters is that your graduate student is successful. Who is your graduate student, by the way?" Ms. Sheehan asked.

"William Butler Boyle."

"Oh, yes, the lad from County Donegal. Came to us from Trinity, didn't he?" asked Dr. Hurley.

"Correct."

"What is his specialty?"

I cringed and lost my voice somewhere deep in my throat. "I'm sorry, I don't know. We're meeting tonight."

"Let's move on with the meeting, Ms. Sheehan," Dr. Sweeney directed.

I met with Ms. Sheehan for thirty minutes following the mentor meeting. She was efficient and sympathetic to my situation. She gave me a series of forms for William to complete and for me to complete. I would have liked to meet the people who design college forms, I thought they all had a twisted sense of humor and knew their work would cause normal people pangs of outrageous pain. One form was titled "Graduate Student Program Evaluation" with a note at the bottom of the page: "Must be completed to be awarded degree." My eyes blurred and I felt myself lose grip on reality.

"Ms. Sheehan, I have no idea how I will complete this form. William won't be completing a standard thesis; he will be directing a play I'm writing. How would you measure success – audience attendance, published critics reviews, review from the Theatre Department faculty, and number of performances? What if the writing is terrible, but the directing is superlative? Also, I don't know when the play will be performed; it might not be until William has completed all his classroom requirements."

Shioban Sheehan put her pen on the table, raised her eyebrows, and trained her blue eyes on me, tapping her fingers on the desk. "What you are undertaking is unique. I know you have the Dean's express permission for this. I suggest you develop a proposal and submit it to Dr. Sweeney in the next week."

"Proposal? I'm not understanding."

Ms. Sheehan took a deep breath and slowly exhaled between her teeth. "You propose how you will determine if William completes the project successfully. I would recommend you have him write a paper describing his experience and what he learned. A self-evaluation if you will. It will be easier on you and make William aware of the learning process."

I felt my heart race and a huge smile broke out on my face. "Ms. Sheehan, you are brilliant!"

"Shioban, please, and you're welcome."

I left with a sense of a huge weight being lifted from my shoulders. The sun had climbed to its apex, but I still needed my Dubarry jacket. I decided to take a brisk walk to Mickey's for lunch, which would help put me in the mood for writing the rest of the afternoon. It wasn't more than a fifteen-minute walk from campus to Mickey's Pub on Patrick Street. I put my hands in my pockets to search for my gloves and found my pipe instead. I took it out, looked at it for a moment, and decided to put it away again. I breathed in the crisp air and coughed. I definitely didn't need to smoke.

I walked along the city streets, not paying attention to my route. Without warning my mind's eye saw a wood-paneled room with a steep ceiling, like an attic. There were no windows, just a desk and a chair at the far end of the room. There wasn't even a carpet on the floor, just worn wooden floor boards. I stopped and rubbed my eyes and looked up at all the buildings surrounding me. I leaned against the nearest building to regain my composure and try to understand what I had seen.

"Are you all right, sir?" a middle-aged man carrying a brief case asked me.

"What?"

"Are you feeling well?"

I straightened myself up and smiled back at the man. "Yes, thank you for asking. I'm fine." The man smiled back and walked down the street.

Things like this had started happening more frequently, though I didn't want to admit it to myself or anyone else, even Mairin. I knew at once the room I envisioned was where I would write my play. I was comfortable reading in my home office, but not writing, and I never wrote in my cramped campus office. Since moving to the home with Mairin, I had not been able to develop a comfortable writing routine. At my age, with the lifelong habit of writing in my cottage in West Cork, any other location was too different, strange even. My subconscious just gave me the answer. I needed to find the room I saw in my vision. The mystery was how to go about the search. It could be in any building in Cork.

I was greeted by Mickey's lunchtime staff, the stalwart Edward. He insisted on being called Edward, not Eddie, not Ed – Edward. "Is himself about today, Edward?" I asked.

"Yes, sir. He's in the kitchen, trying out new recipes." Edward didn't look up and continued polishing the whiskey glasses. "You can go back; he won't mind."

Mickey was in the center of the kitchen with several plates in front of him. "Ian, good to see you. Let me have your opinion on this." He handed me a sandwich. It was a salmon patty with a dill sauce and a hint of some other herb I couldn't identify. The salmon was perfect without breading. I couldn't determine how it had been cooked.

"Well?" Mickey asked.

"It's perfect. You know I love salmon. Are you going to add it to the menu?"

"I am now." Mickey beamed from ear to ear and patted his rounded stomach.

"You're changing the menu. I am in shock. I may need a whiskey. Wait, let me call Mairin and tell her."

"Enough, Ian. I change the menu from time to time."

"Right. The last time might have been 1995."

"I admit, I don't change the menu often. If it sells, why change it, is my motto. It worked for my grandfather and my father."

"So why are you changing it now?"

"Attracts more tourist and it surprises the regulars, like yourself. With this sandwich, I'm guessing you'll stop by more often for lunch."

I laughed out loud and slapped Mickey on the back. "You know me too well. Now, in addition to having another one of these salmon sandwiches and some chips, I need to ask you a special favor."

"Let's go to your table. I'll have Maeve bring your food when it's ready. I'm curious about the favor."

I walked to my regular table. Mickey stopped at the bar and drew two pints for us. "Here, you look thirsty." Mickey sat in the chair opposite me and put his elbows on the table.

"You know I love the house Mairin found for us. The location near campus is perfect. We can both walk to work, but I haven't been able to write in my new office. It's a fine office, mind you, all by itself on the third floor. Mairin was very good about finding a house to allow me to have my private space. Yet, I just can't seem to write there. I was comfortable in my cottage, my writing room was exactly the way I wanted it. In the new house, it's more like an office where people have meetings. Then, walking over here today I had this picture of a room pop into my mind. It was a wood-paneled room, with a wood floor, no windows, like an attic. How can I find a room with that description, Mickey?"

Mickey lifted a single eyebrow and clasped his hand across his mouth. He sucked in his breath and held it. "Blessed Mother Mary, you've just described my Aunt Assumpta's home on Perrott Avenue. We can visit after lunch."

"Here ya are, Mr. Murphy. Yer the first to have our new fancy pub grub. Can I fetch anything else?" Maeve crossed her arms across her chest, not expecting to be asked anything.

"Yes, Maeve you can. Bring your boss and me a Midleton, if you please."

"Oh, I should've known." She turned on her heel and returned in just a moment with the bottle and two Glencairn crystal glasses.

"I could almost believe in miracles."

I finished my sandwich. Mickey and I took our time enjoying the Midleton and then walked to Perrott Ave.

"Shouldn't we call first?" I asked.

"There's no need."

At Mickey's pace it was about a thirty-minute walk. Mickey was never one for the exercise. Mickey's aunt's home was at the end of the street. It was a three-story row house which gave the appearance of being there a long time, maybe fifty years or more.

Mickey walked in without knocking and bellowed, "Assumpta!" at the top of his Irish tenor voice. He looked over his shoulder at me. "She doesn't hear well any longer." Mickey walked straight back into the kitchen and found Assumpta there having her afternoon cup of tea.

A plump lady with snow-white hair and wire-rimmed glasses sat at the kitchen table. "Mickey, what are you doing here in the middle of the day? Who's with you?"

"Aunt Assumpta, this is my friend, Ian Murphy, you know, the writer."

Assumpta adjusted her glasses to focus on me and slurped her tea. "Oh. So why have you come by again?"

"Ian wants to see your attic."

She sat the teacup down with a clink and stared at me. "My attic, you say?"

"Yes."

"You go with him, Mickey darling. I haven't been up there in years. I don't recall if anything is in storage up there or not."

We walked up two flights of stairs. At the top floor there was a narrow hallway with one door on the right-hand side. A rope hung down from the center of the ceiling. Mickey gave the rope a tug. Nothing happened. "All right, Ian, give us a hand."

I grabbed the rope with Mickey and tugged with a grunt. Dust fell on my head but the stairway moved. "One more time, then we'll have it."

We yanked again and the stairway leading to the attic came down. A rope on either side of the narrow stairs served as a railing.

"I'll lead the way," Mickey boasted.

As he took each step, the stairs creaked and moaned. I wasn't confident the stairs would bear his weight. "Come on up, Ian, you're goin' to be surprised."

I swayed back and forth as I climbed and watched my feet so I wouldn't miss a step. I stepped up onto the attic floor and at the far end of the room was a small pine desk. The room was exactly what I had envisioned just a few hours before. "Mickey, I can't believe this. Will she rent it to me?"

"I can't speak for my aunt but I doubt it. She's comfortable. My uncle worked a lifetime on the docks and left her comfortable. She doesn't get out much, never has."

"Well, I wouldn't want to use a room in her home without some compensation. Is there anything she needs or something she's always wanted to do but just didn't have the money?"

Mickey scratched his chin. Well, she's always fancied visiting what's left of her family in Derry. It's such a distance."

I clapped my hands. "Perfect, I'll pay for her to travel to Derry, all expenses paid for as long as she wants. Do you think she might want to be gone for a month? Not to be selfish but it would work well for me."

"Let me talk to her. It will take some convincing for her to be gone long. There isn't anything tying her down here really. When would you like to start?"

"This afternoon?" I asked, knowing the answer.

"I will talk with her and give you a ring."

Two days later Mickey called. His aunt accepted my offer. She would leave on the Saturday train and visit her family for a month. Mickey said she was deeply appreciative. I gave Mickey a check for a thousand Irish pounds. My guess was she knew nothing about the new euro.

CHAPTER 20

I should have anticipated that Mairin wouldn't understand why I needed a space other than the office in our home or my office on campus to work on my script. Although we didn't argue about it or the money I gave Assumpta, Mairin felt inadequate because the house didn't provide the space I needed to write. She worried I shouldn't have sold the cottage. I explained the vision I had of the space I needed. I was just following my muse. Mairin had always been supportive of everything I did, even those times that caused us to be separated, sometimes for weeks at a time. I confess, once I saw the room, I never imagined Mairin's response. When I am focused, I am very self-absorbed.

Mickey stopped by the house early one morning to drop off the key to his Aunt Assumpta's home after he left her at the train station. He guessed I would be eager to get started. Other than Mairin, with Kieran gone, Mickey knew me the best. I have relied on Mickey so many times in the past. I took the key, stashed a few supplies in a backpack, and rode my bike to Perrott Ave. Of course, I didn't plan for rain, which is always a mistake in Cork in January. The morning sky clouded over. As I rode my bike, the fumes from cars and the smell of dampness in the air mingled together into an unpleasant smell. With any luck it would rain and cleanse the urban air of noxious fumes.

I took my bike to the back of the house and tried the key on the back door. The key fit into the lock, but no matter how hard I jiggled, it refused to open. Older homes like these often had different locks for each entrance. My cottage was keyed the same way, but I had it changed within a month of living there. I could never determine why anyone would want separate locks on each entrance; it was a false sense of security. I tried the front door lock. The key slid in easily and the tumbler clicked open with a twist of the key.

Assumpta had left the access ladder to the attic room down. I was grateful for her foresight because of the difficulty Mickey and I had to pull the ladder down and secure it the first time. I climbed the stairs one step at a time and grabbed the ropes on the side to steady my climb. Once at the top of the step, I looked around the room. Everything was the same as it had been several days ago. I doubted if, in her health, Assumpta could have managed the stairs any longer. My guess was it had been years since she had stepped into this room.

The wood paneling and flooring gave the room a warm, comfortable feeling while also having a cave-like affect because there were no windows. I unpacked my bag and sat at the desk. The chair fit me perfectly. I closed my eyes and imagined filling numerous yellow pads with writing.

My solace was disturbed by a loud banging at the front door. At first I didn't move, hoping the visitor would go away when there was no answer. The banging continued and even increased in urgency. I slipped on the bottom stair and caught myself on the ropes to prevent landing face first on the hallway floor. The pounding continued until I opened the front door.

A squat, square woman with a faded scarf tied around her head and face stared up at me.

"Who the hell are you?" she demanded.

"My name is Ian Murphy."

"What are you doing in Assumpta's house? She's on holiday up north. Are ya workin' on somethin' for her? Did that louse of a nephew, Mickey O'Shay, send you here?"

"I'm sorry, I didn't catch your name."

"O'Keefe, Sorcha O'Keefe. This be my neighborhood. I was birthed in the house I live in." Then she stopped and narrowed her eyes. "Clever. Very clever, Mr. got me talkin' about me. Now, in the name of Our Lady, what yous doin' in Assumpta's house?"

"Writing."

"Don't be smart with me, ya ejit."

"I'm renting the attic while Assumpta is visiting her family in Derry. I gave her money for the trip." I reached deep into my pocket and pulled out the house key. I dangled the key in front of Mrs. O'Keefe's nose. "See, I have the key. Mickey gave it to me just this morning."

Sorcha O'Keefe put both hands on her hips and looked me over with distrusting eyes. "Assumpta said nothin' to me about yous or anybody else bein' in her house. I knows her all my life, and she tells me everythin'."

"My impression was she was very excited about her trip. Maybe in her eagerness to get ready for the trip, she forgot to mention our arrangement to you. The fact I have the key to the front door must prove it to you."

She snatched the key from my hand, held it close to her eyes, and studied it for several minutes, then tried it in the lock herself. "This be her key. It ain't no copy; I can tell."

"If it would help, you can talk to Mickey yourself. Come in and use the telephone."

Sorcha O'Keefe pushed me aside and barged through the door into the parlor where the phone was located. I thought it best to leave her alone and waited for her in the kitchen. I noticed she swayed from side to side when she walked into the kitchen.

"Ok, yous are legit, Mickey says. I can still remember the day he was born. I had to check – see – it's my business an all."

"I understand."

"So, how much ya gonna be here?"

"Every day."

"Ok then. I got it."

Sorcha waddled back through the living room and slammed the front door behind her. I looked around the kitchen for tea and a kettle. It took a few minutes, Assumpta was a fastidious woman and everything was tucked into its place. I put a saucer upside down on my cup and carried it back to my *sanctus sanctorum* in the little house on Perrott Ave.

* * * * *

After returning to my new attic writing retreat, I was tempted to pull up the stairs to the room since I thought it possible Mrs. O'Keefe's might wander back into the house to check on me. I let the temptation pass because if she did return, having the stairs pulled up would cause suspicion, and while I like my privacy, I don't like to feel like I'm in a cave.

I lit a pipe, leaned back in my chair, and let my thoughts drift off where they would. I realized I hadn't asked Assumpta if she would mind if I smoked in her house. I also didn't have an ashtray to dump out my pipe when I was finished. I took several pages of my notepad and fashioned them into a makeshift ashtray I could use after the ashes in my pipe went cold.

I set my pipe on the desk and closed my eyes. In a flash the entire play leapt out of my imagination. I knew the first act, first scene and the last act, last scene. I could "see" the entire story arc. I scribbled on my yellow pad:

Act 1 – Joining the IRA

Act 2 – The Green Book

Act 3 - Betrayed

Act 4 – Good Friday Agreement

I had learned from Thomas Murphy I had full liberty to write as few or as many acts in the play as I wanted, the days when stage plays were just three acts was long gone. It was odd to witness my own life unfolding in just four acts. I felt like I was beginning to understand myself in context, in the context of history.

* * * * *

I don't know how long it took me to imagine the play, but my pipe had gone cold and only a few ashes remained in the bowl. I tapped the pipe against my palm and watched the spent tobacco drop into my makeshift paper ashtray. I was very satisfied with my accomplishment for the day. I wanted to rest, maybe take a walk through Fitzgerald Park or Mardyke Walk, and then I remembered I had ridden my bicycle. Those thoughts were fleeting. I stretched my legs and put my hands behind my head and let my mind go empty. My experience has been, when I don't try to corral my inspirations, it is my most creative time.

Dead Reckoning

Act 1

Scene 4

> Timolty's body is laid out in his parents' living room for a traditional Irish wake.

> Ian walks into the room, notices the open window and the clock on the mantle stopped at 6:00.

> Timolty's mother is on her knees beside her son's body. She fumbles with her rosary

Ian: Mrs. Doyle?

Mrs. Doyle: Oh, God, Ian. Oh, God. Did you know?

Ian: Know?

Mrs. Doyle: Did you know that my Timolty went to join
the IRA? Jesus, he told me he wanted to learn a trade. I
didn't understand why he had to go to Belfast. There are
plenty of trades here in Cork – he was headstrong, like
his da was Timolty.

Ian: (hesitates) No, he never said. May I pray with you?

Mrs. Doyle: Pray Ian; pray that his soul is already in
God's hands. You were his only friend you know.

Ian: He was popular, Mrs. Doyle. I wasn't his only friend.

Mrs. Doyle: And where are those friends now, Ian
Murphy? No, you were his friend. We couldn't have
a wake without you.

Ian: Mr. Fitzpatrick brought me from Dublin
straight away.

Mrs. Doyle: Who's Mr. Fitzpatrick? Did my Timolty
know Mr. Fitzpatrick?

Ian: I don't know. I only just met him recently myself.
It doesn't matter. He was kind enough to get me
here, that's all that matters.

Mrs. Doyle: My legs ache. Help me up, Ian. You stay
with Timolty.
Ian watches as she leaves and then turns back to the still
body of his friend.

Ian: (whispering fiercely) Timolty, Timolty, Timolty
didn't I tell you joining the IRA was a foul idea. You
should've stayed on the docks with your da. Now look
what you've done. Your Ma can't be consoled. Did you
know you would sacrifice yourself?

(Pauses and shivers) Jesus, the room is cold; when I
first came into the parlor it wasn't cold. Death is cold,
Timolty. (Jumps up and looks around) What's that? It
felt like someone tapping my shoulder. (The ghost of
Timolty enters the room and stares at Ian) Timolty? Oh,
God, it can't be? I'm hallucinating, I must be. Timolty?
I see your wound. Your shirt and vest are blood-
stained. You're still bleeding. How can that be? (Ian
looks from the ghost to the body on the table.) You're
here on the table, cold and gray, holding your rosary in your hands. (Ian looks back at the ghost whose
lips are moving.) What? I can see your lips moving
but I can't hear you. Mother of God, I'm going stark
raving mad. I won't be going back to Trinity, I'll be
committed someplace. (Ian walks toward the ghost.)
Why are you doing this to me, Timolty? (Ian takes a deep
breath.) I won't look away. I'll look directly into your
face. I can't hear you. My heart is pounding, Timolty, I'm
afraid. I don't understand this.

(Timolthy's ghost whispers louder.)

Ian: (takes a step back) Oh, I hear you now. Yes, I do.
I hear you. Revenge. Revenge? As God is my witness,
my friend, I will revenge your death. I will.
I will.

(Ian faints and falls on the floor)

Close Curtain.

The fountain pen slipped from my sweating palm and crashed
onto the floor. Ink leaked out of the pen and stained the un-
treated wood floor. I stared at the pen, unable to bend down
to pick it up. The ink turned red like blood. I rubbed my eyes.
I pulled the cork out of the whiskey bottle and filled my glass
to the top. I cuddled the glass with both hands to make sure
I didn't drop it too. Its golden liquid was too precious to spill
even a single drop. There was a strong sent of oak from the

years the whiskey had been stored in an Irish stout barrel. I gulped and felt the whiskey burn down my throat. I felt my head become light and my vision blur. Had I forgotten? Did it take the stage play for me to remember? All these years I was sure I joined the IRA for the noble cause – to unify Ireland and expel the British Army from our land. Now I knew different.

I don't remember the events the same way. I distinctly remember telling Mr. Fitzpatrick at the burial ceremony as I threw dirt on Timolty's casket, I would join the IRA. It wasn't out of patriotism or wanting Ireland to be one country again or even to expel the British from our island. I joined for revenge against the IRA. I've lived a lie for thirty years. This was my truth. There was always truth in writing. I would expose myself to the Irish people, to the world. Would I be able to look at myself in the mirror? The man in the mirror today was the same as the one yesterday – but changed. I had been honest with myself for the first time in thirty years. Maybe Kieran was still guiding me, through William. I didn't see Kieran's ghost at his wake.

I sat the empty whiskey glass on the desk with a thud. The attic room felt warm and smaller than before. I had to leave. I needed the wet, fresh air of the River Lee. I needed to free myself from the writing prison I had created.

As I left Assumpta's house, I wasn't sure I would return the next day. Writing the stage play was having unexpected consequences. Truth can be bitter, and as I walked to the river, I had a sharp taste in my mouth.

CHAPTER 21

Sooner than I realized, it was March. I became a hermit, not seeing my sister Caitlin, my new friend Oisen O'Leary, William, or Brianna. I suspect Mairin was my protector. If any of them tried to contact me, she ran interference. I don't know it for a fact but it is so unlikely none of them would contact me in three months. William in particular I'm sure must have been anxious to learn my progress on my stage play because his academic career was in the balance, without the play, he wouldn't be allowed to finish his program.

There were only four students in my spring Irish literature class, which was a relief. I changed the format and required only one paper of at least fifty pages for the term. I confess, it was selfish on my part because the amount of reading I would do was reduced drastically. I also decided the entire group would work on one theme. In the past I didn't focus on a single theme and let the students choose their own direction, a basic foundation in independent learning classes. For this class I selected the theme of betrayal. Betrayal was actually a two-edged sword and in some cases betrayal was actually the moral action.

The spring class was divided equally: two women and two men. I liked the balance. They responded well to working on one theme and were intrigued I choose betrayal. They asked if they could collaborate rather than writing individual papers, and I decided I would let them do as they pleased. As it turned out, two of them decided to collaborate and two elected to write independent papers. I also gave them control over how often we would meet and the location. It was interesting because they were not accustomed to having to make those decisions, but I felt it was a lesson in maturity. Initially we met every week in the classroom but as they became more confident, we met every other week in various locations. I surprised Mairin by offering to meet in our home. In over twenty years of teaching, I never invited students to my home. When I was living in my country cottage alone, it fit my lifestyle. Being married and living in the city, I felt more comfortable and having guests at home was natural.

The first week of April Mairin said it was time we had a conversation. "Having conversation" was our code for having a serious talk. But the subject was not either of us or our marriage but another topic that would need our undivided attention. We relaxed in the parlor with a glass of wine one afternoon after I returned from a day of writing at my retreat in Assumpta's home. I was tired but not exhausted. I was pleased with the stage play, although I had no measure to gauge my progress.

Mairin handed me a glass of wine and sat in the chair opposite me. She didn't sit beside me on the sofa; not a good sign." Listen, Ian, Dr. Sweeney's office has been calling for you. Apparently, the administrative assistant has called several times in an attempt to talk with you."

"I'm not here during the day. You know. Is there a problem?"

Mairin sipped her wine and looked over the top of her glass directly at me. "Today, Dr. Sweeney called me at my office."

"Why?"

"She wants to have a meeting with you. Apparently, you haven't turned in the paper work required from mentors."

"Paperwork? I haven't done any paperwork. I haven't even seen William or Brianna since January."

"Another problem. Did you know, as a mentor, you're required to meet with William once a week and record the outcome of the meeting?"

"Really?"

"My love, you've become so absorbed in writing your stage play, you're ignoring the world. You've made a commitment to help William and you're not fulfilling your role."

"I am helping William. I'm writing the stage play he will direct."

Mairin set her glass on the table next to her and leaned forward on her knees to capture my full attention. "Ian, I've set up an appointment for you to meet with Dr. Sweeney tomorrow morning at nine a.m."

I bolted off the sofa, nearly spilling the small amount of wine still in my glass. "You what?"

"Your heard me, Ian Murphy."

"Absolutely not. Since when did you start making appointments for me? You've gone too far. Where is your respect? I have no intention of going. You can either call Sweeney back or I'll just be a no show. It doesn't matter to me."

Mairin stood and gave me a light hug. "Ian, sit down. Pack your writer's ego away now. Listen to reason. This is for William. You owe it to him. You owe it to Kieran. If it wasn't for William, you would never be challenging yourself with writing a stage play."

I plopped back down on the sofa and looked up at Mairin. "Of course, you're right. I surrender. I'll go to the meeting. But I'm going to tell her to never call you again. If she wants to meet with me, she can contact our department administrator."

"Ian, you don't know that she didn't attempt to schedule a meeting through your department administrator. You have a unique talent for disappearing when you want to. Your hideaway on Perrott Avenue makes you inaccessible, even to me."

I couldn't resist a smile.

"Wipe that grin off your face, Ian Murphy. Now, I would like another glass of wine before dinner. Would you mind?"

* * * * *

I didn't sleep well because I had deep anxiety about meeting with Fion Sweeney. I know she wasn't happy William and I appealed her decision to the dean. She didn't give the impression of being a person to forgive and forget. Sometime, out of exhaustion, I fell into a restless sleep. When I woke the next morning, my night clothes were damp with sweat. It was never a good omen.

I showered as soon as I got up and refused both breakfast and tea. Mairin always noticed when I changed my routine, even in the most minor way. "You're anxious aren't you, dear?"

I didn't reply. I dressed and as I walked out the door, I said, "I'm walking to campus this morning."

I arrived at the theatre department building, and didn't see either students or faculty entering the building. My guess was it wasn't much past eight in the morning. I decided to walk the perimeter of campus both to calm myself and to kill time before the meeting. I could tell what time it was by listening to the campus chime. When the chime rang half-eight, I was just halfway around the campus, so by the time I returned to the theatre building, it would be nine.

I stopped at the administrative assistants' desk to announce myself. Without looking up she instructed me to go through; Dr. Sweeney was waiting for me. I wondered if I might be a few minutes late but even if I was, I really didn't care.

Dr. Sweeney was sitting straight as a board at her desk, reading from a neat stack of papers.

"Good morning, Dr. Sweeney."

"Sit," she ordered without looking up. She didn't offer either coffee or tea, which I considered rude, no matter the circumstances.

She flipped several pages, continuing to read and ignoring my presence. "Dr. Sweeney, you asked to see me. So, I am here."

Dr. Sweeney flipped off her glasses and stared at me. "You are one elusive bastard."

I cleared my throat before responding to her first salvo. "I am a private man."

"I've heard you're slacking off in your senior reading course too."

I could feel blood rise up in my neck, making my cheeks flush. "How I conduct my class is none of your business. Get to the point. Why am I here?"

Dr. Sweeney stood up and leaned forward with her fists on her desk. "You will not take that attitude with me, Mr. Murphy. You have not fulfilled a single requirement of the mentor program. As a result, William is far behind the other students in his progress. I've inquired and learned you haven't even seen William since January. Your behavior is inexcusable. You went behind my back to the dean to be a mentor in my department and now you're ignoring your responsibilities. Think of William. Do you want him to fail? I don't know, nor do I care, what you do with your time. Let me inform you, I am prepared to dismiss William from our graduate program if this is not rectified immediately. When you leave my office, Shiobban will give you the required mentor paperwork. I will give you three days to complete and return it to this office. If you don't comply, William will be expelled from the program immediately. Do you understand?"

I don't recall ever having such a brow beating. "Yes, I understand, but I didn't go behind your back. There is an appeal procedure and I simply followed the procedure. Dr. O'Leary saw things differently."

Dr. Sweeney sat back down and folded her arms across her chest as she spoke. "Oh, yes, Dr. O'Leary. Rumor has it you too are thick as mud. Well, don't get any ideas of trying to use your new friend to get around our department requirements. It won't work."

"No, no I won't. Three days is generous."

"William tells me you're in hiding writing the stage play. Correct?"

"Yes."

"How far along are you?"

"Well, I've completed two acts."

"Do you have any idea how many acts there will be."

"Four."

"Half way. Well, more detail please."

"Detail? It's a stage play. Detail?"

"Oh, you do so try my patience. How many scenes in each act, Mr. Murphy?"

"The first act has five scenes. The second act has three. I suppose there should be an intermission between the second and third act."

Dr. Sweeney stood up and began pacing behind her desk. My right hand had clenched into a vice grip when she began questioning me. I could feel the vein in my neck throbbing. I began to wonder if I would survive her interrogation.

"Five scenes in the first act is a bit heavy. I wonder if they are all necessary."

"Tom Murphy told me I could have as many scenes as I thought necessary to tell the story. He said they are like chapters in a book."

Dr. Sweeney came from around her desk and glared down at me. "Tom Murphy? You've talked with Tom Murphy? Is he any relation of yours?"

"Yes and no."

Dr. Sweeney paced in the space between my chair and the office door. "I shall want to read the first act."

I jumped straight up out of my chair. "No."

"No?"

"You have no authority to review my work. I refuse."

"We will see, Mr. Murphy. You are dismissed."

I sat back down in the chair. "No one, no one, dismisses me."

"Just leave, you arrogant son of a bitch."

Dr. Sweeney walked to the office door and opened it.

"I am waiting, Mr. Murphy."

I stood up, leaned back against her desk, and crossed my arms across my chest. "Dr. Sweeney, it is clear to me you want this project to fail and you would like to exercise some control over me. Neither is going to happen. I will happily complete your boring administrative forms to ensure William continues in the program. That is the extent of my cooperation with you or your department. I have weathered much worse than you in my life. If I were you, I would reconsider making me your enemy. The price you pay may be the dearest thing you have at this university."

"Are you threatening me?"

"I will allow you your own interpretation." I stomped out of her office and stopped by Shiobban's desk, picking up the packet of forms waiting for me.

"Just call if any of these present a problem," she said and winked at me.

CHAPTER 22

I was working on the forms at home for a third day and was totally confused. I called Mairin at work and asked if she could spare a few moments to help a beleaguered writer with forms that were incomprehensible. I refused to ask for help from Dr. Sweeney's administrative assistant because then Sweeney would know I couldn't master them on my own. I wanted to deny her that satisfaction. In exchange for her help, I offered to take Mairin to lunch.

Mairin looked over the forms, shuffled them, and put them in some order that made sense to her. She hid a smile behind her hand and looked at me with sympathetic eyes. "Oh, my dear, I understand your confusion. The Theatre Department is at least ten years behind the rest of the university. I haven't seen these forms for years. If your back is against the wall with Dr. Sweeney, you could point out the department is out of compliance. I'll give you a set of the current mentor forms. My sense is you may need to have this information to defend yourself."

"I'll go get us a cup of tea and let you work on the forms. You do have time for lunch, don't you?" I asked.

"Actually, I'm booked today. How about a nice dinner this evening? I'd like to go to Mutton Lane; I don't think we've ever been there together."

"Mutton Lane? I've never been there, but I do recall it's in the historic district. Give me a time and I'll make reservations."

"How sweet. You are appreciative. I'll need an early dinner; let's say six. You can stop back early this afternoon to pick up these forms. I suggest you hand-deliver them to the Theatre Department. Now, fetch the tea, please."

It was about three in the afternoon when I dropped off the packet of forms. I confess, I didn't look at them before turning them in, although it might have been a mistake.

The department assistant, Shiobban, smiled broadly when I handed her the packet.

"All done, are we? I was expecting you to stop by for some help. Maybe I should glance at these before turning them in to Dr. Sweeney," she said.

"Very kind. I did find them confusing, but I muddled through. Please, take your time."

Shiobban paged through the packet and appeared to check only certain items. A quizzical look passed across her face. She picked up the papers, changed the order, and read through them a second time. "Well now, Mr. Murphy, you've done yourself proud. These all appear to be in order. It wasn't so bad, was it?"

"Being in a British goal for a month would have been easier."

"Mr. Murphy, you exaggerate. Dr. Sweeney will be given the packet yet this afternoon. I'm sure everything will be fine."

I walked home and enjoyed the spring day. My battle with Dr. Sweeney had cost me three days of writing, and I was feeling uneasy. Writing is not a job for me, its living. In the past three days my mind was swirling with ideas for plot development, and lines of dialogue spun around, wanting to find a blank page. I thought it might help me to have a whiskey before picking up Mairin for dinner; it would help me relax. I could spend the next few days writing to recover my sanity.

As I opened the door to our home, I heard the phone ringing. Usually, I would just let it go to the answering machine but for some reason the ring created a sense of urgency. I ran to the phone and mumbled "Hello" slightly out of breath.

"Ian, Ian, it's William. I've just been at Dr. Sweeney's office. I've been expelled. I don't have any idea why."

I dropped the phone and had to pick it up off the floor. "What are you talking about? How can you be expelled?"

"I don't know. I went to her office. She didn't even let me sit down. She stood behind her desk waiting for me. When I walked up to her desk, she shoved a letter toward me. She said, 'Mr. Butler, you're done. You are no longer a graduate student in the Theatre Department. You are to leave immediately.' I couldn't find any words. I swayed back and forth on my feet and felt like I was going to faint. Then she sat down at her desk and began to read something. She looked up at me and scowled, then said, 'Are you still here. I've asked you to leave.' I did an about face and left her office."

"Where are you now, William?"

"At my apartment. I didn't know where else to go."

"Contact Brianna. Have her pick you up and come here as soon as you can. I'm calling Mairin at work. I'm sorry but I believe this is directed at me, not you. You are not to blame for this. Do you understand?"

"Right now, I don't understand anything."

"Bring the letter you were given with you. We will rectify this, don't worry."

* * * * *

"Mairin, my love, I'm sorry but we need to re-schedule dinner. William just called. That bitch Sweeney expelled him from the graduate program. I've asked him to have Brianna bring him over. We need you at home."

I went upstairs to my writing room, slammed the door, and poured myself a full glass of Midleton while I waited for everyone to arrive. The first glass of whiskey disappeared, followed by the second. I don't remember how many times I filled the glass. I hadn't eaten lunch and without food, the effect of the whiskey on my brain was one hundred percent faster than normal. *I had followed Dr. Sweeney's instructions and had the mentor's paperwork in on time. Why would she expel William?* I lost focus and the room began to spin counter clockwise. I leapt onto the sofa and closed my eyes to gain control. I was afraid to open my eyes; the room might be spinning totally out of control. I felt nauseous and not sure if I could avoid vomiting. I plunged deep, deep into the dark place where there is no light and my soul was lost.

I felt something odd on my shoulders. It felt like someone was putting their hands on my shoulders to arouse me or try to pull me up out of the darkness. I felt a sense of warmth shower over my entire body. A soft, yellow light enveloped my body. The darkness disappeared into this light. I opened my eyes; Kieran had his hands on my shoulders and was leaning over me – smiling. "No more darkness, Ian."

I blinked, then rubbed my eyes hard. I felt a burning sensation in my eyes. I was drunk. I was hallucinating. The whiskey had stolen my consciousness. I opened my eyes again and Kieran was still there. "Kieran, you're not here, you're dead."

Kieran's image remained in front of me, and I could feel the warmth of his hands still resting on my shoulders. How many times when he was alive did he console me by placing his hands just like this on my shoulders? Kieran had a talent for calming me and helping me to journey to my center where I could rest and overcome the darkness. Was this a dream or some memory from long, long ago making its way into my whiskey-drenched mind? Maybe I was trying to recall better days when I relied on Kieran being there for me when I needed him.

"Ian. I'm here, now."

I jumped when I heard those words and slipped out from under his hands. I shook my head back and forth and rubbed my eyes again until they stung to the point I couldn't open them. "No, no, no, no. You're dead. Oh, Jesus. Maybe I'm dead. Maybe I have alcohol poisoning – drank myself into the grave."

"Ian! You're not dead."

My body convulsed, choked, and dry heaved. I coughed so hard my stomach curled up into a knot and I couldn't breathe. I felt Kieran put his hand on my head. A wave of warmth cascaded through me, all the way to my feet. The tension in my body snapped back like a rubber band and I fell back into the corner of the sofa. Sweat poured off my forehead, down my cheeks, and into my mustache. I wiped my face with both hands and squinted to see if Kieran was still there. He sat next to me watching my reaction to his apparition.

"How?" I asked.

"Don't ask," Kieran said.

"Why?"

"You disappoint me. You've let William down. I asked you to take care of him. You've botched it. I can't let you fail William. I can't let you fail yourself. You are self-destructive, Ian. I saved you when your mistress betrayed you. I saved you when the IRA wanted you assassinated for treason. Now, here I am again, dragging you back from the final abyss. This is the last time, Ian. Do you understand?"

I hid my face in my hands. "I don't understand what you're saying."

"You can't drink anymore. You're killing yourself. Think of Mairin. The darkness will swallow you at any moment; you're one breath away from no return. It's not about will power. You can't rely on your own will power to pull yourself up out of the darkness; you'll always slip back – always. Learn to know your true self, follow your instincts at all times, and then you will be in harmony with the cosmos and fulfill yourself. Whiskey is the crutch you've used to hide from the world. You can't hide from the world because you are of the world. Look at the pattern of your life. Whiskey has only brought you darkness. I know, you hide in the darkness from what you fear will hurt you. It's the darkness killing you, not the world. This is the last time I can intervene to help you; after this I am no longer still attached to this world. I must move on too. You must let me go, Ian."

"I . . . I . . . I can't just stop; I've lived this way for more than thirty years. My body aches for the sweet taste of Irish whiskey. I need it to write. Whiskey cradles me in the night so I can wake up the next morning."

"Ian, your imagination has created a fantasy world of dependency. You have written a myth, a story you've written for yourself in your vain effort to survive. You have lived in the myth for so many years, you've confused it with reality. You believe the myth you've written for yourself. It only exists in your mind. This is my last attempt to shatter that myth.

"When I first came to you now, I shared the light. The light is the truth, the only truth. You must let the darkness go and make a decision to accept the light in your life."

I slumped back into the sofa. My stomach was empty. It cramped, forcing me to bend over and fold my arms over my stomach to relieve the pain. I tried to ignore Kieran's presence. I grabbed a pillow and buried my head in it. It was impossible to breathe. I sucked in every gulp of air. My head felt light. I sat up and the room circled me. Kieran was still sitting beside me, a scowl replaced his smile.

"You're on the edge of your life, unbalanced, swaying to and fro about to fall off into the darkness for the last time. Depression wants you alone and drunk, Ian, and right now you are both. I'm here so that you're not alone. I gave you a charge and you made a solemn promise in my name you would take care of William. I can't let you fail, both for your sake and William's. Your life and William's are now intertwined as once you and I were.

Muscles throughout my body became loose and supple. I felt my chest rise and fall with each shallow breath. I let go of all my physical senses and felt like I was floating in an ocean. My mind was unable to focus on anything. I tried desperately to remember Kieran's words but they faded away too. I stretched out on the sofa and drifted off to sleep. *Was I dreaming? Was I hallucinating? Mine is a haunted soul. Years ago Timolthy's ghost led me to seek revenge. Kieran's ghost commands me to find myself to conquer the darkness. I am exhausted. I just want to sleep. Is it too much to ask for sleep? Why should I save myself? I know the darkness. Light is foreign to me. Kieran, you always demand something from me, but I'm not sure I have to anything give. Sleep . . . I can't resist.*

* * * * *

I was woken by pounding on my study door. I must have locked it accidentally. "Ian, Jesus, Ian, are you in there. William and Brianna are here. You asked them to come. If you're drunk, I'm sending them home."

I jolted off the sofa and unlocked the door. Mairin rushed in. "You've been drinking already, haven't you? Ian Murphy, I'm ashamed. I'll take William and Brianna out for dinner. You sober up."

I grabbed her wrist. "No, wait. I'm fine. Really. Something incredible just happened to me. Yes, I drank, but I am as sober as a newborn baby. Really. Test me if you want?"

Mairin looked me in my eyes without blinking once. Her stare could whittle me down like a knife through soft pine. "You reek of whiskey."

"I'm here, Mairin. I am. In ways you cannot imagine. I am here and I'm staying here. I'll shower and be right down."

Mairin put her arms around me then pulled back and looked directly into my face. "Something is different, I can sense it. Very odd. I don't understand, Ian, but I believe you. Yes, shower and come down stairs. Later, I want you to share with me what you experienced."

"Kieran Fitzpatrick," I whispered.

"Kieran? What are you talking about?

"Kieran, Kieran was here. Tonight. With me."

"Jesus, I hope you haven't had a drunken hallucination, Ian. I can't tolerate it any longer, I just can't."

I grabbed both of her hands and looked deeply into her eyes. "No, it was real. It happened. He saved me for the third time."

"Now I'm lost. I have no idea what you're talking about. I just need to trust you now. Look, go shower. I'll go try to calm William. Brianna can help, I'm sure."

"He hasn't said anything to you?"

"No, he wanted to but I told him to wait for you."

"I'll dash; I won't be long."

* * * * *

Downstairs Mairin, William, and Brianna were having tea. They had left a cup on the table for me. William fumbled with his teacup as he slurped tea. Brianna had one hand on his leg, trying to comfort him. He looked up at me. Tears swelled in his eyes, then flowed down his cheeks.

William searched through his pockets to find a crumpled-up piece of paper and he handed it to me. It was a fine linen paper with the logo of the Theatre Department at the top. The letter was addressed to Mr. William Butler Boyle. I read it out loud:

> Effective immediately you are expelled from the university of Cork Theatre Department Graduate Program for failure to comply with department requirements in the first quarter.
>
> Department policy mandates those students who do not fulfill the minimum graduate program standards, be expelled.

In my judgment it is highly unlikely you will be successful in the Theatre Department and therefore should not be allowed to continue.

    Respectfully,
    Fion Sweeney, PhD
    Chair, Theatre Department

"William, what is she talking about? Haven't you taken the right courses, turned in assignments?" I asked.

"He has, Uncle Ian, I've helped him with all of them, and I know he turned in all the assignments on time. He hasn't had a single assignment turned back to him for revision or anything," Brianna explained.

"Have you received any grades for the work you've turned in so far?" Mairin asked.

"No, not one." William responded.

"I know what this is about!" I shouted as I stood up. Everyone's eyes turned toward me. "This is retribution for not completing those damn mentor forms. I turned them in. Mairin helped me with them. They were all correct. William, I fear you have paid the price for my insolence. This will not stand, I assure you."

William stood and embraced me, causing me to catch my breath. "I just don't understand?" he said.

"It's a long story, I'm afraid. I'll tell you all about it. Trust me, you will be re-instated, and this damn letter will be purged from your graduate record. Let's all go to dinner and I'll explain the battle between me and Dr. Sweeney, for which, William, you have been the slaughtered lamb."

CHAPTER 23

arrived at Dean O'Leary's office a bit early in hopes of having a few minutes to talk with him before Dr. Sweeney arrived. I wanted to know what he had planned for the meeting. I had William deliver his expulsion letter to his office with a handwritten note asking for a meeting with him. I received a call from his administrative assistant asking me to arrive at his office at nine this morning. I took the meeting as a good sign because, knowing his routine now, I knew a nine o'clock meeting was his first of the day. Whatever he decided, he had done so in less than a day, which, again, I assumed would be positive for William.

When I received the call for the meeting, I asked if William was also invited, and I was told his presence wouldn't be needed. That told me the expulsion would be dealt with by college administration, and while it affected the student, his presence wouldn't influence the final decision. Having lectured at UCC for more than twenty years, even though only an adjunct faculty member, I had learned some of the unique signals within the academic culture.

I walked into the outer office and I was directed into Oisin's office with a hand signal. There was a definite chill in the room. I saw Dr. Sweeney sitting in a chair directly opposite of Dr. O'Leary with her back to me. Dr. O'Leary was busy signing a pile of papers. When he heard the door open, he stood up at once, let his pen fall to the desk, and extended his hand for a handshake.

"Good to see you, Ian."

Fion Sweeney didn't acknowledge my presence. Her hair was pulled back into her usual bun, and her glasses had slipped half way down her nose. She was pale and taking shallow, controlled breaths. She wore a conservative gray suit, and her hands were folded in her lap. I noticed she fumbled with a ring she wore on the thumb of her left hand.

"Pull up a chair, Ian, next to Dr. Sweeney. Yes, fine. Let me finish signing these papers so then I can dispense with the trivial administrative requirements of my job." He took his time to read each page before signing at the bottom. He was careful and I guessed intentionally raising the tension in the room by making us wait. Dr. Sweeney fidgeted in her seat and cleared her throat but didn't speak. I concluded that by signing papers, Oisin was also demonstrating he was in complete control of the situation and he had other duties than to resolve a dispute between staff. He picked up all the papers, shuffled them, and made a neat stack on the right side of his desk. He laid the fountain pen on the desk and looked at each of us.

"Tea?" he asked.

"No," whispered Dr. Sweeney.

"Thanks, I've just had," I said.

Oisin picked up a folder on the left side of his desk. He opened it and read the document inside, then he placed it on the desk in front of Dr. Sweeney. "William Boyle hand delivered this letter to my office yesterday afternoon. A handwritten note was included from Ian Murphy, requesting a meeting. Ian, you didn't ask for any more than a meeting, correct?"

"Yes, correct."

"Did you ask Dr. Sweeney to be invited to me the meeting?"

"No, I didn't."

"Did you expect Dr. Sweeney would be at the meeting today?"

"To be honest, I didn't think about it. I was just pleased you agreed to meet so quickly."

"I want both of you to know I didn't talk with William yesterday. He didn't ask to talk with me, and on a hunch I decided it wouldn't be appropriate for me to talk with him. After reading the contents of this letter, I know I made the right decision. Now, Dr. Sweeney, you are keenly aware expelling any student whether undergraduate or graduate is the most serious action that can be taken."

"Yes, sir, I understand."

"Well, to be honest, I find your letter to William Boyle mysteriously vague. The standard for this type of action has several non-negotiable steps. First, the deficiencies are stated succinctly. Second, an explanation must be provided on the action taken to resolve the deficiencies. Third, the cause for the student's deficiencies must be researched and again stated clearly in the expulsion letter. Are you aware of these requirements, Dr. Sweeney?" Oisin asked.

"Well, I . . . Well, in a general way, yes."

Oisin leaned forward and a crease appeared in his forehead. "It is a simple question, Dr. Sweeney, and I know you understand. The answer is a simple yes or no."

Dr. Sweeney bowed her head. "Yes."

Oisin turned toward me. "Now, Ian, as William Boyle's mentor, were you aware of any deficiencies in his work?"

I sat at up straight. "No. Absolutely not."

"Ian, were you consulted regarding the decision to expel William Boyle?"

"No. It was a complete surprise. I first learned about it when William brought the letter to my home Wednesday night."

"And what was Mr. Boyle's explanation?"

"He didn't have one. He had no idea he was deficient in any course or assignment. My niece, Brianna, who has a post-graduate degree in arts administration, has been helping William, and she confirmed William had completed all his assignments."

Oisin let out a long slow breath. He stood up, turned to look out his window, and held his hands behind his back. As he looked out the window, he continued his inquiry.

"What is this about, Dr. Sweeney. You've been department chair for more than ten years. You know the rules, yet, the letter you gave Mr. Butler is inexplicable."

The room fell silent. The tension was palpable. My hand bound up into a fist so tight my knuckles turned white. I wasn't the one being questioned but Oisin's interrogation even affected me. I didn't look at Dr. Sweeney nor did she look at me. I wanted to bolt out of my chair, run from the office, and forget I ever agreed to be William's mentor. If writing my script had this outcome, I would tear it to shreds the next time I visited my attic hideaway.

Oisin turned on his heel and placed his fist on the desk and leaned toward Dr. Sweeney. "I'm waiting, Dr. Sweeney!"

"The truth is, Dean O'Leary, Ian Murphy is a poor excuse for a mentor. In the first eight weeks of the semester he hasn't met with William Boyle once. I know that for a fact. I had to command his appearance at my office to complete the standard mentor forms, which he successfully ignored. Shiobban even offered her assistance to complete the forms because she knew the process was new to him. He ignored her offer. He gave me no reason, no reason at all for not completing the forms and turning them in on time."

Oisin stood up straight and scratched the back of his head. "Is this true, Ian?"

I cleared my throat and chose my words with caution. "It is true I didn't complete the forms. However, there was no intent on my part to not comply with the mentor requirements. I've been working on my script for the play, and let's just say, I can be self-absorbed when I'm writing."

"Did Dr. Sweeney give you an opportunity to rectify the problem?" Oisin asked.

"Yes, she gave me a three-day extension to complete and return the forms."

Oisin sat back down in his chair. "Well, good. Did you get the forms in within the three days?"

"Yes, only with Mairin's help. I hand delivered them on the afternoon of the third day."

"The expulsion letter is dated the day after you turned in the forms. When did William receive the letter?" Oisin asked.

"The next morning. He was given a note in his first morning class to stop by the department chair's office before his next class."

Oisin leaned back in his chair and stared at the ceiling. He drummed his fingers on his desk. He shook his head and looked directly at Dr. Sweeney.

"Fion, I've known you for years. I don't understand this."

Dr. Sweeney jumped straight out of her chair and screamed. "Ian Murphy refused to let me read the draft of his manuscript. He's never written a stage play in his life. Who does he think he is? I must guarantee the quality of the education students receive in our graduate program. It's unprecedented to allow a novice to serve as a mentor and allow the production of an original play to fulfill graduate requirements and receive a degree. As chair of the department, I have the right to review the script before the play goes to casting and rehearsal."

"Sit down, Dr. Sweeney," Dean O'Leary commanded.

"The fog is beginning to lift, isn't it?" He looked back and forth at Dr. Sweeney and me.

"I need to make some phone calls. I want both of you back in my office at one this afternoon."

We both got up and nearly knocked each other down in our haste to leave the office. I've never been kicked out of a dean's office, and I hope I never again have the experience in my life. Out of habit, I walked to my office. I was shaken and couldn't focus. I slammed the office door behind me. I needed a good smoke. I was grateful no one saw me enter the building. I didn't want to see anyone while waiting to return to Oisin's office. At some level I wanted to visit Mairin at her office but I stopped myself because I didn't want to waste more of her time with the situation I had created. *Why didn't I just give Sweeney the damned manuscript? Who cares? Even if she would ask for changes, it doesn't mean I need to accept them. I've failed William completely, me and my extraordinary ego. What would Kieran say if he was here? Kieran would have a more direct solution. He would convince Dr. Sweeney it was in her best interest to leave University College Cork.*

I can't stay cooped up in this office.

I spent the rest of the morning roaming around Fitzgerald Park and listening for the clock tower chime so I would return to Oisin's office at the appointed time. I worked very hard to control my emotions and to stop my mind from racing through the variety of potential outcomes. I let myself absorb the spring fauna as the fresh fragrance of spring arrived and winter passed. I forgot a jacket at my office and walked at a fast pace to stave off the spring chill. By the time I heard the clock tower chime half twelve, I was sweating and realized I had to walk faster to make in back in time for the one o'clock meeting.

* * * * *

I heard the campus tower chime one o'clock just as I opened the door to Dean O'Leary's office.

"I was hoping you weren't going to be late," said the administrative assistant, with a faint smile.

Dr. Sweeney was pacing back and forth and didn't acknowledge me when I entered the outer office.

"Now that you're both here, you can go right in. Dean O'Leary is waiting for you." And motioned toward his closed door.

Dr. Sweeney jumped in front of me, bolting through the door. She walked directly to Dr. O'Leary's desk and placed both hands on her hips.

"Well, don't waste my time, Oisin, let's have it."

"Would either of you like some tea? Please, both of you, sit down."

I sat down but Dr. Sweeney continued to stand. "Yes, I've been for a long walk, a cup of tea would be perfect, Dean O'Leary." I said this in part just to agitate Dr. Sweeney, whose behavior was demanding and rude, not good for a person in her position.

"The tea won't take a moment. Please, Dr. Sweeney, please have a seat. It will be in your interest, I assure you."

Fion Sweeney scowled at me and sat down like a feather floating to the floor. As before, she folded her hands on her lap and sat up stiffly on the edge of the chair. The tea arrived as if by magic.

Oisin had a very stern look on his face when he spoke. "I want you to know I've considered William Butler's expulsion, talked with faculty in the Theatre Department, and talked with the chancellor. I will review my findings and then share my decision, which, by the way, is completely supported by the chancellor.

"All of the faculty members were unaware and even astounded William had been expelled. They were curious why he didn't attend classes today because his attendance record is impeccable. I queried all of his professors and not one indicated he was deficient in his performance in any way. In fact, quite the opposite, they find him engaging, curious, and anxious to learn.

"Based on these interviews I find the statements in the expulsion letter are at best inaccurate and potentially intentionally false. Next, I talked with Shiobban to confirm Ian did turn in the mentor forms in within the deadline you set, Fion. She confirmed the forms were turned in. I also asked if she had had the opportunity to review the forms for accuracy. She said there wasn't a single error. I believe you have Mairin to thank, Ian.

"Fion, when you identified a deficiency, it was completely corrected within the guidelines you yourself provided.

"I have decided the expulsion will be expunged from William's official record as if it had never happened. The expulsion was unprofessional, reprehensible, and violates professional ethics. There is evidence your motive was vindictiveness toward Mr. Murphy.

"Dr. Sweeney, as of today your contract is null and void; you are no longer a member of the University of Cork faculty. Do not return to your office. Shiobban is packing your personal belongings, which will be sent to the address on file as your residence. You are directed to not have any contact with any UCC faculty for one year. You will not receive a recommendation for any position you pursue in the future. Your personnel file will be sealed for one year. After that, you or any potential employer can have access to the complete file upon written request.

"On a personal note, Fion, I am ashamed of your behavior. You have tarnished the reputation of the Theatre Department and the University."

Tears streamed down Dr. Sweeney's checks. She leaned forward and hid her face in her hands. Her body shook violently. "Oh, God, I am so sorry, I, I, I . . ."

Oisin stood up and motioned toward the door. "It is too late, Dr. Sweeney. Please leave."

I sat petrified in my chair. The tea had grown cold. I didn't know what to say. I couldn't image why I had been allowed to stay in the office to witness the end of Dr. Sweeney's career. I looked at Oisin and hunched my shoulders.

"Ian, I want you to be the first to know the chancellor has asked me to step in as the interim chair of the Theatre Department. I certainly don't need the extra workload but I understand his position. I will be visiting the department later this afternoon to make the announcement. We will, of course, put together a search committee sometime next week and let the new chair have a fresh start in the fall term. The chancellor has asked me to chair the search committee and recommended you also serve on the search committee, having a non-academic and a non-theatre staff member would be refreshing. You will agree, won't you?"

I leaned back in my chair, taking my time to search for just the right words. "Well, it's impossible to turn down the chancellor, isn't it?"

"Now, Ian, there is one more issue to address. I believe Fion was right in wanting you to accept some guidance in writing your stage play. I know you work with an editor when writing your fiction."

I smiled, "Oh, yes, I've been blessed with the same editor for twenty years."

Oisin got up and stretched his back. "So, I suggest you contact Tom Murphy and ask him to serve the role of editor or creative consultant as you develop the play. It will be a writer-to-writer relationship. Can your ego bear it?"

The tension in my shoulders melted off like running water in a hot morning shower. "It would be an honor to work with Tom Murphy. I hope he isn't insulted and has the time?"

Oisin winked at me. "Oh, I think you'll find him receptive. One more thing. Start working with William and Brianna on the technical aspects of the play – costumes, sets, casting, etc., etc. All right?"

I stood up and shook Oisin's hand as a friend would. "Of course. Of course."

Oisin pointed toward the door. "Now, out with you. Go find William and tell him he has his life back. Express my apologies for this entire affair."

CHAPTER 24

I walked out of Oisin's office in a daze, unable to comprehend what had just transpired. I strolled off campus, not paying any attention to where I was walking, nor did I have a destination in mind. I had been witness to a volcanic upheaval in the academic life of University College Cork. I worried faculty may blame me for the eruption. While I wasn't the cause, I may have been the catalyst. My thoughts wandered as much as I did through the streets of Cork. I knew I needed to call William. For a late morning, the sidewalks were filled with people looking stern and purposeful. I don't have any idea how long I walked, long enough to feel my stomach growl. Still unable to ground myself, I walked unconsciously until I found myself at the front door of Mickey's Pub.

"What a surprise! You've haven't been by in mid-afternoon in so long, I just can't remember. Ian, you don't look yourself. Are ya fine?" Mickey continued to wipe down the bar as he spoke.

"To be honest, my friend, I'm not sure."

"Need a snack? I have a good lamb stew today. It will warm your insides. How about I fetch you a mug of black tea?" Mickey looked at me as if I were a stranger.

I pulled out the stool and sat opposite of where Mickey was still cleaning the bar. "Stew and tea would be fine."

The hot tea started to revive my senses and the stew brought me back to life and filled me with warmth as Mickey had promised. My spoon rattled in the bowl after taking the last bite. I realized what I must do next. "Mickey!" I shouted into the kitchen. Mickey flipped a white bar towel over his shoulder as he limped out of the kitchen toward the bar. "Mickey, you're limping. What happened?"

Mickey wiped his face with the towel as he looked at me. "Old age happened, Ian. I can't stand on worn wooden floors like I once did. Why did you shout?"

"I need to have a banquet, Mickey. Can you handle ten or more for dinner?"

Mickey slapped his hand flat on the bar. "Does the sun rise in the east? When do you want to have your banquet?"

I scratched my head, "Well, tonight would be too soon for most people, but I don't want to wait too long. How about tomorrow? Thursday night?"

"Done. What do you want for food?"

"Your salmon for sure. The lamb stew was excellent."

"For so many people, you should have another main dish, Ian."

"Just surprise me, Mickey."

Mickey smiled with satisfaction. "What time?"

"Let's say early. We may talk late into the evening. We might even close you, my friend. Yes, early."

"Six o'clock then. I'll have a few starters ready as people arrive. You can let me know when you want the main courses served. What about drinks?"

"Mickey, I want an open bar. It's all on my tab. I also want at least two bottles of Midleton on the table. I want everyone to experience the joy of a glass of Midleton."

Mickey leaned down and searched behind the bar for something. He grumbled as he moved things around. In a minute he surfaced with a scrap of paper and a pencil. "I best write this down. The memory isn't what it once was." Mickey scribbled something only he could read. "Ok, got it. I'll be ready, my friend. What's the occasion?"

I finished my tea and set the mug on the bar with a thud. "Another?

"It's a meeting, Mickey. This group of people is helping me and William with my stage play. I've been remiss. It takes a lot of people to produce a play and I've only been concentrating on writing. I need to connect with everyone who will breathe life into my words."

Mickey blushed. "It is an honor to host your meeting, Ian. You can make my pub the official location for all yer meetings and parties and so forth."

Feeling stiff, I eased my way off the barstool. "I need to start making calls. I'll see you tomorrow night, my friend." *I ordered Midleton. Why did I do that? Habit?*

* * * * *

After meeting with Mickey, my first call was to William to let him know he had been re-instated and could attend class that afternoon, if he had one. He told me Dr. Sweeney's dismissal was already old news in the Theatre Department. Classes were canceled in the afternoon so the faculty could meet with Dr. O'Leary. The faculty hoped one of them would be selected as interim director so it would be someone they knew and were familiar working with. I decided it wasn't my place to tell William that O'Leary would take the role or that I was going to be a member of the search committee for Dr. Sweeney's replacement. William had enough concerns and didn't need to burden himself with obtuse academic politics. I asked William to prepare a list of questions/concerns/challenges he had in preparing for the stage production of my memoir.

"You must have had something to do with Dr. Sweeney getting fired. It's the way my Uncle Kieran would have taken care of things. Sometimes, you do remind me of my Uncle Kieran, Ian. It's totally unexpected. I suspect you two were more alike than the world knows."

"Trust me when I tell you, William, I had no part in Dr. Sweeney's demise. She was the architect of her own tragedy. She allowed anger and her demand to control the situation taint her judgment. Expelling you wasn't acceptable to anyone. I admit, I was surprised her dismissal was immediate. My guess would have been they would not renew her contract and she would have been allowed to leave at the end of the term. Who knows? Let's focus on our job at hand."

"Do you have a name for your play, Ian?"

"*Dead Reckoning.*"

"Interesting. The title could be interpreted several ways; it's ambiguous. Even on the phone, I can tell you're smiling, Ian."

"I admit, you caught me. Yes, I'm smiling. As you've guessed, the ambiguity in the title is intentional. Goodbye, see you tomorrow night. Oh, would you mind calling Brianna; it would save me a call."

"No, of course not. Could I invite someone I'm considering for stage manager? Do you want to approve the stage manager?"

"Of course, invite the person. All staffing decisions are for you and Brianna. I don't have the inclination or the talent to recruit staff. I have other calls to make. Good afternoon, William."

* * * * *

As usual, Mairin's judgment on arriving early was the right thing to do. She made sure enough tables and chairs were set up in my corner and even went into the kitchen to ask for the starters to be brought out, and she checked on the progress of our dinner. Mairin was pleased Mickey was directing the staff himself, although he left the cooking to the chef from Galway he recently hired. She instructed the kitchen staff to bring out the main courses at half six so dinner would end at a reasonable time and the conversation could begin in earnest. I had

182

needed someone like Mairin in my life for years but I was simply unaware or ignorant. I am not sure which or maybe both.

By six o'clock all the guests had arrived, ordered drinks, and were enjoying corned beef spread on rounds, stuffed baby red potatoes, a dilly-cheese ring with spinach dip, and a variety of Irish cheeses. Mairin tugged at my sleeve and told me to do the introductions. I banged my glass with a spoon to get everyone's attention.

"Excuse me, I don't have a reputation for social graces, but I've been instructed to make just a brief comment. First, I want to thank everyone for sacrificing your Thursday evening to kick-off our endeavor to present a memoir play and to give William Butler Boyle the opportunity to complete his graduate studies in the UCC Theatre Department." There was clapping.

William stood up. "By the way, I am William Boyle, not Willie, not Bill, please just William."

"Oh, yes, I know everyone but you don't all know each other. The expedient thing is to have you introduce yourselves. Satisfactory, Mairin?" Mairin nodded her head.

"I will start. I am Mairin Murphy. I am an administrator at UCC and the love of Ian's life."

Everyone chuckled.

Oisin stood, straightened his bow tie, and took a sip of whiskey before speaking. "I am Ian and Mairin's friend, Oisin O'Leary. I am sorry my wife could not join us this evening; she had a previous engagement. You will meet her at another event, I'm sure. I too am an administrator at UCC and the interim director of the Theatre Department. You must all try the Midleton whiskey Ian is providing; it's exquisite."

Oisin sat down and there was a pause in the room. People looked at each other and no one was willing to speak up. Caitlin jumped up, nearly toppling her Guinness. "I am Caitlin

Lourigan, Ian's sister, and this is my fiancé, Rory. Guess what? We both work at UCC. Are you all noticing something?"

I pointed to Rory to stand and introduce himself, but he shook his head and pointed to Brianna, who took the cue. "I am Brianna Lourigan, Ian's niece. I hold a master's degree in fine art from Trinity and have the privilege of being your producer. Nothing could be better than helping bring a work of my uncle's to life while at the same time collaborating with William to help him on his artistic path. I would like to introduce the person I've selected to be our stage manager, a dear friend Ealga O'Halahan."

I couldn't resist standing up to welcome Ealga. "Attention everyone, did you notice her name? Ealga is the ancient name for our beloved green isle. Bless your parents for bestowing such an elegant and historic name. And we all know the O'Halahan's have been in County Cork since it was founded." Mairin tugged at my sleeve so I would sit down.

When Ealga rose to speak, she stood not more than five-foot tall with short brown hair swept to one side. When she spoke, it was clear and bold beyond her physical height. "I'm thrilled Brianna asked me to stage direct this show. We have worked together for years, and I can say we have deep professional respect for each other in addition to being friends. I should warn you, the final week before the first performance, tech week, the show is mine. In time William will have his say on the acting and when we concentrate on the staging. Thank you. I'll sit down now. Oh, yes, the whiskey is extraordinary."

Just as Ealga was taking her seat, Mickey arrived with great fanfare. He carried a large tray with a gigantic salmon fillet swimming in butter and the Galway chef was right behind him with a second salmon fillet. "Let me introduce you to our chef this evening, Anna Taggart from County Galway. As you can imagine, being from Galway, she has a delicate touch with the beautiful salmon." Several kitchen staff lined up behind Chef Taggart, each carried another dish. Mickey rushed back into the kitchen and returned with a cart with new dinnerware. "I will have Chef Taggart serve you tonight!" Mickey explained.

All my adult life I have been a regular customer at Mickey's Pub and that's what it was, a pub with pub food. Tonight, Mickey's Pub could compete with any of the five-star restaurants in Cork. Hiring a chef rather than a cook must have been expensive for Mickey, and it was out of character for him to want his pub to be anything more than a traditional Irish pub that would attract both the locals and a few tourists. Mickey wore his pride on his sleeve. He had more energy and enthusiasm than I had seen in years. I wondered what brought about his transformation but decided it wasn't necessary to know the details. Enjoying him perform and take obvious pleasure in serving fine food, was enough.

"Mickey, Chef Taggart, I know it isn't protocol, but please join us. It will bring all of us joy to share this magnificent meal with you both," I said.

Chef Taggart started to back away and Mickey caught the edge of her apron to stop her retreat. He wiped the sweat from his cheeks, smiled at her, and motioned her toward the table. She shook her head back and forth vigorously protesting the invitation. "Please?"

Mickey somehow pulled a chair up and grabbed Chef Taggart around the waist to guide her into the chair. He found another nearby chair and sat down next to the chef.

"You are a gracious friend, Ian. I should have mentioned, this is Chef Taggart's first night, and you have given her a Cork welcome. Thank you. Now, everyone, time to craic!"

We took our time and devoured every morsel put on the table. Mairin leaned in and whispered, "Darling, this has been wonderful, but remember we have serious work tonight.

William, Brianna, and now Ealga need direction. Maybe you should turn the evening over to Brianna. She can do it and my guess is she wants to but would never want to impose herself, especially with you here."

I threw my napkin on my plate and scowled at Mairin. "Sometimes, just sometimes, I tire of you being right all the time. It must get boring for you." Mairin laughed and gave me a peck on the cheek.

I stood up, putting my fists on the table and leaning around so I could garner everyone's intention. "In addition to sharing one of the finest meals of my life, we have another purpose in gathering. It has been pointed out to me, in recent months I've behaved like a hermit, hiding out in a location not to be revealed, drafting the first manuscript of my play. Oh, God, is it called a manuscript? Well, tonight I want to focus on the requirements of putting on a stage play, an undertaking in which I have absolutely no experience but am anxious to learn. I will turn this meeting over to Brianna, as our producer. And I've asked William to develop a list of questions, and from my vantage point, I can see a notebook hidden behind his back so he is prepared."

Brianna sat up straight and gave an outline of the steps to stage a play. I noticed Caitlin did not hide her pride and admiration for her daughter. William appeared in near rapture when Brianna spoke. In the few months he had been in Cork, he and Brianna spent a great deal of time together. Of course, being less than observant about such things, Mairin pointed out to me they were on the path to having a relationship. I hadn't paid attention before but watching the two of them during our meeting, it was clear they shared a fondness for each other beyond two young people working together for the first time. While it would never be appropriate to intervene, I wasn't certain about having them engage in a relationship while they were working on presenting my play. Mairin assured me such sentiments were totally selfish on my part. "Let them be," she told me. "All you need to worry about is writing the script."

I was drawn out of my own thoughts by a series of questions from Brianna and I shared my vision of the play for the first time. "The story will begin with attending Timolty's wake and end with the referendum on the 1998 Good Friday Agreement. I will show how I made the transformation from an IRA operative to one of the architects of the peace agreement and my battle with depression and alcoholism. I need to reveal the truth, even if I don't want to admit it to myself, I have buried many memories, and they are just reaching the surface of my consciousness now."

There was a communal gasp. Shock registered on both Mairin's and Caitlin's face. Mairin reached under the table and squeezed my hand. "This is a memoir, not a biography, and honesty is essential. The truth is, I like to drink, often too much. I know I need to be blunt and honest with the people of Ireland and explain my view of both the Troubles and my troubles."

The group grew quiet; no one spoke for a few minutes. Brianna broke the mood by asking detail questions, like the number of acts and scenes, number of actors and roles, a preliminary list of characters, costuming, and how I wanted to participate in the production. "The production belongs to you, William and Ealga.

"My vision is the play begins with the curtains closed. I sit at a desk in front of the curtains on the corner of the stage. I have my writing pad, pipe, and a bottle of whiskey. The image is that I'm writing the play – curtains open and I disappear off the stage. No lines for me, of course."

"I like it, Ian." William said.

I looked into Mairin's eyes, hoping to find reassurance. Instead she gave me a puzzled look. Under the table she took my hand and squeezed. I remembered one other announcement I promised myself to make. I jumped up and wobbled as I leaned over the table to balance myself.

"Oh, I apologize, I am not graceful. I have never been known to be graceful but that was embarrassing." I glanced down at Mairin and she shook her head. I couldn't tell if it meant disapproval or curiosity. I knew I had to forge on. "Well now, I've admitted I'm blundering my way through the manuscript, and Dean O'Leary has been gracious enough to recruit some help for me. Today I talked with dramatist Tom Murphy and he has agreed to collaborate with me on this play. In fact, he will be arriving tomorrow and staying for, well, I don't know how long he'll be staying." I looked down at Mairin for approval and her face was a blank slate. "Yes, in fact, Tom will be staying at our home."

"Ian!" Mairin shouted.

"I, I, know, I didn't have a chance to talk to you about it. Tom has a reputation for being very intense and I wanted to be able to work anytime of the day or night. Oh, God, I do hope you understand."

Mairin pulled on my arm and I plopped down next to her. "We will talk about this at home," she whispered into my ear.

"Ian, I'm thrilled Tom will be working with you. You are fortunate, and this is definitely the right path," Oisin said.

"I have to meet him while he's staying with you; I must," William demanded.

"Tom Murphy and my uncle, Ian Murphy, working together; it doesn't get any better. I have a lot of questions for him, especially about his play *Wake*. I wrote a paper about that play in graduate school.

"Don't forget me," Ealga chimed in.

"He's not here for a symposium. We have hard work to do. And I don't know how long he can stay. I forgot to ask."

"We understand, Ian. His visit presents such opportunity, forgive us, please. Yes, the first task at hand is to polish up your manuscript," Oisin said.

"I am tired and you are all looking like it has been a long evening. Thank you for coming. It took a lot for me to share with you tonight; exposing my inner life is a challenge. Thank you for listening. We are undertaking a very special project. It will take everyone here and more to be successful. My first lesson in theatre is it builds community."

CHAPTER 25

Tom Murphy arrived on Friday afternoon with a shabby brown valise. He noticed my focus on his bag. "I've had the damn thing since college. It's all I need. If I need more than one bag to travel, I'd give up traveling."

We both laughed, and I invited him to sit down. "I'd rather stretch a bit. The train was crowded this morning and I didn't have a lot of room. Still, it's better than driving."

"I didn't know you were taking the train. I could have collected you at the station," I said.

"No matter. I didn't want to inconvenience you."

Mairin walked into the room with a broad smile and offered Tom her hand. "I thought I heard voices. Mr. Murphy, you are so generous for helping Ian. I'm Mairin, often called his better half."

"Oh, God, call me Tom. I am happy to meet you, and I'm not surprised you are Ian's better half."

"Please, do sit. I'll get us some tea." Mairin glided out of the room.

Tom gravitated to the Tuam chair and leaned his elbows on his knees, looking at me directly for a few minutes. "Now, Ian, I want to be clear with you from the start. My job here is to be sure your work is stage worthy. Novels and plays really have only two things in common, dialogue and the general story structure. When you write knowing an actor will breathe life into your words, it changes the writer's perspective in unimaginable ways."

"I admit, when I started writing, I was beyond naive, I was ignorant. I began believing relying on dialogue and the plot I could pull this off. The truth is, I know I can't. How do we start?"

Mairin arrived with a tray and three mugs of steaming tea. "I didn't intend to be rude; I didn't ask you about the tea. Ian only takes Barry's. I hope that's all right, Tom."

"Of course, tea is tea, isn't it?"

"May I offer you a tea cake or maybe a scone?"

"No, thank you, Mairin, I had a nibble on the train and that's enough for me. You are so gracious. I don't want to impose on you. But Mairin, I must be honest about my visit. I don't know how long I will be here. I'm here for the work and until it's done, well, I guess I'm your house guest."

Mairin sat her tea on the tray. "You are very generous, Tom. I'm thrilled you are helping Ian. Our home is open to you, period."

Tom looked over at me and winked. "You are a damn lucky man, Ian Murphy."

"I am and I know it."

"Mairin, I was just explaining to Ian, I really have only one job here, to make his play stage worthy."

"Well, I'm the only one in the room who isn't a writer. I don't think I know what you mean by stage worthy."

"Actually, I was going to ask the same question. The best I can do is compare it to when a publisher says a book is ready for publication," I offered.

"Again, the difference is a play is written words intended to be spoken and acted."

My stomach seized up into a cramp and my right hand clenched. I felt hot all over my body. I doubled over in the chair. Mairin sprang out of her chair and started rubbing my shoulders.

"Jesus, man, are you ill?" Tom asked.

I tried to focus on Tom's face but I my eyes were blurred.

"I . . . I . . . I think it's a panic attack."

"You have panic attacks?"

"He does," Mairin said.

"Writers have our own crosses to bear. I have mine, too. I've fought the darkness all my life. Listen, Ian, the first time you see your stage play rehearsed, you'll understand what I mean. It's where the actor meets the words. You'll see how the actor interprets your words with voice and emotion. It's magic, really. You'll re-write after you've watched your play rehearsed, I guarantee it. I generally don't begin to feel comfortable until after the fourth draft. It's a process. You know that. I'm sure writing your novels is a process too."

While Tom was explaining what he meant, Mairin stroked my hair and practiced slow, deliberate breathing with me. "I'll be fine. Where do we start, Tom?"

Tom finished his tea before answering. "I want to spend the afternoon reading your manuscript. Then let's have dinner. After dinner you and I can begin talking. Do you have someplace we can work?"

With Mairin's help I was able to sit back in the chair and breathe normally. "Yes, the third floor is my office. I have Mairin to thank. It's quiet and private."

Mairin returned to her seat and took a sip of tea. "Of course, you'll want to go to Mickey's, Ian."

"Mickey's? Sounds local," Tom said.

"It's been my pub for thirty years," I explained.

"Thank you for the tea, Mairin. Ian, let's retreat to your office. I'll read through the manuscript there."

CHAPTER 26

Tom Murphy stayed for seven days. Those days were, all in all, the most intense, creative days of my life, which is a lot to say for a writer my age. The first day, after Tom's read through, was the most brutal and most honest. I will never forget his first words: "Ian, we have some work to do."

That week was a crash course in how to write a stage play. We shared a reputation for enjoying a drink or two. That week, the only time any alcohol passed either my lips or Tom's was when we were having dinner. I had a case of Midleton hidden in my office, and we spent entire days alone in the office and I didn't offer him a drink, not once.

It took all my concentration to craft the stage play scene by scene and character by character. My first lesson was how stage play dialogue and novel dialogue differ. Stage play dialogue requires more depth, and the intent is to elicit an immediate audience response. As a novelist, I never knew what the response of the reader was to a scene or a character. When I started out as a writer, I did attend a few book club sessions and learned how some readers responded to my work. In those days my books were given away free to book groups to try to build readership.

My publisher warned me not to respond negatively to any comment or viewpoint a reader might have. It was like being a caged animal because some of the comments were bizarre, and some readers totally missed the point. My days of attending book groups only lasted a few years. Had I been required to continue with book groups, I may have given up writing for almost any other career. I suppose I could have survived financially on a college lecturer's salary.

Tom Murphy radically changed my point of view on how to write dialogue. Tom also taught me more about characterization in a week than had learned in thirty years of publishing fiction. On stage a character must be larger than life; the audience must learn to know the person in less than two hours. A character's transformation must be bold and emotional, in an effort to draw the audience into the life of the character, even if only for two or two and a half hours.

To be honest, I had never worked so hard in my life. I knew for the rest of my life my fiction writing would be driven by my experience creating a stage play. I never imagined I would have such a profound creative experience by volunteering to mentor William in his creative journey. I labored on the stage play for three weeks after Tom returned to Dublin. He promised to attend the premier, whenever it would be.

"Hello, William, the play is ready to meet the actors." There was silence at the end of the line. I waited. "Hello, hello, William, are you there?"

"I'm here. I'm here. We've been waiting. It's unexpected. Well, it's not unexpected, we didn't know. We've been working on scenery, costumes, lighting based on the outline of acts you gave us several months ago. It's been slow but steady. With Brianna's help, I've learned a lot about technical theatre. What did you say again?"

"I said the play is ready to meet the actors."

"What a unique way to express it. You do mean to schedule rehearsals, don't you?"

"Yes, William, schedule rehearsals. I want to attend all the rehearsals. I want everyone to know I'm willing to re-write based on rehearsals."

"You are?"

"Yes. Tom Murphy told me it was a necessary. He has done it his entire career."

"Does that include actors, Ian?"

"I will listen and consider everyone's creative critique, but there is no promise I will change words. I accept the final work the audience will see is a complete collaboration. I will also listen to you, Brianna, and Eagla."

* * * * *

William sent me the rehearsal schedule by messenger the next day.

I gave copies of the draft script to both Mairin and Oisin and asked them to read for content. I also invited them to attend any rehearsal. After considering for several days, I elected to not send a script to Tom Murphy. I didn't want to be a burden. He had devoted a great deal of time to me and I felt guilty asking him to devote more time to my project.

The schedule called for rehearsing six days a week from seven until ten. Brianna told me technical rehearsals wouldn't require my presence. I had the full weekend off before rehearsals would begin on Monday. William told me he, Brianna, and Eagla would spend the weekend with the script and didn't want to be bothered with socializing. It was clear William was learning independence at light speed.

I had to be honest with myself; I wasn't devoting any time to mentoring William, at least not in the traditional sense of an academic counselor. I wasn't sure about Kieran's wisdom in choosing me to mentor William and the past few months hadn't changed my initial reaction.

* * * * *

"I'm not mentoring William at all. Brianna and Eagla are mentoring him. How arrogant of me to even agree to be his mentor. I'm a joke." I swallowed the remainder of the wine and filled my glass again. I offered the bottle to Mairin but she shook her head no.

"Ian, you are giving him the gift of your stage play. Without your play, how would be get his degree? He is learning the entire creative process at one time. You are teaching him how to write by watching your process. Anyone can learn to direct by copying the work already done on some overproduced play. You're also mentoring him on how to work with other creative people to produce a single work. There is no greater lesson, Ian."

I rolled the wine glass between my hands and noted the rich fragrance, like a summer day in Provence. "My mind says you are right, my love, but the sentiment lingers."

"Ian, this may not make sense to you but in your case, you often should ignore your own emotions, at least reactions to circumstances; they cloud your judgment."

"Says you?"

"Look Ian, talk to Oisin about this. In his role as department head, he can give you an answer. Now, you've been secluded with the damn play long enough. I'm calling Caitlin to invite her and Rory to a session at Mickey's tomorrow night – it will do you good. I want you to give Oisin a call and suggest the four of us go out to dinner Sunday night. I'll even approve if you and Oisin talk shop, for a few minutes at least."

I broke into a smile and giggled under my breath. "Is it any wonder I'm madly in love with you? I'm going to call Oisin now."

"Before you do, I have a question for you, my dear."

"Yes?"

"I've sensed a change in you. A bit of comfort in your own skin or something. It's odd, but something has changed, not for the worse, just changed."

I flew out of my chair and offered to take Mairin's glass to the kitchen as I went up to my office.

"Ian, you're ignoring me!"

I glanced back over my shoulder as I entered the kitchen. "Yes, I am, I am indeed."

I climbed the stairs two at a time and vanished.

CHAPTER 27

I arrived at the theatre just before seven. Walking through the lobby, I followed the cacophony of voices. Several tables were pushed together on stage with at least fifteen people squeezed next to each other. Everyone at the table had a three-ring binder, which I guessed held my script. A ring of chairs surrounded those at the table. There were enough chairs in the outer ring for at least twenty people, maybe more, I couldn't tell for sure. There were only a few people sitting in the outer ring. A number of people crisscrossed the stage having conversations with people I couldn't see. I strained to see a familiar face, like William or Brianna. In the confusion I couldn't quite remember what Ealga looked like. That's odd for a writer; it's odd for me because writers are among the most observant people on earth.

I heard shouting from a distance. "Ian, come up on stage." I squinted to try to see where the voice came from. It was a mystery, so I followed instructions. Once on stage, a hand tugged at my arm. "I'm here, Uncle Ian; the lights must be confusing you." I recognized Brianna's voice. She guided me to the table and gently eased me down onto a chair. "Just wait here. It will be just a few minutes." No one at the table noticed I had joined them. There were at least ten conversations going on simultaneously. I twisted on the hardwood chair. My back was beginning to ache and I had just sat down.

All at once the chairs at the table were taken, and from what I could see all the chairs in the outer circle were filled too. "You're going to enjoy this tonight, Ian," a familiar voice on my right said. William sat next to me. He leaned across me. "Are you ready? You should introduce Ian, I think." I turned to look at who he was talking to and there sat Brianna. I was surrounded.

"Ok, everybody, let's get started. I'm sure you're all anxious to start reading. First, I need to introduce our playwright and my uncle, Ian Murphy. Stand up, Uncle Ian, say a few words."

I took my time to stand because the chairs were so close and I didn't want to get tangled with one of the chairs next to me. "Well, uh, I'm new at this. I told Brianna and William I wanted to attend rehearsals – you know – in case re-writing is needed. I . . . I need your help with this. I'm a novice, not at writing but at writing for the stage. I've gotten some good advice from someone you all know, Tom Murphy – no family connection – we think. I didn't know what to expect tonight. I confess I have no idea what we're doing."

I sat down with a thud to a round of applause and laughter. "Uncle Ian, this is called a table read. All the people at the table are the actors cast for this show. The people sitting outside the table are the technical crew. The whole purpose for this evening is to give your play its first public reading."

I glanced around the table to see a variety of people from college age to one or two at least my age or older. They were dressed in interesting, flamboyant clothes. Quite a few wore scarves with the loose knot, both men and women, like the French.

Brianna dressed very casual with torn denim jeans, a baggy t-shirt, and a vest, which might have been mine once upon a time. William wore a V-neck pullover sweater with corduroy slacks. Several men and women wore necklaces or something that resembled a necklace. One woman had cut-off sleeves with a large 'RA' tattoo on her right arm. She could never have crossed the border into Northern Ireland unless it was completely covered.

I scratched my head and gave my mustache a twirl. "So this isn't rehearsal?"

"Not yet. Eagla and William haven't had the script long enough to begin blocking, so tonight we're just going to read."

"Blocking?" I looked at William and saw Eagla sitting next to him.

William cleared his throat. "Yes, we have our own language too. Blocking is the movement actors have on stage. We need to choreograph the movement with the words and the actors with each other and the set and props."

"I'll watch. I'll learn. Tom suggested I not write in any, any, any . . ."

"Stage direction." Eagla completed my sentence. "It was a good suggestion, especially for your first script."

"All we will do tonight is read the script out loud. With this group of rowdy actors, there's likely to be some interpreting going on, even at first reading," Brianna explained.

"Some novelists read their own work out loud as they work," I said. "They claim it helps. I've never done it."

"Well, this is the first meeting of the actors and your words. Let's begin. Further introductions can come another night." Brianna sat down.

The first actor spoke in a clear resonating baritone voice, which I instantly admired, especially when I realized he was playing me. Many of the actors experimented with both voice and gestures as they read. The hair on the back of my neck tingled as I listened to my words jump off the page, into the world, and onto the stage. My heart raced and my breathing became erratic. Brianna put her hand on top of mine and looked with alarm at me.

"All right? Is this too much for you? Would you like to leave?"

"Leave? Absolutely not. This is exhilarating, and the most frightening experience of my life."

Brianna leaned in close to me. "Let's just be safe." She stood up, "Great job everyone. Let's take five."

Brianna looked toward William and with extreme gentleness they picked me up, guided me back through the lobby, and out onto the street. "Uncle Ian, why don't you have a pipe? William will stay here with you and have a smoke."

William gave Brianna a puzzled look but followed her instructions. "What do you think so far, Ian?"

"It's a miracle. Words are so different when they're spoken out loud. The woman you cast to be Eileen has an uncanny resemblance to the real Eileen Donohue; she actually makes me a bit nervous."

William drew heavily on his cigarette and chocked as he laughed out loud. "Yes, it was lucky casting. Her name is Evelyn, and it's the only role she tried out for. I think she's a natural."

I fiddled with lighting my pipe, deciding how honest I wanted to be with William. I was honest when I told Brianna that hearing my words interpreted by total strangers was exhilarating and frightening but I failed to tell anyone it was mostly frightening. I backed up against the wall of the building. My right hand bound up into a fist, and my pipe dropped to the walk, spattering red ember tobacco.

"Ian!" William leapt in my direction, crushing the tobacco under his shoe.

"I . . . I . . . I'm just having a moment. I'll be fine. God, I could use a whiskey. I don't know how I'm going to get through this. Seeing my life in front of me is a special kind torture. I had no idea it would be this way, no idea."

Brianna and Eagla joined us outside. Alarm spread across Brianna's face when she saw me propped up against the building.

"I'm not sure this is a good idea," Brianna said.

Eagla stiffened visibly. "What's not a good idea?"

William gripped my arm so hard that I felt the blood circulation stop. I shook free from him.

"I hope you don't mean what I think you mean," William shouted into Brianna's face, even though she stood less than a foot away from him.

Brianna bristled. "We're talking family, William. I will not risk Ian's health for this project. We can do something else."

"Dear Jesus . . ." Eagla mumbled.

I straightened up and jerked myself free from William. "Don't you dare talk about me as if I wasn't here. I said I was fine and I am. How would any of you like to see your short lives played out in front of you by a group of strangers? I will get through this, I must, and I've made a promise. I've promised Mairin; I've promised William; but most important I've promised myself. I will drag myself out of the darkness, I will. I have tried to atone for the harm I've caused others but found my efforts to date hollow. No, Mairin, as usual, is right. This is my path. If I am nothing, I'm a man of words. Playwriting is so different from writing a novel, so different. I . . . I . . . I'm learning but it is painful. Our five minutes must be up. Let's not hold up the actors any longer."

Brianna, William, and Eagla lowered their heads. William threw his cigarette onto the pavement and crushed it with the heel of his shoe. The three of them walked back into the theatre without saying a word to me. I kicked at the pipe tobacco trying to scatter it, hoping the breeze would help. I took a deep breath, ran my hands through my hair, and took long strides down the aisle and took my seat.

Brianna looked at me and winked as she patted my shoulder. "Ok, let's finish the reading. Nice work everyone. We are all impressed."

CHAPTER 28

Mairin was sipping a glass of wine and reading when I arrived home. "You're awake? Are you waiting for me?"

A coy smile crossed her lips. "How did it go?"

I took off my hat and coat tossing them onto a nearby chair. I shrugged and fell into the chair next to hers. I bent over putting my face in my hands.

"Oh, my dear, dear Ian. I shouldn't offer but would you like a whiskey?"

I looked up at her in disbelief. Mairin tolerated my drinking with her own special stoicism. She was determined not to be judgmental, but in the three years we had been together, she had never offered me a whiskey. I didn't know how to answer. In some ways it felt like a trap. I sat up and crossed my arms in front of my chest to stare at her. I couldn't detect any duplicity. I caught myself mid-thought, *I love this woman. She would never, never deceive me or try to trick me.* "No, I don't want a drink, as surprising as it might sound. I need to absorb the night in a very slow, deliberate way."

"I can understand. I have to ask you something I have been reluctant to ask but . . ."

"My love, you can always ask anything."

"Well, why didn't you let me read the script before you gave it to Brianna and William? You usually have me read draft work, just for my perspective – no critique intended or implied."

I looked at her and screwed my face into a question mark. I sat in silence repeating the question to myself. *Why didn't I show the script to Mairin? Why didn't I show the script to Mairin?*

"My love, where are you? You've drifted off somewhere."

I cleared my throat several times, waiting for the words to find their way out. "The truth is, I don't know. To be honest, I never even thought about it until you just asked. You know, you're not in it; the play, I mean."

The muscles in Mairin's jaw flexed. She sat her wine glass on the table next to her chair with extreme deliberateness. She tossed her head back then looked me directly in the eyes. "What do you mean I'm not in the play? How can I not be in the play?"

"Simple. The play ends after the Good Friday Agreement ratification in 1998."

"Oh, I see."

I didn't feel like our conversation was going well. I had told the truth. I really didn't consider writing about my struggles or Northern Ireland's dismal attempt at self-governance.

"Did you talk with Tom Murphy about this?"

"No, I didn't. Of course he offered to read the script. I didn't want to bother him anymore. He gave me enough of his time. I don't want to abuse him."

Mairin took her goblet and sipped the wine. "I could use more wine – would you mind?"

I smiled, walked to the kitchen, and filled her glass to the rim.

"Aren't you generous tonight? Want to get me drunk?"

I sat closer to her on the sofa. "No, of course not. You don't have to drink it all."

Mairin sat back in the chair and finished half the glass. She rolled the glass in her hands and then held it to the light to check on the wine's legs. Without looking at me she asked, "So did you write about the Donohue woman?" Mairin turned toward me and leaned close to my face.

"I damn near ended up in a British gaol because of Eileen Donohue. Yes, I did. It happened."

"Honest. How honest were you, dear?"

I squirmed in my seat. "How honest?"

"Don't be sly, Ian. Is there a sex scene in this play?"

I shot out of the chair. I stared down at Mairin, the blood rushed to my face and for a moment I thought I would lose my balance. "Jesus Christ, is that what you care about? No, there is no sex scene in the play. My relationship with her shows how gullible and naïve I was when it came to relationships with women. It's also about how I was betrayed. To this very moment I don't know if she was honest with me. I suspect I was used throughout the relationship. I'm not even sure she knows. When I was in hiding at Kieran's' cabin, I came treacherously close to diving into the Atlantic."

Tears streamed down Mairin's face. She stood slowly and embraced me, tucking her head underneath my chin. A shiver seized me and I shook, unable to control myself. I came to understand the effect on my life of writing the play. I let my mind go blank and soaked in Mairin's warmth.

"The play is like watching a PBS documentary of your life; it tries to be non-judgmental, but it's just not possible. When I listened to the words tonight, I lost all awareness I had written them. I had lived the life being portrayed. The actors are so creative; they transform the words into gestures and emotions right before my eyes. Frankly, they display the emotions I should have had. Maybe, if I would have been more emotionally vested in my own life, some things would have turned out differently. While listening to them read, I found myself wondering who the play was about. Makes no sense, does it?

"I must tell you something that makes even less sense. In a way I am learning how I came to be, as I am right now, with you, in this moment. The power to look back on your life is frightening. Is my memory crystal clear or is it foggy, unreliable, maybe even fictitious? How can a person know? I don't understand why I did some of the things I did. What possessed me to write *The Green Book*? I can't even guess how many died because they read my little green terrorist manual. I've abused the gift I was given.

"Maybe after this play fades away into the nether land of a graduate library bookshelf, I will not write again. Do I need to write? I've always told myself writing is akin to breathing in my life. Have I deluded myself? Oh, Mairin, you are going to regret marrying me, you are."

Mairin couldn't stop sobbing. I didn't understand why she was crying so much. Maybe I was so self-absorbed I couldn't break out of the prison that was me to comprehend her empathy. I closed my eyes tight and held her. I imagined what a strange sight this must be, two middle-aged folks standing in their living room, embracing each other, bound by tears. The writer in me wanted to capture the essence of the moment. To capture the moment in words would steal this time, it would be dead and hollow.

The line from T.S. Eliot floated through my mind, '*The world is too much with us now.*' I felt the weight of so many bad decisions, stomping down the wrong path, having the innocence to believe simplistic nationalistic ideas. Beliefs bind our lives into knots, in Ireland's case, Celtic knots which can never be unraveled. I am also the prisoner of our history, allowing history to dictate the actions we take in the present. How does a person break the shackles of history? Does any generation learn from history? It hasn't happened in Ireland for many generations.

"Ian, we should go to bed," Mairin whispered in my ear as she wiped her face.

"I don't think I will be able to sleep tonight."

"Please, oh, please, my love, don't drink. There's nothing in the bottle of whiskey for you."

"You offered me a whiskey earlier. Now, you tell me not to drink. I couldn't be more confused."

"I was wrong to offer you whiskey."

I squeezed her tight. "You know tonight, during the break, I was desperate for a drink but instead I went inside and listened to the rest of the table read. I . . . I . . . don't want a drink. I said it out loud. I don't want a drink. I've never had that feeling before. It's scary."

Mairin slipped her hand to the back of my neck, bringing my head down to kiss. Her lips invited me to share the joy and passion of love. When you find love later in life, as I had, it was different.

"Tea then?" Mairin asked as she stroked the back of my neck.

"Tea would be nice. You don't need to stay up with me."

"I want to be by your side. I won't promise I can stay awake all night but I will stay awake as long as I can. If you want, I can call in tomorrow. There's nothing on my schedule that can't be changed."

"Mairin, my love, I don't deserve you. No, go to work tomorrow. I need to prepare myself for tomorrow's rehearsal. I'll help you make tea."

CHAPTER 29

I sat quietly through the first full week of rehearsal. Brianna and William would whisper back and forth to each other, then both scribbled on their note pads. I found their whispering distracting so I would sit several aisles away from them. They didn't notice I moved or if they did, nothing was ever said to me. Eagla was a mystery. She would sit with her feet up on the seat in front of her and the script balanced in her lap. She scribbled in the script but said nothing.

At the end of the scene William would shout "notes." The actors would stop and turn toward William and Brianna. William would start and review the notes he had taken. "Cara, you need to project more, and when you're not facing the audience, we lose you totally. Have you had voice instruction?"

I could see Cara's mouth move but her voice didn't make it to aisle fourteen, where I was sitting.

"What?" William shouted. Everyone laughed, except Cara. I guessed she hadn't taken any voice instruction, which I was learning was an essential for every stage actor. On the live stage, a voice is the actor's tool and gives a true depth of performance.

After rehearsal, William and Brianna asked to meet with me after the cast left for the evening. "Is something wrong?" I asked. Both William and Brianna shook their heads as they read their notes; William continued to scribble on the page. He looked up at me as he put his pencil in his mouth sideways then he looked at Brianna.

"Well, Uncle Ian, William and I have doubts about Cara. In auditions she was fine, it was a smaller room, but on stage she's just not projecting. You heard us today; we tried to work with her."

"I agree you tried. I noticed even in the second scene her voice was hard to hear."

"I'm worried she can't take instruction," William said after taking the pencil out of his mouth.

"Oh, what an interesting way of expressing it," I said. "Brianna?"

"I completely agree with William. We have several choices. We could just cut Cara now and review our casting notes to replace her. Or we could double cast and ask another female to take her role. We can use make-up to show the different characters – a wig and a little stage make-up is magic."

"The third choice would be to hold a quick audition to cast the role," William explained.

I stroked my beard and asked, "Why are you talking to me about this?"

William and Brianna looked at each other and then at me. "We just wanted to include you," William said.

"I don't feel qualified to even express an opinion, except it is clear, Cara doesn't know how to project her voice. I do wonder if she can learn to over the next few weeks of rehearsal. By the way, why isn't Eagla in this meeting?"

"In a word, she doesn't care. The show becomes hers in the very last week of rehearsal, the technical rehearsal – we call it tech week. You will understand when the time comes." Brianna taught me another theatre lesson.

"What would you both like to do?" I asked.

"It's only the first week of rehearsal, we have time. I think we should do an audition the day after tomorrow. William?" Brianna asked.

"I'm always nervous about auditions, but I trust your judgment. I will ask Cara to come in before rehearsal tomorrow night and tell her our decision. I want her to understand it isn't a question of her talent or her capability, it's really a technical issue – she just needs to learn to project."

"It's settled then. I'll put out a notice and schedule the audition for the day after tomorrow," Brianna said, closing her binder. I want to attend the meeting with Cara just to be supportive. We can move on with rehearsal because the next three scenes don't have that character."

I shuffled my feet and twisted in my chair to get more comfortable. "How will the other actors respond to Cara being let go?" I asked.

"Oh, not a problem. Most will be expecting it. They know she wasn't projecting. Things like this happen in the theatre world," Brianna explained.

"Uncle Ian, you look tired. Let's call it a night. Poor Mairin will be wondering what happened to you. I know you walked tonight. I'll drive you home."

"Thank you, Brianna."

* * * * *

The second week of rehearsals everything changed – for the worse. The young man cast to be me was named Lugan, a very traditional Irish name. In Irish mythology, there was a god Lug, the god of the arts, and its rough translation also meant brilliant. Unfortunately, the young man was well aware of the heritage of his name and thought it was also descriptive of his acting ability. I didn't want to express my view during the first week of rehearsals. William and Brianna explained the first week would be rough with actors reading from the script, learning the character, and learning where to move on stage all at the same time. I confessed, it was a daunting task to take and all involved skills I didn't have. They also told me in the second week the actors would begin to work much harder on character.

Lugan did put a lot of work into being me on stage. The work was all in the wrong direction. As I watched him on stage, it was painfully clear from the page to the stage was a transition he didn't understand in portraying my life. He didn't appear to comprehend my motivation for many of the things I did, so to me, his portrayal just wasn't right – it didn't ring true. The important aspect of the play being a memoir format was to share with the audience my motivation for my decisions and actions.

After the third day of rehearsal during the second week, I couldn't restrain myself any longer. At the first break I demanded William and Brianna meet with me. I marched them to a small practice room on second floor and shut the door behind us.

"Please sit." Brianna and William looked surprised and confused. "Look, there is no easy way for me to say this but Lugan just isn't getting it. He is missing my motivation. He comes off as if I just floated from event to event in my life almost in a daze, letting circumstances make decisions for me."

"Uncle Ian, you're upset."

"Brianna, you're stating the obvious. However, Ian, I'm glad you're comfortable telling us this. Right now Lugan is just reading the script."

I paced back and forth in front of them. Again, my right fist rolled up into a clenched fist and I winced. "That's my point – he is just reading the words. I'm not even sure he understands the words. Can you two work with him? Brianna, have you seen him on stage?"

"No, I haven't seen him on stage. His reputation is quite good. Although, I believe he has performed more comedy than drama. I'm not understanding your concern."

"I'm not bragging but I'm not a simple man. I'm a complex man and the stage performance is flat, one-dimensional."

"He can only say what you wrote," William said.

I could feel the blood surge to my face and my right hand squeezed into a fist so tight it would take Mairin thirty minutes of massage to regain use of my hand. "The words!" I screamed at William and Brianna.

Both of them gave me a pensive look, but they didn't back down. "You said you would be willing to re-write, Uncle Ian. If you've changed your mind, well, then we will have to come up with another approach."

Having my own words thrown back at me was like being slapped hard across the face. My breathing became calm and thoughts buzzed around my head. I had agreed to re-writing because Tom Murphy told me it was part of the evolution of a play from the page to the stage. "Right, I did. Of course, I am a man of my word, so I will re-write. Do you have any suggestions?"

"Whew." William wiped his face and forced a little smile. Brianna smiled broadly.

"Uncle Ian, a reader internalizes what you write and has a solitary experience of the emotions and conflict. An actor must externalize the experience and show the audience the emotions and the conflict. The words must inspire the actor to express emotion. Oh, gosh, it's pretty technical – like a graduate course in acting. I may not be making any sense. What do you want the actor to show the audience?"

I brushed back my hair with both my hands and pulled at my mustache. "I want the audience to see my original motivation to join the IRA was revenge for Timolty's death but soon evolved into a nationalistic fervor to re-unite Ireland and throw the British out of our country."

"Fair enough, revenge is classic, we can work with Lugan. The transition is much more difficult. Brianna, why don't you and I work together. In the meantime, let's release the cast and work only with Lugan this evening. Ian, how much time will you need for re-writes?"

I sat up, cleared my throat. "Through the end of the weekend. I can have them for you Monday next."

Brianna and William looked at each other. "Ok," they said.

I stood up and stretched. "It's been a long night. I'm going home. I will have script revisions delivered to you Monday morning. Let's see how this goes. But I must tell you both, my confidence in Lugan remains low. He has to prove a lot to me."

"We understand clearly, Uncle Ian. Good night. Thank you for giving us all a chance."

* * * * *

I shared the night's experience with Mairin when I got home as she massaged my hand back to normal. I made us a cup of tea and intentionally changed the topic and asked how her day had gone. I ran the risk of being self-centered if Mairin shared my world more than I shared hers. I needed to be more conscious of this weakness because I never wanted her to feel I didn't value the activities she is passionate about. Her world as an academic librarian was a mystery to me. The library was an integral part of the academic community but with computers and online research, their role had changed. Mairin believed the role of the research librarian was in a period of dramatic change.

We enjoyed our tea, and I told her I didn't want to talk about the damn play anymore, I needed some psychological distance from it. We ended our evening talking about a variety of subjects and then crawled into bed together and snuggled until I drifted off to sleep.

CHAPTER 30

I went into seclusion in my office to re-write the lines of my character in the first act. It was critical to both the play and to the expression of my life that my motives for joining the IRA be very clear. I am not and never was an idealistic youth. I wanted revenge, when I agreed to join the 'RA, I wasn't sure who to blame for Timolty's death, the IRA or the British. In recalling those years, it was blurry. My first impression was the volunteers were responsible for accepting the services of a young man, providing little training, and then pushing him into harm's way. Joining the IRA was an act of subversion.

The actor portraying me didn't appear to understand my underlying motive for volunteering for the IRA and how it changed within a few months. Growing up in Cork I had no idea how the British actually ruled Northern Ireland, the only solution was reunification to establish one Ireland and turn back the history of 1921when Northern Ireland joined the United Kingdom.

I spent the first day reading act one out loud, over and over. I wanted to hear the words myself and I wanted to "act out" what I intended. The original script didn't capture the emotion and confusion I felt when I was in my twenties and overcome with grief at losing my best friend to a British soldier. I'm sure Timolty didn't intend to sacrifice himself. General Patton is supposed to have said, "You don't win a war dying for your country. You win a war by making the other son of a bitch die for his country." The IRA was founded on that principle, and knowing him as I did, I'm sure Timolty believed that with his whole heart. Timolty felt stuck in Cork, and he didn't want the life his father had.

The first scene of the play began with Timolty's wake, to show the audience how I became radicalized. Even though Kieran recruited me, it was my choice, and I didn't make my decision until the car ride back to Dublin after burying my friend.

I changed the first scene to take out most of the lines for my character allowing other characters tell the story of the wake. The actor would need to rely on expressing emotion through his body and I wasn't sure Lugan was capable of that type of acting. Watching him for nearly two weeks, he seemed to be in love with his own voice, and his range was impressive. So far he hadn't jumped into my skin to understand me or my motivation. Lines were taken out of the first act for my character both to make the scene more stark and to test Lugan.

Is it fair to test an actor with changes in the script? The thought passed away without any serious consideration.

Mairin yanked me out of my world. "Ian, Ian, who are you talking to? I want to come in."

"I'm not talking to anyone – except maybe myself – come in, of course."

Mairin looked around the room as if she had lost something and was looking for it. "You're not drinking."

I sat behind my desk and tossed the pages of the script on top of my desk. "No, I'm not. What made you think I was drinking?"

Mairin sat on the edge of the desk. "I heard all this chatter, and it sounded like people pacing back and forth."

I leaned back and put my hands behind my head. "No, it was only your crazy husband deep in one of those creative frenzies."

"Oh, God, I hope I haven't interrupted you."

"What time is it?"

Nearly five p.m. I just got home."

"That explains why my stomach is growling at me. I don't think I had lunch. No, I'm sure I didn't have lunch."

"Darling, you must be famished. Let me throw some appetizers together."

"Why did you ask if I was drinking?"

"Well, from down the hall it sounded like there were several people in your office. I don't know . . . maybe William and Brianna were here with you working on the script."

I leaned forward to look Mairin directly in the eyes. "It doesn't explain why you asked about drinking."

"Oh, this is embarrassing. With all the noise, I just jumped to the conclusion you were drinking with friends, not working on the stage play."

I leaned back in the chair and rubbed my hands together. "Based on my past I can understand how you would come to that conclusion. No, this play is, well, it's changing me. Somehow writing about my life in the past is having a real impact on my present. I can't pretend to understand it."

Mairin leaned down and hugged my shoulders and whispered into my ear, "You're not angry with me?"

I brought her closer to me and whispered back to her, "No reason to be."

Mairin got up, as she walked out of the office, she said she would return in a few minutes with tea and sandwiches until we decided what to do for dinner.

I wasn't drinking. All my life, as I've written my novels, I've had a bottle of whiskey on my desk, at my elbow. I'm not drinking. What's changed? Have I shattered a habit? I still love the taste of a fine whiskey, especially a peated whiskey. Where did time go today? I feel like Mairin left for work just a few minutes ago but now it's late afternoon and she's back. I never left this room — not once. Something is happening. I don't understand. . . .

"Ian, come open the door."

Mairin's command jolted me out of my own head. I opened the door with a broad smile and took the tray with tea and sandwiches. The fragrant tea was alluring; I grabbed a sandwich, stuffing the whole thing in my mouth. My favorite, brie with pear.

"Ian, don't be uncouth."

I held my hands in front of my mouth to hide my chomping. I swallowed hard then blurted out a question. "Do you think it's fair to write lines to test an actor?"

Mairin turned her head to one side with a questioning look on her face. "An odd question."

I ate the next sandwich, taking small, deliberate bites (a favorite – sharp cheddar). "I was just wondering."

Mairin sipped her tea and looked over the teacup at me. "In general, I don't believe in 'testing' people. Can you explain yourself; I know you don't like Lugan."

"Mairin, it's not a matter of liking or not liking. So far he hasn't demonstrated to me he can handle the role. I've written some very demanding lines for him. He has to convince the audience why I joined the IRA in the first place and how my reasons evolved over a few months."

"You know, dear, you should really talk to William and Brianna about this. I don't know anything about stage acting. Let's go to Mickey's tonight – someplace familiar and friendly."

* * * * *

At dinner I warned Mairin I would need to have a working weekend and wouldn't be available. She understood my writing process and didn't make any demands of me. I huddled in my office both Saturday and Sunday, completely re-writing the first act and increased the conflict of my character in acts two, three, and four and intensified the language the character used. The re-write was cathartic for me. For the first time in my life

I accepted my own past and my role in the Troubles. I also understood why Mairin had been insistent I write my memoir; the stage play served the same purpose.

Sunday evening I was spent. I went to my secret stash of whiskey and poured myself a tall glass. I set the glass on my desk and enjoyed the fragrance. My head was light and the whiskey took me away to a warm peat bog in western Ireland. I stared at the glass but didn't drink it and I fell back into my chair too exhausted to move. I decided to call William early Monday morning to have someone pick up the new script so there would be time for it to be reproduced for the cast and crew. I knew they would all be surprised at the extent of the changes.

I left the glass of whiskey on my desk – untouched. I tossed and turned all night long, worrying I might wake Mairin and I got up, made myself a cup of tea and a cheddar sandwich.

The re-write made the stage play stronger, more honest, even if it meant exposing myself to Ireland. Based on his work in previous rehearsals, I felt Lugan wouldn't be up to portraying my character as presented in the re-write. The re-write began as a test for him but it evolved into a more in depth, brutally honest portrayal of my past. I prepared to make the case to Brianna and William that Lugan didn't have the talent to portray me. There was a remote chance he could meet the challenge, but if he did, it would be evidence that to date he hadn't been devoted to the role. My plan was to deliver a copy of the re-write to Oisin myself and have a courier deliver a copy to Tom Murphy. I would leave a note with the script asking each of them to share their reaction to the revised script. They would be my litmus test. I finished my tea and sandwich, putting the dishes in the sink and finally relaxed enough to curl up next to Mairin and get a few hours' sleep.

CHAPTER 31

The next morning I offered to make porridge with clotted cream for breakfast. Mairin's expression alone was worth the offer. We ate together, making small talk so I could avoid talking about the play or evening rehearsal. As she left, Mairin turned toward me and shared a warm embrace, filling me with the confidence I knew I would need for the day.

"Love you," I whispered. "Don't wait up for me tonight."

"Ian – really." She winked at me.

"I know, I know, you'll want a blow-by-blow description of the battle this evening. Of course, I can't keep anything from you. It does make our relationship honest – the only way to be."

"Do you really expect a battle, my love?"

"I *expect* Armageddon."

"Don't project, my dear. It's not becoming and a waste of your time."

"Yes dear. I'm going to drop by Oisin's office this morning. Maybe he'll be free for lunch."

"A good idea. I'm sorry I can't join you. Today is our monthly lunch social and I really should attend."

"I wouldn't want it any other way – please enjoy. I'll be going to rehearsal early, so I won't see you until late tonight."

Mairin kissed me with tenderness and held my face in her hands. "I love *you*, Ian Murphy. You are the love of my life, have a good day, and don't worry about me, not even for a single second."

I helped Mairin slip on her coat, she left, throwing me a kiss as she opened the car door, then she was gone.

The house was empty. A wave of anxiety overcame me when I realized I was alone. I rang the courier to deliver manuscripts to Tom Murphy, William, and Brianna. I busied myself with cleaning up after breakfast to endure the wait. The courier arrived in less than twenty minutes. For an extra fee he agreed to deliver Tom Murphy's personally in Dublin and promised to have the delivery to William and Brianna no later than nine that morning. For such excellent service, I gave him a generous tip and offered to call his boss to explain that he wouldn't be available during the day because of his trip to Dublin. "It would make my day, Mr. Murphy. Any time you need a delivery, ask for me, I'm your man. My name is Molony, Tom Molony." Tom shook my hand with such strength, I felt my knuckles crack. I winced and pulled my hand out of his vice grip.

"I'll do that."

* * * * *

I walked to campus both to kill time and to tire myself. I felt a rumbling in my stomach as I walked upstairs to Oisin's office and couldn't decide if it was hunger or my growing anticipation of the rehearsal in the evening. I walked into the outer office, which was empty, sat on the couch and waited. It would be impolite to knock on his door or worse yet just to barge in. A few minutes passed and the longer I waited, the more unusual it was Ailis was not at her post. I stood and paced in front of her desk. Just then the door flew open and Ailis stomped past me and sat down at her desk. She looked up – startled. "Mr. Murphy!"

"I've been waiting." I said in the calmest voice I could muster.

"I don't believe you were expected. Let me check the calendar." She ruffled through the calendar book on her desk.

"No, no, I'm not on his calendar. Is he in?"

Oisin's office guard dog sat up straight. "Stop pacing. He is in but he isn't."

I stopped directly in front of her and leaned in close. "What does that mean?"

She crossed her arms in front of her and gave me a stern look. "It means, Mr. Murphy, he is in the office today but at this moment he's attending the dean's weekly meeting. He's working hard on recruiting our new theatre department chair."

I stood up and took several steps back from her desk. "Oh, now I understand. Will he be back for lunch?"

"Let me check the calendar. Well, he doesn't have anyone scheduled for lunch. Sometimes Dr. Oisin and Dean O'Kane go to lunch after their meeting and sometimes they have carry-out brought in. I really have no way of knowing."

I stood in front of her and tried to process the information she shared. Thoughts spun around in my head and I was incapable of making a decision. Yet it wasn't difficult. I would either wait for Oisin to return or leave – just two choices.

"Would you like to wait, Mr. Murphy? I could get you a cup of tea."

Her question jolted me into action. "No, I'll go. Thank you."

"Should I tell Dr. Oisin you stopped by?"

"Just give this to him. Tell him it's a re-write."

I turned on my heel and walked out of the office and down the stairs. When I reached the exit, my stomach erupted again and this time I knew it wasn't hunger. I decided to walk to Mickey's for some lunch and pass the afternoon with my friend, he wouldn't mind me staying at the pub for the afternoon. I walked the long route to the pub so I wouldn't arrive until after the lunch crowd was gone. I didn't want to distract my friend when he was trying to make a living. The pub had provided his family and his father's family before him with a modest but regular income.

"Ian, it's odd to see you in the middle of the afternoon. Are you hungry?" Mickey asked.

"Hello old friend. Your face always brings me cheer."

Mickey's forehead wrinkled. He tossed the towel from his shoulder onto the bar and walked to my side. He put his arm around my shoulder. "Let's go back to my office; I'll have Mary bring lunch in. The special is potato leek soup."

"Your soup would be perfect." Mickey guided me to his office. He shoved some papers to the side of his desk so there would be room for the bowl of soup. We made small talk for a few minutes until the soup arrived. Mickey watched me take small spoonfuls of soup until I finished the bowl.

"Ian, it's clear something is rattling your cage today. What's the problem?" Mickey leaned back in his chair as if he had nothing better to do than spend the afternoon with me.

"Do you think I'm a mean person, Mickey? Am I cunning or spiteful or underhanded?"

Mickey leaned forward in his chair. "Whoa! Where do all those questions come from?"

"I . . . I just."

Mickey slammed the palm of his hand on the desk hard. I jumped in my chair. "No. You are not any of those things. Is the darkness creeping up on you again? Where does this come from?"

"It's the damn play. The actor portraying me is all wrong. His head is as big as the Rock of Gibraltar. Rather than giving more direction to the actor, William and Brianna asked me for a re-write. As I continued to write, something changed and I found myself pouring heart and soul into the play. Tonight is the first rehearsal with the re-write, and I can feel fury building up inside me. I've never felt this way before. I'm sorry to admit but it is personal, the actor portraying me doesn't fit; he doesn't have the talent. We've rehearsed for two weeks and I'm terrified Brianna and William will insist it's too late to change actors." I collapsed back into my chair, short of breath.

"You need a proper cup of tea. Just sit there. I'll get it and be right back."

* * * * *

Mickey didn't rush to speak but gave me time to become calm and let the tea do its job. I averted my eyes and didn't want to look Mickey in the face. A cocktail of emotions brewing inside me: anger, anxiety, and angst.

"Listen, Ian, I don't know nothin' about this theatre business, but it seems to me the play is about your life and you should be able to decide which actor is right for the role."

My head fell to my chest, and I rubbed my hands together. "William and Brianna did the casting. I've never had any experience with the theatre. I wanted them to make the choices; it's their field, and I trusted them."

"Did you tell them the actor was wrong?"

"I waited a few weeks. Last week I finally insisted he go. They challenged me. They told me he could only read the words I wrote and maybe a re-write was needed. Tom Murphy, he's the playwright in Dublin, told me to expect re-writes — it's normal, it's how theatre works. At first I was ashamed of myself for writing to try to get rid of the actor, but it changed. For the first time I'm being brutally honest. Ireland will be surprised at my life and my motivations." I slumped in my chair. "More tea?"

"Ian, I can recall the first day you walked into my pub looking for a hot meal. We struck it up the first day. Your life is no mystery to me. Sure, I don't know all the details but I know what went on. I'm not stupid. You're a man with strong convictions, I know. I'm sure you did what you thought was right for Ireland. Things change. You changed. I remember what happened to you when Brianna was injured. I was in the hospital with you, remember? It changed everything when Eileen Donohue betrayed you. You're just like any man – you do what you think is right – you make mistakes – you go on. That's it."

I looked at Mickey, who was red in the face. "Do you mind if I stay here until I go to rehearsal?"

"Of course not. Can I get you anything?"

"No, just a few hours alone."

Mickey filled the mug with tea again and put the cozy on the pot in case I wanted a cup later. He closed the door behind him without making a sound. I stretched out my legs and massaged my neck.

I need a strategy if I'm going to survive the rehearsal. I'll arrive promptly at seven, take my regular seat, and not say anything. I hope William will have them start at scene one, act one. My strategy is to let it play out – I'm sure Lugan won't be able to bring the emotion needed for the first scene. I doubt if he's ever been to the wake of a friend; he won't have any background for it. The re-write is very clear about my experience at Timolty's wake. I've got to control myself. I've got to remain composed in front of the cast, William, and Brianna. I'll use the cloak of the dark theatre to hide my cocktail of emotions.

CHAPTER 32

The theatre was dark when I walked in and sat two aisles behind William and Brianna. Brianna got up and kneeled beside my seat. "Uncle Ian, your re-write is amazing. I . . . I never knew. Oh, I don't want to miss this." She kissed me on the cheek and returned to her seat next to William. I didn't understand what was going on, no actors were on stage. They must have been making technical adjustments I didn't understand. I was thankful for the darkness because it helped me cloak my feelings. There was a murmur from someplace back stage, not arguing, but an undercurrent, maybe between the technical staff and the actors. I watched for a reaction from William or Brianna but they sat calmly in their seats. William appeared to be reading the script while Brianna sat with a pad and pencil ready to take notes.

The curtains closed and the spotlight revealed Lugan sitting at the desk on the left side of the stage. I still didn't understand why it was called stage right; everything was always from the actor's perspective. I suppose it was for actors to learn how to move around the stage and be given direction, it had to be that way. He sat at the desk and stared into the blackness, an empty theatre. *Why is he looking out into the audience? That isn't realistic. I'm sure I wrote in the notes — Ian scribbles intently on a yellow pad.* This was not a good start to the evening. Then he began fidgeting with his fake mustache, and he combed his hair back with his hands. Was this his interpretation of me? At least he could have asked what it was like to sit in a room in a small cottage in the country writing all day. Instead he made me look vain and not able to concentrate on my writing. Brianna convinced me being on stage myself would be a mistake. *Maybe I should have insisted on opening the play myself.*

I could feel my right hand begin to twitch and then clench into a fist. My knuckles turned white. I felt a stinging pain in the back of my neck. I rubbed my neck but it only irritated my cramped muscles even more. The curtain opened to the scene of Timolty's wake. The set designer completely understood what Timolty's parents' home looked like. For a moment I was transported back almost forty years to the wake vigil. *Where is the actor portraying me?* Timolty's mother was on her knees crying with her back to the audience. Her body language shouted out her grief at the death of her only son. Lugan, the actor portraying me, appeared on the stage, ignored the tearful Mrs. Doyle, and walked behind Timolty's body stretched out on the dining room table. *What is he doing?*

A soft light focused on the actor's face. He looked out toward the audience. *He's playing to the audience! He doesn't understand the scene at all. The scene isn't about him.* I looked left and right for someplace to escape. My skin tingled with beads of sweat around my shirt collar.

I bolted out of my seat, tripped on the chair in front of me and caught myself with both hands in the middle of the aisle. "Stop!" I shouted. "In the name of all that is holy stop! Stop right now." I ran past William and Brianna without looking in their direction to gauge their reaction. I ran up the aisle to the stairs on the left side of the stage where the prop desk had been minutes before. I ran directly to Lugan, just missing the actor on her knees portraying Mrs. Doyle. My voice cracked when I shouted, "What are you doing? Haven't you ever been to a wake? Why are you facing the audience?"

Lugan stepped back as I ran toward him. "Hey, why are you interrupting rehearsal – you have no right!"

"This is my life and these are my words in the play – I have the right, young man!"

"Like hell," he said under his breath.

I felt William on my left and Brianna on my right next to me. William put his hand across my shoulder. Neither of them was looking at me; they were staring at Lugan.

"Why are you facing the audience?" I asked in the most controlled voice I could muster.

"I'm showing the audience the depth of my grief for my friend Timolty," Lugan snorted.

"Look at how Sinead is showing grief in the scene. She doesn't need to face the audience. Her body language is howling grief. William, Brianna, has Sinead convinced you of her grief?"

"Yes, it's very effective," William said.

"Actually, it's quite amazing how she does it," Brianna added.

"Well, I need to show the audience I'm exhausted, forlorn, and confused. I can only demonstrate it if I face the audience."

"And who decided to give you the lighting in this part of the scene? William? Brianna?" I asked. Both of them shook their heads no.

"Oh, I talked to the lighting guy backstage earlier," Lugan said.

"You what?" William asked in amazement.

"Well, I'm so far from the front of the stage and behind the corpse, I felt my face needed some lighting."

"Get out! Now! You're fired," I shouted. "You will never be in my play. I will shut this whole play down and burn the manuscript before you appear on this stage. You're a self-absorbed, menial actor, totally out of your depth. I won't have it. I won't."

My entire body was shaking. There wasn't a single sound in the theatre; I could only hear my heavy breathing. I felt my knees start to buckle as I slumped. William and Brianna braced me under the arms. Lugan stared at me. He looked at William and Brianna expecting support. Their silence was deafening. Lugan bared his teeth.

"I quit. This play isn't worth my talent. It will never make it to Dublin. I doubt if it lasts a single weekend in Cork. The critics will shred it to pieces. I don't want my name associated with this self-serving piece of trash. Brianna, I want my check by Friday."

Lugan ran past me, jumped off the stage, and stumbled into the front row seats. He scrambled over the seat and ran toward the exit. The door slammed against the wall, shattering the glass as he careened out of the theatre.

"Take the cost of repairing the door out of his pay," William shouted.

"All right. All right. We've had enough drama for tonight. I'm sure you will all agree. We will rehearse tomorrow night – usual time. Cathal, this is why we have understudies – be ready tomorrow night." Brianna gave battle instructions like Churchill.

I was only able to continue standing with William and Brianna's help. Sinead walked up to me with tears streaming down her face. "It was very brave, Mr. Murphy. You are right, Lugan is self-absorbed, and a bully too. He's not liked or respected in the actors' guild. Cathal will be marvelous – just wait and see."

"Cathal, have you met Ian Murphy?" William asked.

A slim young man with high cheekbones and a mustache too big for his narrow face stepped out of the shadow from somewhere back stage. He held the script with both hands. "Mr. Murphy, I am Cathal Bracken." He bowed from the waist as he introduced himself.

"No need for that, young man. Where are you from? Your accent is familiar but not a Cork accent, which is fine," I responded.

"County Dingle."

"I have family in County Dingle. Have you read the re-write, Cathal?"

"Yes. Several times. I can be off book in a week."

"Thank you. I'm looking forward to watching you work tomorrow night."

Everyone shuffled off stage. I still couldn't find the energy to walk on my own. "William, Brianna, I can't move."

They each took an arm and tucked themselves under me to form a human bridge. In unison they turned around and took careful steps back stage where they planted me on a prop couch. My body was like a rubber band. As I landed on the couch, my voice froze and I was unable to speak a single word.

Never in my life have I exposed raw emotions. I wasn't embarrassed but I also wasn't proud of my outburst, even though for the rest of my life I will feel I did the right thing. I have always felt some conflict in my life over doing the right thing. Leaving the IRA was the right action, even though it took Brianna's injury to jolt me into action. Working on the Good Friday Agreement was the right action, even though it put both my life and Kieran Fitzpatrick's life in jeopardy.

My attempt to quell the violence from the Real Irish Republication Army was correct, although incredibly naive and foolish. Finally, changing my position about construction of additional walls in Belfast in the days following the resolution on the Good Friday Agreement was still an internal conflict for me. Several principles I cherish were in direct opposition; the principle that people have the right to make decisions about their own lives versus an action that segregated those same people and allowed them to ignore the problems between them. I've had to acknowledge that security for Catholic families won the day. It was a mystery why all these unconnected thoughts swirled through my mind in a rampant stream of consciousness.

Brianna hovered over me. "How long have you been there, dear?"

"Just a moment, Uncle Ian. I thought you needed a moment. I didn't want to disturb you."

"Let me try to stand."

"Let's go to Mickey's for a drink. I, for one could use a large glass of wine," Brianna suggested.

I smiled as I tested my legs. "Not for me, dear. I need to go home. I need to be with Mairin. Tell Mickey to put it on my tab. Take the whole company out, if you want. I owe everyone."

Brianna held her hand to my forehead. "I don't feel a temperature. You don't want a whiskey?"

"No, I don't. I know it must be a surprise. I'm spent. I need Mairin. Now, take me home, please."

* * * * *

I don't remember the drive home at all. It took both William and Brianna to pull me out of the front seat and help me into the house. Mairin wasn't home. It wasn't unusual for her to have her own activities while we were in rehearsal.

"Just let me stay on the sofa. Mairin will be home soon." I told William and Brianna.

"I'm not sure we should leave you alone," Brianna said.

"I won't delay your trip to Mickey's; you both deserve a whiskey tonight after my fiasco. Oh, God, I am so sorry, William. I'm ruining this for you."

William looked at me with cool, stern eyes. "You haven't ruined anything. Quite the opposite. You've saved the play. I shouldn't have cast Lugan. It was his reputation, which I'm beginning to suspect is self-aggrandizement. Can I get you anything before we leave?"

I fell back into the couch and covered my face with my hands. "A proper cup of tea."

CHAPTER 33

The next evening Mairin drove me to the theatre. "I really wouldn't mind watching the rehearsal, Ian," she said as she pulled the car up to the curb. "I can see the parking lot from here."

I stared out the window, the outside lights were off, there was only a faint glow from the lobby without any sign a rehearsal was about to begin. I rubbed my knees and pulled the door handle before the car came to a full stop. "Ian, are you listening to me?" the agitation in Mairin's question was undeniable.

"I'm sorry, I . . . I . . . I'm preoccupied. Thank you for delivering me. I'll have Brianna bring me home."

"As you wish."

I shut the car door with a thud. The wheels squealed as Mairin left me clutching my script to my chest. The theatre lights were dim. It took me several minutes to adjust my sight and find my regular seat. William and Brianna were not in their seats so I assumed they were talking with the cast. Without warning, the house went black.

Dead Reckoning
A Memoir Play
By
Ian Padraic Murphy

Act 1

Scene 1 – The desk

    Spotlight on Ian Murphy, sitting at a table on stage right. Ian writes on a yellow pad, he blows puffs of smoke from his pipe toward the ceiling. A bottle of whiskey sits on one corner of the desk, a whiskey tumbler on the other. An ashtray filled with spent pipe tobacco rests in the front center of the table.

Someone had added a pile of books on the floor next to the desk. I gasped, my eyes widened, I felt my heart jump. Cathal wore a brown aran-shawl-collar cardigan and held the smoldering pipe in his left hand as he wrote with a fountain pen on the yellow pad. I didn't expect him to wear make-up at his first rehearsal but he had re-created my mustache with amazing attention to detail. He reached down, picked up the book on top of the stack, thumbed through it and then put it back. He twirled his mustache the same way I do. Watching him was unnerving. He continued to write on the yellow pad, then set the pen down on the desk and poured himself a short whiskey. He leaned back in the chair, sipped the whiskey, and shook his head left and right. He sat the half-finished glass on the desk and then turned to his left to watch the curtains begin to open. I felt myself transported back into my history. *How could Cathal know such detail about my mannerisms? Did Brianna coach him? I am enthralled.*

Scene 2 – Timolty's Wake
A body rests on top of the dining room table. The only light provided by a series of column candles around the room and at the head and foot of the body. A floor clock behind the body is stopped, showing the time of death. Stage left a window is open for Timoltly's soul to take flight. Ian, 23, dressed in all black, enters from stage right. Ian takes a few steps into the room. Halts as he approaches the body. Covers his face with his hands. Steps up next to the body and stares down at his friend's corpse. Ian's back is to the audience.

Ian: Oh, God, Timolty, oh, God. That's the suit you wore at graduation. You hated that suit. You told me it was the first suit you had ever worn and your ma insisted. The girls made fun of you – called you a prissy dandy – they did, just three years ago.

Cathal began to sob. *It wasn't in the stage direction, at least not the stage direction I wrote.* I was taken in, Cathal was right; crying at this point was perfect. In the first two scenes he was proving to be an insightful actor.

Ian: I should have stopped you when you visited me at Trinity. You were so forlorn. I know you hated the idea of spending your life on the docks like your da. Is this better, then? Did you die for a cause? Whose life is better because you died? Where is everyone? I expected someone to be here – your ma? Your da? Why am I the only one here? Is death lonely Timolty? Surely, this is the only time you're quiet. How many times did I ask you to pipe down or just shut up? I regret each time now. I would give anything to hear that cackle laugh of yours again. You left me alone, damn you. I'm left without a single friend in the world. Did you think about it when you volunteered? Jesus, we're from Cork, Timolty; it's not our fight up there in Northern Ireland. Let those bastards kill themselves.

Ian moves to his right around the head of the body. He touches Timolty's hair.

Ian: Who combed your hair like this – all filled with Bryl Cream and slicked back? You never did that. Why didn't your ma say something to the undertaker? You would hate how you look now, Timolty – but it's going to be that way to eternity.

Ian moves around to stand behind the body. He stares at the rosary in Timolty's folded hands. He touches the top of Timolty's hand.

Ian: The rosary. I'm sure your ma had them do that. I remember the day we took our confirmation vows together and our parents gave each of us a rosary to commemorate the occasion. My da gave me my first drink; he said I was a man. He gave you a drink too. Do you remember finding my da's cigarette's sitting on the kitchen counter with no one around? We took one each and hid in the alley to take our first smoke. Wasn't it horrible? Do you remember choking and spitting out the terrible taste? We laughed so hard our knees buckled. Well, it changed, didn't it? We both took up the smokes anyway. At Trinity I took up the pipe, being a college man. You were so surprised to see me with a pipe when you visited. You called me snooty. I guess you were right. I have a pipe in my pocket now, Timolty.

Ian strokes his friend's hand and wipes tears off his cheeks.

Ian: (Screaming) Why did you die you son of a bitch? Were you careless? Did you get enough training? Did you volunteer to go on the raid or was it an order? Or were you just stupid?
(Whispering) Did it hurt? Did you feel yourself dying? Did you know you were dying? Oh, God, my life will never be the same – never.

Ian walks back around Timolty's head and kneels at his side with his back facing the audience.

Ian: I will write a keen for you my friend. I'm the only one who can. I should ask your da and ma first. I will, don't worry. I will stay with you tonight, I will not sleep. I have a lifetime to sleep and you, you have eternity.

Scene 3: Timolty's burial
The casket is at the head of the church, closed, near the altar. The tricolor is draped over the coffin. The church is filled with mourners. Timolty's father and mother along with Ian and his father and mother sit in the front pew. The priest is finishing the high mass and eulogy.

Priest: Come forward now to carry our brother, our son, to his eternal resting place.

There is a commotion from the rear of the church, four young men march to the front of the church, two by two and take places around the casket. Ian and Mr. Doyle look back toward the men and watch them surround the casket. They look at each other in dismay. Mr. Doyle steps out first and takes Ian's arm to guide him to a position opposite him at the head of the casket.'

Mr. Doyle: Up then.

In unison the six men raise the casket, placing it on their shoulders, turning and walking down the aisle, out of the church and into the graveyard. The men carry the coffin to a section of the graveyard reserved for Ireland's heroes. Tears stream down Mr. Doyle's face when he realizes where his son will lie."

Mr. Doyle: Down, boys.

Parishioners file behind the casket and form a half circle around the casket. The casket can be seen on stage. The priest stands in the center behind the casket with the Doyle's and Murphy's on either side.

Priest: We come now to place Timolty in his final resting place. This place is sacred to the Holy Mother Church and to God, the Father, the Son and the Holy Ghost.

Everyone makes the sign of the cross.

Priest: In the sweat of they face thou shalt eat bread, till thou return until the ground; for out of it wast thou taken; for dust thou art, and unto dust thou shalt return. For as much as it hath pleased Almighty God of his great mercy to take unto himself the soul of our dear brother, Timolty, here departed, we therefore commit his body to the ground, earth to earth, ashes to ashes, dust to dust, in sure and certain hope of the resurrection to eternal life, through our Lord Jesus Christ, who shall change our vile body, that it may be like unto his glorious body, according to the mighty working, whereby he is able to subdue all things to himself.

The casket is lowered into the grave. The priest bends over, takes a handful of clay and throws it on the casket. Mr. Doyle, Mrs. Doyle, Mr. Murphy, Mrs. Murphy, Ian Murphy do the same in turn.

Ian: May God have mercy on Timolty's soul. May God have mercy on all our souls.

All: Amen

All make the sign of the cross. Curtain closes.

The house went dark. The theatre reeked with silence. I could hear myself in labored breathing. I grabbed the script with both my hands, which curled in my sweaty palms. My head fell on my chest. It was if I had had an out-of-body experience watching myself thirty-five years ago at Timolty's funeral. I bolted out of my chair and clapped once. The crack of sound bounced off the theatre walls. The curtains opened. The cast stood on stage where they finished the scene. I clapped again, then again. William and Brianna turned and gawked at me. *Was I inappropriate?*

Brianna and William both broke out into broad smiles and began laughing. They clapped, too. They turned toward the actors, raising their hands over their heads as they applauded.

I fell back into my seat exhausted. "Let's take five," William shouted to the cast.

No notes. There couldn't possibly be any notes. Just a break to take a breath. What can I say?"

"Outstanding, truly outstanding – all of you. Cathal, I'm impressed you have the first act off-book – well done. I think Mr. Murphy's response says it all. We'll move on to act two after the break."

"Cathal, Cathal, Cathal," I repeated over and over.

"Are you staying for the rest of rehearsal, Uncle Ian?" Brianna asked.

I rubbed the tears out of my eyes and brushed my hair back with my hands. "I suppose. I don't want to call Mairin; it's not fair to her. I don't want to take the bus home and I don't think my old, tired body could make the trip to walk. No, I'll stay. It will be fine. Everything's going to be fine, isn't it?"

I looked up into William and Brianna's fresh faces. "Yes it is. Everything is going to be just fine," Brianna said.

CHAPTER 34

The next morning I slept in until the smell of the morning cup of tea woke me. Mairin smiled and set the tray with toast and jam on the side table and handed me a mug. As she did, she leaned over and kissed my forehead. "It must have gone well last night; you haven't slept like this in months. Do you even know the time?"

"Do I ever?"

"Well, my love, it's half seven and I must be off soon. What are your plans for the day?"

I sat up in bed, stretched, and sipped the hot tea. I looked at Mairin for a moment to gather the courage to share my plans for next week with her. "Come sit next to me in bed for just a few minutes before you go. This is important." Mairin's mouth fell open as she gasped. She trotted around the bed and slid in close to me.

"It went well. The actor portraying me now, Cathal, is extraordinary. He's managed to get into my head somehow. It's uncanny and uncomfortable. I can't watch anymore. I need to wait until opening night; it's only five weeks away."

"Won't they need you to make script changes or something?"

I scratched my beard as I considered her question. "I doubt it, but I should ask Brianna and William."

Mairin put her arm around me and tucked her head under my chin. "So what are you planning, my mystery man."

I took a few moments to gather the words together before speaking. I whispered, "I need to go to Dingle. There are side effects, things I didn't expect, ugly things. It's just happened and I'm experiencing life differently than I have for years. I need to learn to cope. I need to learn how to be alive."

Mairin raised her head and looked deeply into my eyes for a very long time. She stroked my beard and kissed me open mouthed with her unique passion. My beard dampened with tears.

"You could see a doctor. There are drugs that can help."

"No. No drugs. I don't want to substitute one drug for another. I'm not strong enough, I know I'm not. I have another plan. You know what it is; you know me better than myself some days."

"You're off to Dingle."

I smiled to myself and was relieved to not have to utter the words myself.

"Will you stay with your aunt and uncle?"

"Definitely not. I'll stay on the west side of the peninsula, Ballydavid maybe, so I can be near water. I have a great notion to climb Mount Brandon. I haven't climbed since I was in my twenties. It's the challenge I need, both physical and mental."

Mairin hugged me so hard it was difficult to breath. She buried her head in my chest. I wasn't sure she would let go. "Weren't you off to work?"

She slapped my shoulder. "Avoiding me, aren't you?"

"No, never, my love."

"When are you leaving?"

"Haven't decided. In the next few days."

Mairin jerked straight up and took my face in both of her hands. "Before you go, do your research. Study the hiking map. Have a plan; make sure to take food with you and the right clothes. Share your plan with me, won't you?"

"Of course, dear heart, I'll start researching today and I'll call William and Brianna to let them know – they shouldn't have any surprises at this point. You do understand, don't you?"

"Yes, I understand. I would like to be with you but you haven't asked me to join you, I know what that means. I won't pretend loving you isn't sometimes a chore, and this will be one. I've wanted you to come to terms with your drinking for so long. I can't judge your path to sobriety but I can pray for you every day." She kissed me again full on the lips then slid off the bed. "I should be home no later than half five tonight. I'll pick something up; let's dine alone tonight – all right?"

"Perfect. The jam and toast look inviting, thank you."

* * * * *

I visited the map store and purchased the most recent hiking maps for the Dingle Peninsula and Mount Brandon. I also stopped by the outfitter's to get new hiking boots and rain gear. The owner, Sean, was in the shop alone, which meant I would receive uninterrupted, personal attention. Sean was a small man with close-cropped white hair and a light complexion. His face was very angular. While small in stature, he was quite fit and wore hiking clothes. He looked like he could walk out the door and return in a month without a second thought.

When I shared my plan to hike Mount Brandon, he insisted I purchase Meindl Alpine boots. He pointed out he was wearing a pair of their shoes. I tried on several sizes until Sean was satisfied it was the perfect fit. I have flat feet, which makes finding comfortable shoes a challenge. The boots I purchased had a very high arch. I lost my breath when I saw the price of the boots but decided this was no time to worry about a bit of expense. *Wasn't I worth it?* Next, I asked for Sean's suggestion on clothes. "Here's the thing Mr. Murphy."

"Ian, please."

"If you insist. Ian, in the hill country you have to be prepared for anything. Hiking Brandon is at least a half day hike and the weather could change three or four times. Rain will be your worst enemy; if you get wet, the wind will chill you to near hypothermia in minutes, minutes I tell you. If the sun shines bright all day, you can sweat and then get chilled from trapping body heat in the clothes you wear. Oh, yes, it's a challenge."

"When I was younger, I just threw on a jacket and whatever boots I had and off I went."

"To be honest, Ian, it was foolish. It's about layers. There are three: wicking, insulation, and shell: the modern way."

"I had no idea. Well, I have all day. Show me what I need."

I spent hours in the store and was confident I could climb any mountain in Ireland or Scotland with the assortment of clothes and other gear I was the new proud owner of. In addition to the clothes, I bought a day pack, a metal water container, dried fruit, jerky, and healthy bars to eat.

"Now, Ian, listen to me. Make sure to make yourself a peanut butter sandwich and take along a chocolate bar for instant energy."

I shook my head in disbelief. "Peanut butter sandwich?"

"Great protein and carbs all in one. Perfect."

"Speaking of food, I'm famished. All I had for breakfast was toast and jam. I'm off to Mickey's Pub for lunch. Want to join me?"

"Do you see anyone else here? I appreciate your kindness but I'll stay in the shop. My wife made me an egg sandwich today. A cup of tea is all I need."

Sean opened the door for me; my arms were full. "Wish me well. Good-bye. My wife will be proud of my purchases. I couldn't have done it without you."

"God speed, Ian Murphy."

* * * * *

It took me another day to organize myself for the trip. I had Brianna and William stop at the house before rehearsal to share my plan. As expected, they were confident I wouldn't

be needed for re-writing. I can't say they were completely supportive of my solo hiking plans. They worried I might injure
myself and be without aide for hours. I found their concern
touching but unfounded. I promised to be in touch with
Mairin every day and if they would need me, they could contact me through her. I was pleased they didn't cross-examine
me about my reasons for the trip. William might have guessed
and Brianna knew hiking in the Dingle Peninsula was one of
my regular activities.

On the third day Mairin made a huge Irish breakfast, in-
spected my packing, and sent me off with all the love she could
give. I insisted she go off to work while I stayed behind and
cleaned up after our meal. I set off by mid-morning, taking the
N22 to Killarney where I stopped for a cup of tea and a scone.
I studied the map of the Dingle Peninsula to decide where I
would stay. Recently the Official Language Act took effect and
the town took back its Irish name, Baile na nGall. This was the
perfect village for me to stay, even if it would mean a short
drive to Mount Brandon.

The village was on the edge of the ocean and was small
enough not to attract tourists in March. It was also likely my
face wouldn't be noticed in Baile na nGall, especially now that
I sported a full beard. I finished my tea, folded the map back
neatly, and continued west toward Dingle. In Dingle I turned
north on the R559 toward Murreagh. The road was posted for
80 kph, which felt a little fast as I toured on. About half way
to Baile na nGall I stopped completely to let a herd of wooly
sheep cross the road. Each sheep had a large blue cross painted
on its back to show the herdsman who they belonged to. The
herdsman waved wildly after getting his flock safely to the other side of the road. I guessed he appreciated I wasn't impatient
and hadn't honked at the crossing, which would have disturbed
the sheep and lengthened the time it took them to cross. As I

passed by them at a crawl, I waved back and gained cruising speed again.

Baile na nGall sat on the edge of the Atlantic with a small sand beach. The village was near Gallarus Castle, a fifteenth-century relic of feudal Ireland. It was also home to the more historically significant Gallarus Oratory. For years it was thought to be the oldest Christian church in Ireland, though I have always thought that unlikely. Recent scholarship focused on the Gaelic name *"gallarus,"* which roughly translates into "shelter for foreigners," which was a more romantic and historic purpose for the stone building. The structure overlooked the harbor in one of the most stunning settings on the peninsula.

I drove through the village and found the An Riasc Bed and Breakfast, a two-story stone building with a classic view of Mount Brandon. It was mid-afternoon and not a single car was parked in their lot. This time of year it was possible I could be the only guest. I was welcomed by the owner, Owen Campbell, who offered me tea before I could ask if there was a room available. He led me to the dining room with a spectacular view of the ocean, set a plate of scones and jam on the table, then brought us both a cup of tea.

"I was hoping to get a room for a few days – maybe a week." The scone melted in my mouth and the tea was strong enough to need a bit of milk but I wasn't bold enough to ask.

"A week? It would be grand. You can have the room of your choice, depends on what view you would like."

"This scone is delicious. I stopped for tea and a bite in Killarney and didn't realize how hungry I am."

"Ah, you're a man from Cork, aren't you?"

"My Cork accent gave me away again. Yes, Ian Murphy. I drove over today."

"Murphy? Are you related to the Dingle Murphy's?"

"I am."

"And you're not staying in Dingle?"

"Well, this is not a family visit sort of trip. Not a vacation really – more of a pilgrimage. I plan on spending time on Mount Brandon and it's seemed more convenient here. I'm also taken with the wild Atlantic region."

Owen Campbell looked at me for what felt like ten minutes without saying a word and scratched at the hairy stubble on his face – maybe it had been two days since he shaved. "Well, we don't have any other lodgers. The place looks big from the outside but we only rent four rooms. At our age it's all the missus and I can handle."

"You don't appear that old, Mr. Campbell."

"Next month I turn seventy, and I can tell you, I don't know how much longer I want to run this business. The missus and I haven't taken a vacation in years; I can't even remember how many years. Although I do enjoy our guests. The missus says the world comes to our doorstep so we can just stay put."

I laughed out loud at his straightforward truth and finished off my scone. "I will pay you in advance for seven days. If I leave sooner, we can just settle up."

"It's generous of you, Mr. Murphy. Do you want a view of the Atlantic or the Mount?"

"The Atlantic."

"Breakfast, of course, comes with the room rate. Other meals are offered at a reasonable charge. My missus is a real gourmet cook. She's got quite the reputation in this area; you won't be disappointed if you intend to take your other meals with us."

"Mr. Campbell, you can count on me. When do you serve breakfast?"

Owen Campbell looked to his left then his right, leaned close to me and whispered, "When do you want it?"

"I would like to be off for Mount Brandon by seven. The weather is most likely to be calm then, even if it's cool."

"Seven it is, Mr. Murphy. Now don't tell the missus I gave you a choice. She tells me we serve breakfast at eight and at nine. I'll tell her you're a special case, paying a week in advance and all. Listen, if you're hiking, we have a very special smoked salmon and egg breakfast that will be perfect before your hike."

My mouth watered at the mention of smoked salmon. "Salmon is one of my favorites. Listen, I wonder if your missus could make me two peanut butter sandwiches, a scone, and tea for me to take up the mountain for lunch – I'll pay the regular lunch fee, of course."

"Not a problem. Now, you go take a walk through our village and in thirty minutes your room will be ready. I'll ask the missus what she plans on making for dinner. What time do you want dinner?"

"Whenever your missus has it ready."

CHAPTER 35

I called Mairin and shared my plan to use the Pilgrim's Path to the summit of Mount Brandon. She warned me hiking alone at my age might not be a wise decision, she presented several arguments for me to take The Saints Road.

"The Saints Road doesn't lead to the summit, dear!" I reminded her.

"And you have a need to hike the summit? Oh, I wish I were with you. It was a mistake to let you out on your own. I know, maybe I'll send William over to check on you."

"Please do no such thing. I've hiked in these hills all my life; it's my second home. I'll be fine. I'm *so* glad I shared my plans with you."

"Ian Padraic Murphy, don't be sarcastic with me. It's only because I love you dearly."

"I know, I know. I'll carry a phone, I promise. I'm outfitted for it. It's just something I have to do right now, before opening night of the play."

"Well, thank you for sharing. I'll look forward to your call early this evening. I'll be home by five. Call as soon as you can. I love you with all of my heart, Ian."

"Thank you for understanding. You are the joy in my life. Goodbye."

* * * * *

Mr. Campbell gave excellent directions to the car park at Faha Grotto. I arrived by half seven and was the only car in the lot. The trail followed the Faha Ridge and took just over four hours. My plan was to have a private lunch at the summit and return to one of Mrs. Campbell's gourmet dinners, then sleep the sleep of the dead.

As I drove to the car park, a fine mist descended, the kind of mist that makes the rocks slippery and the hike dangerous. From the Grotto, the path was easy to follow and rose gradually along the Faha Ridge. As I walked, my face was showered, tiny drops of mist lodging in my beard. Several times I tried wiping my face but to no avail. I walked along the lower path, just under the ridge, until I came to the twin lakes, Paternoster and Coumaknock Lough. The lake water was pristine, blue crystalline filled with pan fish. The valley hasd been created by a glacier that left daunting steep slopes. From the valley, I glanced up and doubted my ability to make the climb to the summit. I felt I had failed, an old man's silly sojourn. I sat down on an outcrop and poured myself a cup of tea. The steam from the tea warmed my face. I pulled the map out of my inside pocket and studied it carefully. The map clearly indicated a winding path to the Col and from there the path to the summit would be manageable.

I was thankful I listened to all the recommendations the outfitter made, especially the clothing. The wicking effect was a miracle because in even the gentle phase of the hike, I sweat a great deal. I have not walked like that in years and my muscles were no longer accustomed to the challenges I faced today. I guessed I had been walking for three hours, which meant I had at least an hour to the summit.

There was no sign of other hikers in any direction. There were no trees to break up the landscape, just rock jutting out here and there with a whiff of snow in the valley — a snow which would not melt until next spring. I felt alone for the first time on my hike. I wondered if there might be others on the trail behind me. Hikers more fit would catch up with me, speak for a few moments, and then jog up to the summit before I could stand up again. I strained to look down the trail, and there was no one in sight. I told myself I wanted to be alone and I was fulfilling my wish – maybe too well.

I pulled myself up off the rock and took a few minutes to stretch before facing the challenge to the Col. I put my head down and watched each step, not wanting to focus on how far up the mountain I was climbing. One step in front of the other, step after step, I felt myself slip into a walking meditation. There was only me and this path in the whole world. The ache in my calves melted away or I learned to ignore it, I don't know which. Then, I was at the Col. I took a moment to check my map again, then took the path to the left. The path glided to the summit at maybe a four- or five-degree angle; not bad but enough to know it was an ascent to the top.

After a few minutes, the trail become a rocky ledge. I took my eyes off the trail to look around. *I made it!* I was on the summit. I imagined centuries ago the navigator Brandon looking out over the Atlantic Ocean and imagining his voyage to the west. Everyone in Ireland knows Brandon found the shore of North America long before the imposter Columbus. In fact, our legend says Columbus relied on the charts Brandon made to cross the Atlantic.

The mist blurred my view in all directions. I sat down on the ridge and ate the sandwiches Mrs. Campbell had made and finished the tea. As I sat, the breeze turned into a constant wind, and I could feel the droplets in my beard turn to ice. I reached inside my coat pocket and pulled out a silver flask. I unscrewed the lid and took in a deep breath of peated Midleton whiskey. The sweet fragrance made my head light. I closed my eyes. My body ached to raise the flask to my lips and consume its contents in one long drink. Tears clouded my eyes, and I couldn't see more than a few feet in front of me. I began to shake all over and some of the whiskey bounced out of the flask. By pure instinct I brought the flask to my lips, wanting to lick off the few drops sliding down the outside of the flask. I stopped and raised the flask to eye level where I could see bloodshot eyes staring back at me. From the first sentence of my first book, I had a bottle of whiskey on the desk. It was cheap whiskey in the beginning and often made my stomach curdle. As success and money came to me, my taste in whiskey improved and now I drank only Ireland's finest. How many times had Kieran and I shared a bottle? I miss him; I miss our friendship. It was also the whiskey that gave me the misguided bravery to drive my car into a British barricade. I can't imagine a life without whiskey, but I am committed to try and find out.

I turned the flask upside down and watched the wind bend the stream of whiskey as it hit the rocks and splattered in all directions. I pulled my knees up to my chest and buried my face in my arms. I let the flask slip out of my hand and bounce on the jagged rocks and cried until I could cry no more, tears off my face. Fog was rolling in off the Atlantic. It was time to get off the summit. I picked up the empty flask and tucked it back inside my jacket pocket. When I stood, I lost my balance and caught myself with both hands to prevent falling down the side of the ridge. I took my time to right myself and stretch to full height. No one was in sight. I had met my demon and tossed it down the mountainside. My head flew back into a hearty laughter.

As I descended, the energy in my body grew. Each step brought me greater assurance. By the time I reached the car, I felt like I had the strength of the Cork hero Michael Collins. I had given myself the gift of exuberance and self-confidence.

* * * * *

Mr. Campbell greeted me at the entrance of the bed-and-breakfast as he had the previous day and again offered tea and cake. I was famished from my hike and didn't want to wait for dinner.

"Oh, yes, I almost for forgot, there's a young man waiting for you in the parlor. Nice young man."

"There is?"

"Yes, I believe he said his name was William, William Boyle."

I walked into the parlor where William was enjoying a smoke and reading the local newspaper. "Mairin sent you, didn't she?"

William looked up from the newspaper, folded it, and set it on the table next to his chair. He smiled.

"I should have guessed. I'm sorry she sent you on this goose chase, or should I say Ian chase."

William stood and embraced me with such strength I lost my breath for a moment. "One hell of a bear hug, young man; remember, I'm old and fragile."

"Trust me, Ian, you are neither old nor fragile, but I'm glad you're safe. Mairin convinced both me Brianna that hiking by yourself you would fall off the ridge and never be seen again."

"So between you and Brianna I guess you drew the short straw."

"Something like that."

"I have tea and cake coming. Would you like some? Will you drive back this evening to catch the last half of rehearsal?"

"I'm supposed to stay the night, but if you think it would be ok for me to drive back to Cork yet tonight, I'll do it."

"I will call Mairin and tell her I insisted you return for rehearsal. Speaking of rehearsal, how's it going? Need any further re-writes."

William sat back down in his chair and Mrs. Campbell brought us the food. "It turns out, in addition to being a fine actor, Cathal is quite the leader. He's working closely with all the actors. He has an uncanny sense of the play. He's actually teaching me how to direct, how to collaborate with actors to turn your words into theatrical magic. It's amazing, really it is."

I took a bite of cake and a few crumbs fell into my tea and I picked up the teacup and slurped up the morsels before they were noticed. "Well, I confess I haven't been a mentor to you in the traditional sense. My kind of mentoring is to give you the keys to the car and say 'have at it,' you'll learn your own way. You do see the metaphor there, don't you?"

William couldn't restrain his laughter. "Yes, Ian, you've made your point, and I do understand the metaphor. What was this hiking trip of yours all about?"

"Oh, William, sometimes actions become habits and then habits become addictions and a person loses control over their own lives. We have such wonderful minds; we can rationalize anything, anything at all. The simple truth is I am addicted to alcohol – to Midleton Irish whiskey. This frail body of mine became dependent on a daily dose of booze. In some miraculous way, with writing this stage play, I broke a link or two in my chain of addiction. I needed to do more. I needed to cast the chain away and free myself."

William sat staring at me for a few minutes. I couldn't tell if he was just at a loss for words or didn't believe me. After a few minutes, he smiled and then chuckled to himself. "Uncle Kieran would have been proud."

"Mmm, yes, I suppose he would. Now, you be on your way back to Cork. I need to call my dear wife before she explodes from anxiety. Thank you for coming, William."

* * * * *

"Hello, Mairin? Listen, I just sent William off. There's absolutely no need for him to miss the entire rehearsal this evening. . . ."

251

CHAPTER 36

I begged several cigarettes from William at the final cast meeting prior to the show opening. He was as nervous as I was while Brianna remained calm and composed; it was difficult to imagine Brianna was my niece. I had an intense empty feeling in the pit of my stomach. In a matter of minutes my life would be exposed and my secrets revealed. My words had brought death to the untold innocent Irish. *How can I survive this night?*

Backstage, the actors had unique routines to focus and direct their energy before curtains opened. The lead actor, Cathal, stood in a corner jumping up and down on his toes; it was distracting but William didn't rein him in. Watching the actors, my stomach clenched in fear. I had to leave. I stomped away without saying the traditional "break a leg" to the cast.

Mairin didn't want to attend the cast meeting because she wanted to meet the O'Learys in the lobby. While Mairin waited inside, I paced in the alley behind the theatre chain smoking the cigarettes I bummed from William. Stray cups, discarded newspapers, and food wrappers littered the alley. The trash bins overflowed, reeking of rotten food. When I inhaled, the stench entered my throat. I dry heaved. I didn't want to watch the play. I skipped dress rehearsal because I just couldn't spend another evening looking in a mirror. Tonight, I didn't have a choice. After tonight, I wouldn't have any secrets. *What if I would just catch a cab home? I can't abandon William and Brianna. Hell, I can't abandon myself. Who will they say that I am?*

"Ian, you reek of cheap cigarettes!" Mairin shouted.

I took her arm and walked into the theatre.

"Yes, well, so what?" I mumbled under my foul breath.

I asked to be seated late to avoid both well-wishers and potential critics. *I will be judged tonight. I'm certain I will.* As we were escorted to our seats, the house lights dimmed. I grabbed Mairin's arm to avoid stumbling. A low hum of a hundred whispered conversations enveloped me as I wiggled into my seat. From the row in front of me the odor of cheap, French gardenia perfume co-mingled with Patrick's men's cologne — a disgusting concoction. I held my hands over my nose and mouth to prevent vomiting.

Without warning the theatre went black. Mairin took my hand and held it tightly. My heart fluttered out of rhythm. I sucked air through my mouth deep into my lungs and held my breath a few moments to prevent hyperventilation. I turned toward Mairin for comfort and could just make out her lips curling into a smile as she stroked my hand.

The opening scene framed the entire play for the audience. One of my greatest lessons from working on this production was how theatre expressed a scene through action. It was an advantage over writing fiction, which was limited only to words.

I watched my life unfold before my eyes, acted by people I didn't know, trusting them to translate the words I wrote for them into a portrayal of my life that was authentic and grounded in truth, or at least my truth, as I lived it. Brianna had convinced me to stage the production without an intermission. "Did your life have an intermission, Uncle Ian?" she challenged me. Of course not. Most dramatic productions had at least one fifteen-minute intermission. I worried the audience would become weary sitting for two hours. *Could my story keep their attention for that long — was it worth their attention?"*

The anguish I felt was clear on stage. Cathal was able to show how I felt when I touched the crucifix Timolty held in his unmoving hands. Cathal swayed back and forth, and then leaned over and whispered to Timolty. Cathal walked in front of the body lying on the dining room table, fell to his knees, and cried out, "Timolty, Timolty!" When I swore revenge for his death, the audience gasped. Curtains closed.

Words became mystical in a stage play. It felt intoxicating in a way I had never before experienced. I was riveted to the action on stage and was oblivious to the audience's response or to Mairin sitting next to me still clutching my hand in her lap.

The scene when I attempted taking my own life was handled with restraint and without judgment. Cathal understood how my mind had swirled in a cesspool of self-destruction when I learned children were dying in Belfast because of my words; when I drove my car into a British barricade. I hid my face with a mask, which on stage appeared comical. Could anyone recognize a crazed Irishman ramming a barricade at midnight under just a few dismal streetlights? *Was I hiding from myself?* The truth was I had never been reflective about those days. After the crash, Kieran provided a safe house. I had to challenge death to realize I wanted to live, regardless of the pain I endured. I couldn't imagine myself dead. I was pathetic in those days; it was a miracle I recovered emotionally, even though I was slamming down a bottle of whiskey a day. And now everyone knew it.

Cathal and Evelyn, who portrayed Eileen Donohue, exposed my naiveté in love. I could feel myself blush during those scenes. I wondered what it was like for Mairin to watch "me" on stage have a love affair with another woman. Of course, Mairin knew about my affair with Eileen; she had agreed not to ask questions as I agreed to not ask about her relationship with her former husband. I was curious what it was like for her to stay at his side in hospice. I didn't want to risk offending her or prying into difficult memories. I never imagined she would be curious about my relationship with Eileen. It was embarrassing to watch myself fail at love.

Cathal and Evelyn captured my anger and sense of betrayal in the scene where Eileen and I saw each other for the last time. Cathal even captured the physical expression of my pain as my stomach cramped and I nearly fell to my knees. I didn't recall writing any stage direction for the scene but somehow the words leapt off the page and onto the stage and captured the quintessence of that moment in my life. To this day, I could not look Eileen Donohue in the eyes. She never understood how writing those articles for the *Irish Times* about my days in the IRA put me at risk of spending years in a British gaol.

The scene with the priest instructing me before he could absolve my sins was poignant. I shivered when I saw myself on stage stuffed into the confessional. I didn't wander into the cathedral to ask for absolution; I wanted guidance, which the priest accepted. I recalled an enormous sense of relief because, after years of misdirection, I learned the path to restore my soul was atonement.

While I was working on the stage play, I was uncertain how to portray my role in drafting the Good Friday Agreement. To be honest, my recollection of those days was blurry. I drank every night I worked on the agreement. I convinced myself binge drinking was the only way I could sleep. I made a choice to betray the IRA; it was the only way I could save myself and hope to cleanse my blood-stained soul. Watching the actors, it was clear as a day on Mount Brandon I was desperate to atone for my IRA volunteer days. I revealed the truth—my work on the Good Friday Agreement was selfish, not altruistic and how much I relied on the drink to make it through. I must confess, I didn't comprehend how self-absorbed I was until I saw it on stage. Now, I was ashamed of my hubris. I had learned in theatre a great deal can be expressed by subtext or what isn't said, sometimes revealing even more than dialogue.

This evening, watching the actors, they brought my words to life. My original motivation to write the play was to give William something to work with and serve as my gift to mentor him through his graduate program. Now I realized it was much more.

Yes, "dead reckoning" was an old nautical term that navigators used to describe how to calculate their current position by knowing where they had been. But for me, it was much more. This evening I watched my past unfold in front of me, and I understood how I came to this point in my life and where I needed to go. The stage play was my dead reckoning and my compass home.

The final scene was fraught with tension and conflict when I grasped the idea that my lifelong friend, Kieran Fitzpatrick, had been sent by the IRA to assassinate me for betraying the cause.

Kieran was conflicted. He had to choose between his loyalty to the IRA and our bond of friendship. I drowned myself in a bottle of Midleton that night to avoid facing death a second time. I could re-play Kieran's confession in my mind as if it happened yesterday; the actors captured the intensity and truthfulness of the night. When I watched the scene on stage, I wasn't sure Kieran apologized for recruiting me into the IRA or if it was a construct of my imagination. *If I remember it happened, does it mean it is an objective fact?* Seeing it on stage, it was out of character for Kieran to apologize. Yes, he might have felt regret, but to apologize – I'm not sure.

Before passing out, I told Kieran, "I will go to my grave with blood on my hands. I pray to God two misguided soldiers like you and I are granted the gift of redemption, to save our immortal souls."

With those words the curtains closed, then re-opened immediately to an empty stage with the revolver sitting on the table. As the stage lights faded to gray the spotlight came up on stage right with Cathal again sitting at the desk. He was concentrating on writing on a yellow pad. He turned back toward his left to look at the empty room. He finished off the glass of whiskey and walked off stage as the curtains closed. Someone added the final scene with Cathal at the desk; I hadn't written it, and I hoped William had. Having my character on stage writing in the first and last scene was like a pair of bookends.

The tension I felt throughout the performance melted. I stretched my legs out as far as I could under the seat in front of me. I shook my shoulders. Mairin raised my hand to her lips and kissed it. When the house lights came up, everyone jumped out of their seats, giving a standing ovation with whistles and catcalls. People cheered and cried. Mairin crushed me in her arms. She whispered into my ear, "I love you, Ian Padraic Murphy."

The curtains opened to reveal the cast standing across the stage in a single row. After their third bow, they pointed toward me. Someone grabbed my arm and led me to the stairs to join the actors on stage.

I froze, looking out over a sea of smiling faces. A wave of relief surged through my body.

Cathal and Evelyn locked their arms behind my back to help me take a bow. Blood rushed to my face. After a deep bow, they pulled me up, bracing me like a wood soldier at attention. As they waved to the crowd, Cathal shouted into my ear, "Wave, Mr. Murphy, this is for you." The clapping went on and on.

I wanted time to stop. The play gave me the incredible gift of insight; I knew exactly who I was and the purpose of the play. I had bared it all. All Ireland ever wanted from me was the truth, to no longer hide behind the charade of an innocent author. Now I knew that I created my own darkness, whiskey clouded my mind. I've leapt out of the darkness into the light by the power of my own words. I was unbound.

I took a step in front of the actors and raised my hand to silence the audience. It took a few minutes for them to understand I wanted them to be quiet.

While waiting, my knees felt weak; I worried I might fall on my face before addressing the crowd.

My mouth was dry; words flooded my mind but lodged in my throat. In an eruption of courage, I blurted out, "Ireland, I offer *Dead Reckoning* as my act of public contrition."

THE END

ABOUT THE AUTHOR

Inspired by Irish newspaper reports on children injured in the Peace Zone in Belfast, Rex Owens began the story that became his first novel *Murphy's Troubles*. Unexpectedly laid off from his management job in a healthcare organization, Rex took this as sign from the universe that it was time to move forward with the story.

Murphy's Troubles explores the complexity of "The Troubles" in Ireland through the eyes of fictional Ian Murphy, an IRA volunteer and writer, who comes to question the decisions he's made. *Out of Darkness*, book two in the *Irish Troubles Series*, published in June 2015, continues the story for Ian to conquer his demons while working for peace in Northern Ireland.

Owens is a devoted history buff and natural storyteller who states that writing is his path to express his creativity and liberate his imagination. "I believe writing is about storytelling and throughout history stories have served many purposes," says Owens. His fiction explores people's motives when making life changing decisions and searches for common themes in our lifetime journey.

Rex posts a blog each week at www.rexowens.us. In addition to writing, Owens hosts a radio show "My World and Welcome to It" on 103.5 FM The Sun Radio on the 2nd and 4th Tuesdays of the month at 9:30 a.m. The program is streamed live and archived at: http://sunprairiemediacenter.com/